The
Forbidden
Caller

Books by Shelley Shepard Gray

A Season in Pinecraft

Her Heart's Desire

Her Only Wish

Her Secret Hope

The Amish Widows Club

The Unexpected Caller

The Forbidden Caller

Unforgiven

Unforgotten

Unshaken

the
AMISH WIDOWS CLUB

BOOK 2

The Forbidden Caller

SHELLEY SHEPARD GRAY

Revell
a division of Baker Publishing Group
Grand Rapids, Michigan

Published by Revell
a division of Baker Publishing Group
Grand Rapids, Michigan
RevellBooks.com

Printed in the United States of America

Library of Congress Cataloging-in-Publication Data

Names: Gray, Shelley Shepard author
Title: The forbidden caller / Shelley Shepard Gray.
Description: Grand Rapids, Michigan : Revell, a division of Baker Publishing Group, 2026. | Series: The Amish widows club ; 2
Identifiers: LCCN 2026009737 | ISBN 9780800747275 paperback | ISBN 9781493455553 ebook
Subjects: LCSH: Amish | Widows | Grief | LCGFT: Romance fiction | Christian fiction | Novels
Classification: LCC PS3607.R3966 F66 2026
LC record available at https://lccn.loc.gov/2026009737

Cover design and photograph by Laura Klynstra

The author is represented by The Seymour Agency.

Baker Publishing Group publications use paper produced from sustainable forestry practices and postconsumer waste whenever possible.

26 27 28 29 30 31 32 7 6 5 4 3 2 1

For Kristin, editor extraordinaire.
Thank you for continuing to make my books
better than I could have imagined.

Open my eyes to see the wonderful truths in your instructions.

PSALM 119:18

The best way to be understood is to be understanding.

AMISH PROVERB

Prologue

Was there a worse month than October? Jenna Graber didn't think so. As far as she was concerned, October was such a middling thing. No longer warm, not really cold. The vegetables in her garden had been harvested, washed, and canned. But the field where they once grew looked ravaged. The formerly neat rows were unkempt and the ground was empty.

Barren.

Jenna swallowed as she realized that she hadn't been looking at her garden but the spot on the hill where Jimmy was buried. The dirt covering his casket was still not smooth.

It was Jimmy's *grave* that looked unkempt and scarred. It was much like her insides felt. So twisted and pained.

She wondered if they always would.

"I think that's everything, Jenna."

Startled, she focused on the present again. Atle Weaver was walking along her front walkway wearing a somber expression.

"I made sure to tell the boys to pick up every piece of

trash and carry it off with them," he continued. "Don't you worry about that none."

Atle's wife, Rebeccah, strode to his side. "I put all the leftovers in containers and placed them in your refrigerator, dear," she said with a pleased-looking smile. "Why, you won't have to worry about feeding Katie for the next week."

The couple were now standing directly in front of her. Realizing they were waiting for a response, Jenna stood up. She'd been sitting on the front steps of her porch ever since the auction ended. She wanted to stay out of the way while friends, neighbors, and strangers carted off Jimmy's things. In a matter of hours all his tools and clothes had been purchased. So had his fancy courting buggy and Lightning, that cantankerous gelding she'd never liked.

She drew a breath, then stopped. Stared at the couple. What was she supposed to say now? She had no idea.

As another second passed, some of the light in Rebeccah's kind gray eyes faded. "Jenna? Are you okay?"

No, she was not. Jimmy had died in an accident at the lumber mill where he worked. She was twenty-four, a widow, and mother to a grieving four-year-old daughter. In addition, the last of Jimmy's personal belongings had just been sold at an auction barely a week after she'd buried him in the ground.

All she had left of her husband was the flannel shirt she'd tucked under her pillow and a heart full of memories. That was it. So she was far from okay.

But no one wanted to hear that.

"Yes, I'm fine," she lied. "Thank you for everything you've done. I'm grateful."

"It's what Jimmy would've wanted us to do," Atle said. "He would've hated it if no one was looking out for you."

"Yes." It felt as if she had cotton in her mouth. Talking was an effort.

Rebeccah fussed with the edge of her dress's apron as she continued to study Jenna's expression. "Where is Katie?"

"She is with Jimmy's parents. They took her home with them early." Katie had been bored and kept asking why everyone was playing with her father's tools.

"Oh. That was probably better."

"Jah." Realizing they were seeking a sign that she was all right so they could leave, Jenna cleared her throat. "It has been a long day. I . . . I think I'd like to lay down for a spell. If you don't mind."

Relief lit Atle's eyes. "Of course not. We should get on home ourselves."

"Indeed. Why, the kinner are probably wondering why I'm not working on supper." Rebeccah smiled at Jenna. "Children are always hungry."

Jenna folded her arms across her chest. Wished that she was wearing one of Jimmy's old sweatshirts over her dress like she used to do. He'd loved that.

So had she.

The couple turned around and at last walked to their buggy, which Atle had parked on her drive. Jenna watched Atle help Rebeccah in then loosen the horse's leads before climbing in as well.

Moments later, the horse was leading them toward the road. Jimmy's old coat, boots, and a set of screwdrivers were in the back of the buggy. Jenna had heard all of it was for their eldest son, who'd just turned sixteen.

Alone at last, Jenna scanned the area one last time. The tent that had been raised was gone. The tables holding refreshments had been put away. And, true to his word, Atle had made sure there wasn't a speck of trash to be seen. The field was empty.

Grateful to still be feeling numb, Jenna walked back up the five front-porch steps, through the entryway, and into the living room. It was dark and silent.

She lived in a cozy house. There was one sitting area, one dining area, and a serviceable kitchen on the bottom floor. Upstairs were two bedrooms and a bathroom. She and Jimmy used to joke that their house was big enough for three but far too small for four. He'd promised to add another room when she got pregnant again.

Now there wouldn't be a need for that.

For the first time, she wished Jimmy had gone ahead and built that extra bedroom they'd talked about. She hadn't been able to sleep in their bed yet. Instead, she rested as much as she could on the couch.

After slipping off her tennis shoes, Jenna unfolded an old quilt, wrapped it around herself, and lay down. Closed her eyes. Prayed for sleep.

It didn't come. Instead, she tried to think of something to look forward to. Maybe the first snow? A piece of her mother's pumpkin pie? Katie's darling chatter? She so loved to ask questions about things Jenna didn't know the answers to.

Jenna was still attempting to think of something to lift

her spirits when she heard footsteps on her porch. A pause and then, at last, two knocks on the door.

She didn't want to answer it but didn't want anyone to look in the window and see her lying on the couch either. People would talk.

Shaking her dress out as she hurried to the door, she tried not to care that her white kapp was likely wrinkled and crushed. She'd forgotten to unpin it before she lay down.

"Yes?" she asked as she pulled open the door and, far too belatedly, attempted to collect herself. "Oh. Mr. Harper! I'm sorry. Hello." Her cheeks heated. She knew better than to greet Jimmy's boss with such poor manners.

"It's Nelson, Jenna. Please." Before she could respond, he held up a paper bag with handles. The name of a fancy English grocery store was printed on the side. "I hope you don't mind, but I brought you a care package of sorts."

When Jenna reached for it, he shook his head. "Oh no. It's heavy. If you'll allow me, I'll put it on your kitchen counter."

She stepped backward to let him enter. "The kitchen is right over there." She cringed in embarrassment yet again. It was obvious where the kitchen was.

Without a word, Nelson carried the bag in, walked it to the counter, and then turned back to where Jenna stood in the doorway.

"There's chips, pretzels, dried fruit, chocolate, and a slice of apple spice cake." He frowned. "Oh, there's a coloring book, crayons, two cans of soda, and a magazine inside too."

The contents he listed were so random, Jenna was almost

tempted to smile. "All of that sounds very un-Amish-like, Nelson."

He looked down at his feet as he chuckled softly. "I took a guess and thought that there might come a day in the next week or so when the last thing you want is another casserole."

He was right. "That is thoughtful of you. Thank you for thinking of me."

Nelson met her gaze before averting his eyes yet again. "There's no need to thank me. You've been on my mind."

"Oh?"

"I mean because of the auction." Looking pained, he added, "I meant to say, I heard Jimmy's auction was today."

"It was."

His hazel eyes scanned her face. Seemed to see something he liked. "It's a relief to have it over, yes?" he asked in a gentle tone. "I mean, it's just a memory now, right?"

She nodded. "It is a relief. To be honest, I've been dreading this morning for days."

"I would feel the same way." In a soft voice, he added, "You'll be glad to not worry about it when you wake up tomorrow morning."

"I imagine so."

Nelson scanned her face again. Swallowed. "Well . . . I should let you go." After shooting her a soft, sad smile, he turned and headed down the steps.

"Wait. Ah, Nelson, was that the only reason you came by? To drop off the food?"

Turning to face her, he shook his head. "No. I wanted

to check on you too. I know you aren't okay, but I wanted to make sure that auction didn't get the best of you."

"Thank you for thinking of me."

Pure compassion filled his features before he seemed to collect himself again. "Please take care, Jenna. And remember, if you need anything—*anything* at all—I'm just a phone call away."

"I won't forget."

He smiled at her again before he got in his big gray truck and started the ignition.

She watched him carefully turn his vehicle around then head back down the drive.

After she closed the door, lay back down, and stared off into nothing once again, Jenna realized that at long last, she'd found something to look forward to.

Nelson had been right. The auction was no longer looming in the distance. It was over. Tomorrow might feel a little bit easier than today.

It wasn't much, but it was enough.

chapter one

NINETEEN MONTHS LATER
MAY

Jenna and Katie had developed a routine of sorts. Every morning after Jenna got up, got dressed, and had a cup of coffee, she would get Katie out of bed. They'd have breakfast together and she'd walk her five-year-old to the Amish school a little less than a mile away. After placing her precious daughter into the care of Miss Trudy, she'd go for a walk.

Sometimes she'd stop at the grocer's and get a few basics. Sometimes she'd take a walk in the park or stop into the library. Most of the time, however, Jenna would go home, make two beds, run a dustcloth over things that were already clean, and write letters.

For some reason—she wasn't quite sure why—she had always been a prolific letter writer. She'd had four pen pals for almost ten years. They were from all walks of life, and they lived all over the world. One lived in Germany, another was a missionary in Mexico, yet another was a widow who lived in Pinecraft, and the last was a teacher in England. Three were women, one was a man. Only two of them were Amish. They were all different ages too. Sometimes she thought that the only thing she had in common with them all was the fact that they enjoyed writing letters as much as she did.

That didn't matter to Jenna. What did was the fact that they'd become part of her lifeline since Jimmy had passed on to heaven.

Well, their correspondence and Nelson Harper's visits once a week.

No matter how many times she'd tried to tell Nelson that he wasn't responsible for Jimmy's death and surely didn't need to bring her care packages, he still did. He'd also provided her with a sounding board when she hinted that she was thinking about selling her chickens and cows. Not only had he agreed with her desire to simplify her life and buy milk and eggs at the store, but he'd also helped her sell the animals and the henhouse.

"You are going to be okay," she whispered to herself as she fixed herself a cup of hot tea and walked to her writing desk. Jimmy had built it for her when they were engaged. He never completely understood her need for her pen pals, but he'd loved her enough to give her a place to organize her letters and write everyone back.

When the morning's mail delivery brought her not one but two letters, Jenna hurriedly made the beds before sitting at her desk and opening Liam's letter from Germany.

Hello Jenna!

I hope this note finds you well. How are you en-

joying your store-bought eggs? I shared all the news about your henhouse sale with Annabelle and she asked me to convey her best wishes. She thinks you should put the money toward a plane flight here. Ha! I can practically see you shaking your head in wonder. I understand how you feel. My Annabelle keeps forgetting about you not being able to get on an airplane. If your circumstances ever change, however, please keep us first on your list.

So . . . are you ready to hear about the latest happenings at the office?

Jenna giggled as Liam continued his chatty, breezy note, filling her in on gossipy coworkers, a problem he'd had with one of his clients, and finally a story about their son Mark, who was in high school.

When she folded the note again, Jenna realized that she was smiling. She wasn't surprised. Liam's letters from Germany usually did inspire good feelings. He seemed like such a kind man, and his dear, ditzy Annabelle reminded her in many ways of Jimmy. Jimmy had never been ditzy, but he did seem to be blissfully ignorant of the things that were out of his comfort zone. He never completely understood how Jenna could be friends with someone who she would likely never meet in person.

She supposed he had a point, but it didn't matter to her. She enjoyed Liam's letters tremendously and felt as if they were good friends. Just because their friendship was an untraditional one didn't mean it was wrong.

She'd just started to open the second letter when she heard two raps at her door.

Was Nelson already paying her a call? Excited about the possibility, she hurried to the door and opened it up.

And saw Doreen Beachy standing on her front stoop with a jar of peanut butter fluff in one hand and a rather weighty-looking purse in the other.

"Hi there, Jenna," she said in a bright tone. "I was hoping you'd answer. Now I can give you this. Here." She thrust the jar of peanut butter fluff into Jenna's hands.

Jenna clutched it to her chest so she wouldn't drop it.

Doreen beamed. "I'm so glad it's in your hands and out of mine. I've been carrying around this stuff for two days."

Jenna wasn't sure which was odder, Doreen showing up or her presentation of the large jar of fluff. As one second passed into two, she remembered her voice. "Danke?"

Doreen laughed heartily. It made the tails of her kapp swing with motion. "You have every right to be confused about my gift, but don't worry. I didn't make it. I bought it at Wolf's."

"The market?" For some reason, she felt as if she was a beat behind.

"None other," Doreen said as she walked right inside and closed the door behind her. "I hope you won't mind if I come in for a few minutes."

"Nee. I mean, not at all."

"Danke. I promise I won't stay long."

Feeling as if she was a guest in her own house, Jenna followed Doreen into the living room. As she stood beside the little desk where she'd been sitting, the space looked stark and empty. Kind of how her heart had been for the last year and a half.

Doreen seemed to take in everything that Jenna was

experiencing within a few scant minutes. She didn't sit down. "When was the last time you relaxed, dear? When was the last time you sat down on this couch and put your feet up?"

Her feet up? "I don't know," Jenna admitted before the memory returned. "It was the last time my in-laws came over. It was Katie's birthday." She actually hadn't taken off her shoes and propped her feet on the edge of the coffee table until their buggy was out of sight. But there was no need to share that.

"She turned five, I think?"

"Jah." She was surprised that Doreen knew such a thing. The woman lived on her own so far out that she joined several different church districts throughout the year for services. It was all very irregular, but Doreen seemed to be the type of person who never arrived empty-handed and always had a smile for other people. She was well-liked.

They'd certainly never been close, though.

The woman's startling hazel eyes darted her way. "Would you mind if I suggested we visit in your kitchen after all? It's your choice, of course, but I've always considered kitchen visits to be the coziest."

"Nee, I wouldn't mind." She led the way into the kitchen, mentally thanking herself for wiping the counters after she'd finished washing the morning dishes. "The kettle is warm. I could make some coffee. Or perhaps you'd rather have tea?"

"Kaffi would be welcome. Even though it's May, the weather still seems to think winter just passed."

"Jah. It is chilly out today." Fussing with the percolator, she emptied the old grounds, added fresh ones, and poured in cool water. When she placed it on the stove, it began to brew. "It will be done in a few moments."

"I reckon so." Doreen's voice gentled. "Have a seat, child. I don't want to cause you any worries."

Jenna did as she asked, though she was beginning to feel more than a little impatient. Doreen's "quick" visit didn't feel very quick at all. She wished she'd get to the point so she could go back to her letters. "Is there something I might be able to help you with?"

"Perhaps." After studying Jenna's face for another moment, Doreen opened her handbag, pulled out a card, and placed it on the table.

Curious, Jenna picked it up and read the inscription.

Amish Widows Club

She looked at Doreen in confusion. "I'm afraid I don't understand."

"I started this group almost fifteen years ago, dear. It's comprised of Amish and Mennonite women of all ages and backgrounds. We meet every so often at each other's houses or at a mutually agreeable place, such as the back room of a store or in a town library. When we get together, we foster friendship."

"Foster friendship?" It had a nice ring to it, but she wasn't very interested.

Doreen waved a hand. "Sometimes widows feel pressured to marry again because they are lonely."

"I don't want to marry again." She'd loved Jimmy.

"I understand. But not everyone in a widow's life understands what we are going through. In our club, you can cry or share frustrations or laugh or be however you would like to be. No one will judge you." She smiled softly. "I think you would be an excellent addition."

"Thank you, but I don't know . . ."

"Oh?"

"Yes. You see . . . I already have friends. And family." She had her parents and Jimmy's parents. And Katie. She also had all of her pen pals. And Nelson too. "I am not lonely."

"I'd like some kaffi now."

Becoming even more frustrated with her unexpected guest, Jenna stood up, poured two cups of coffee, added a small carton of cream and a jar of sugar to a tray, and carried it all to the table. With an ease she'd perfected in the six months after Jimmy's death when she'd had callers almost daily, Jenna placed the cup and saucer, napkin, and teaspoon in front of Doreen and then did the same with her own place setting.

Doreen sipped the coffee. "Goodness. This is a wonderful cup of coffee, dear."

"Danke."

"What coffee brand do you use?"

She realized then that she got a package of coffee from Nelson almost once a month. "I'm not sure. A friend gives me a package of coffee from time to time."

After taking another sip from her cup, Doreen set it on the kitchen table. "Well, next time you get a package, keep the container. I'd love to get some for myself. It is that good."

"Yes. I mean, I'll be happy to do that."

Doreen smiled at her as she finished her cup. Glanced at it longingly.

"May I get you another cup?"

"As much as I'd love one, I better not." Her eyes lit up. "Next thing you know, I'll be having to use the restroom. We can't have that."

Jenna blinked but said nothing.

Tapping the card with one finger, Doreen added, "My only wish is to bring you comfort and support, dear Jenna. We could all use a little bit more of that, ain't so?"

"Yes."

Looking pleased, Doreen stood up. "If you change your mind, flip the card over. It will tell you how to find the next meeting."

"Thank you for letting me know," Jenna said as politely as she was able as she followed Doreen back to the front door.

Holding the door handle, the older woman looked back at her. "If I approach you next time our paths cross at church, please don't worry. If I come up to you, I'll likely only be hoping to get that coffee brand's name. It really is delicious."

"I'll look forward to telling you about it."

Doreen chuckled as she opened the door. "Wishing you many blessings today, dear Jenna. Oh! And enjoy that peanut butter fluff! Good day!"

"Jah. Um, gut matin."

But Doreen was already halfway down the front walkway. It was unlikely she'd heard Jenna's reply.

In fact, she never even looked back. A couple of minutes later, the woman was out of sight.

Relieved to close the door and return to her correspondence, Jenna walked into the living room. Then the kitchen. Except for some new dishes in the sink and a very large jar of fluff decorating the counter, everything was still and silent. Almost empty.

Why, it was almost as if no one had come over at all.

It was all so strange.

chapter two

Nelson Harper figured he was the only person in the state of Ohio who looked forward to Mondays. So much so, he sometimes found himself pacing on Sunday evenings as his impatience got the best of him.

The thing of it was, he wasn't a workaholic. Not anything close to that. He loved his job. Alliance Millworks was his family's pride and joy. It had been started by his grandfather, was handed down to his father and uncle to run, and now it was in his hands.

His father and uncle had handed it over to him to run about ten years ago. His mother wanted to see all the national parks and even visit Disneyland and Universal Studios in California. Dad had confided that he thought she'd waited long enough to take all the vacations she'd dreamed about, and Nelson didn't disagree. He wanted his parents to take some time off and relax while they were still young enough to enjoy themselves.

Though every day wasn't easy, Nelson felt well prepared to run the business. He'd worked there in some capacity from the time he was old enough to sweep floors and wipe down the office furniture.

Aside from Jimmy's accident—which he still had nightmares about—Nelson was happy to go to work on Monday mornings and continue to do his part for the mill and his family's legacy.

But the reason he looked forward to Mondays was because of what he did on Monday evenings at five thirty. That was when he paid a call on Jenna and Katie Graber.

Once a week, he'd bring them a box filled with items that he thought they would enjoy. Fresh fruit. A package of chicken on sale. Flowers. A new coloring book or stuffed animal for Katie. Once, he'd even brought Jenna five yards of pretty pink fabric. Jenna had flushed with pleasure when she ran a hand along the smooth cloth before attempting to hand it back.

Only when he said that a relative had been about to toss it in the ragbag did she go ahead and keep it. Later, she admitted that she'd made both a spring dress and a set of curtains for Katie's room out of it.

Nelson was pretty sure that he'd been as happy about that as little Katie had been. He loved making Jenna's life brighter.

It was only when he was by himself late in the night that Nelson admitted he had selfish reasons for continually looking out for Jenna and her daughter. Every time he did something that made Jenna smile, it alleviated some of the guilt he felt about Jimmy's death.

Sure, more than a handful of men at the plant had respectfully shared their opinions on Jimmy's accident. Lots of the guys had said Jimmy Graber was impatient. He was also a talker and, at times, didn't pay as much careful attention to the machines as he should have. He was also too cocky. There were guidelines for operating the planer, and the most important one was that men needed to work in pairs. Jimmy had ignored that rule on the day he died. The guys had privately confided that Jimmy could've done a lot of things differently that day.

Nelson didn't disagree.

However, it was still one of the plant's machines that he'd been using. Someone had to take the blame, and Nelson had accepted that it would be him—even though he'd gotten every machine reviewed and checked just weeks before Jimmy's death.

So he'd accepted the blame and did his best never to say a word that wasn't respectful about Jimmy to anyone outside of the company. Not to Jimmy's parents and not to Jimmy's widow.

Nelson was at peace about that too. Even if Jimmy could've handled things differently, it didn't change Jenna's reality, which was that she'd become a widow at twenty-four, and her sweet little daughter, Katie, was growing up without her dad.

Hating to think about that as he pulled up to Jenna's house, Nelson shook his head a bit to clear it, got out of his truck, and lifted a box into his arms.

He was bringing something special today.

Jenna's door opened before he was halfway there. But it wasn't Jenna's pretty face peering through the screen door. No, it was little Katie instead. Katie, who he'd nicknamed "Kitty" when she was pretending to be a barn cat one afternoon when he'd decided to sweep their barn floor.

"Hiya, Nelson!"

"Hiya, Kitty," he replied to her through the screen. "How are you today?"

She wrinkled her nose. "It's evening, Nelson. Because it's after five o'clock."

"Goodness." He looked up at the sky and frowned. "I suppose it is."

"Mei teacher taught us all about the proper greetings this morning," she explained with a bit of self-important flair. "On account of Cale telling her 'good afternoon' when it was only a quarter past eleven."

It all sounded rather picky, but who was he to say? Sometimes Nelson had to remind himself what day of the week it was. "My, aren't we growing up?" he teased.

"Uh-huh. Hey, what's in the box?"

"Something special." In fact, his "something special" had just taken that moment to mew. He needed to get it out onto solid ground before it got too restless.

Katie's eyes widened. "What is it?"

"I'm sorry, but I can't tell you that without your mother being here." He tilted his head in a half-baked attempt to see past her. "Where is she?"

"In the kitchen."

"Nee, Katie. I'm right here!" Jenna called out as she hurried toward them.

Today Jenna was wearing a gray dress that still hung loose on her. He knew it well. She'd worn it several of the times he'd visited.

He'd never liked it. The shade seemed to wash out any hint of color from her face, and it didn't fit well. She once told him she'd made it when she had gained a little bit of weight when Katie turned three. As she mourned her husband, it hung looser and looser on her frame.

Now it fit slightly better but was rather the worse for wear. Nelson didn't know if she kept wearing it because it was comfortable, because she didn't care how she looked anymore, or because she couldn't afford to make herself new clothes. He hoped it was the first reason.

Jenna's eyes widened as she got closer. "Katie, you haven't let our guest in yet?"

"Nee, Mamm. You said I wasn't supposed to."

"Jah, but this is our friend Nelson," she chided.

"I'm glad she waited for you, Jenna," he interrupted quickly. "That's safer, I think."

"I suppose . . ."

"Look, Mamm!" Katie chirped. "Nelson brought us a big box."

"Oh my word. It looks heavy. Move out of the way, child." Jenna reached for the door handle and ushered him inside. "Nelson, I'm sorry you had to wait."

"No reason to apologize."

She frowned as she looked down at the front of her dress. "Obviously, I was making bread."

"Obviously?"

Jenna waved a hand across her front. "Look at me! I'm practically covered in flour."

"Covered" was a bit of a strong way to describe her state. She did have some dabs of flour on her dress. "I hadn't noticed."

She chuckled. "Nelson Harper, what am I going to do with you?"

His heart skipped a beat. "What do you mean by that?"

"It means that when you start dating one of the Englisher girls in earnest, she's gonna get her feelings hurt when you don't notice things like that."

"That's not going to be a problem because I'm not dating any Englisher girl at the moment." Especially not in earnest. Especially not since he couldn't seem to focus on anything besides Jenna.

To his chagrin.

"*Meew.*"

Jenna narrowed her eyes. "What was that?"

"Your surprise."

Katie jumped up and down. "Nelson, that sounds like a kitty."

He finally set the box down. "Do you think so?"

"Jah." She nodded her head. "I heard it meow."

"I don't know, Katie. Are you sure? The only Kitty I know talks a mile a minute," he teased.

Lifting one of the box's flaps, he murmured, "We should probably see what's inside, though." When he peered down, the sweet face of a black-and-white kitten stared back at him from its little bed. "Well. My goodness. Would you look at that?"

As he'd hoped, Katie edged closer, then finally curved her fingertips around the edge. She looked in and then turned to her mama with a slack-jawed expression. "There's a kitten in there!"

"Truly?" Jenna peered in. "Oh! Aren't you sweet?" Before Nelson could offer to reach for the cat himself, Jenna bent down and lifted it out. "So precious and tiny," she whispered.

When she straightened, the kitten was curled in her arms like it had finally come home.

"Mamm, I think it likes you," Katie said.

"I reckon kittens like everyone, don't you?" Jenna glanced at Nelson before smiling down at her daughter.

"Maybe," he said. "I'm not sure."

Katie was still gazing at the kitten with wonder. "Can I touch it?" she asked.

"You may, but let's sit down first," Jenna answered.

The moment Jenna sat down on the couch, Katie scrambled next to her. And the kitten . . . well, it raised a paw and batted at Jenna's hand before doing the same with Katie.

Katie's laughter rang out like a beautiful chime, bringing much-needed happiness into the room. And to his heart. He was right. This tiny kitten was just what Jenna and Katie needed.

Still standing at a distance, Nelson continued to smile as he watched both Katie and Jenna focus completely on the cat. It was obvious that the three of them had already formed a connection.

After playing with the kitten for a few moments, Katie whispered, "Nelson, who's the kitten for?"

The hint of wonder—and worry—in her voice made his heart break. This little girl was far too young to already be preparing herself for disappointment. "It's for you and your mother, Katie."

Her eyes were wide when she turned to look at him. "You brought us our very own cat?"

Almost afraid to meet Jenna's eyes, Nelson nodded. "A worker of mine found a stray mother cat and her kittens on his property. He found a home for the mama cat and the other two kittens. There was just this little guy left. He needed a home." Feeling more awkward as each second passed, he finished up the story. "So, I got to thinking that maybe you two wouldn't mind giving it one."

"Nelson," Jenna chided. "This is mighty kind of you but not necessary."

Ah, but there was a wealth of unsaid words in her tone. Words about him overstepping. Offering Katie a pet without thinking of consequences.

Maybe simply just making a general nuisance of himself.

But he refused to feel guilty. Not when Katie's eyes were lit up and happiness glowed in her cheeks. He'd do a lot to see such a sight.

"I know bringing it here without asking you first was a bit cheeky, but maybe you wouldn't mind having it? After all, kittens aren't that much work." When Jenna narrowed her eyes, he blurted, "Not compared to a puppy."

"It really likes my mamm." Katie's eyes widened. "And it licked me with its scratchy tongue!" Turning to her mother, the little girl's eyes looked worried. "I bet this kitten wouldn't be too hard to take care of. He's tiny too."

"Kittens grow, child," Jenna murmured. But she was petting it while she was talking.

"If he caught a mouse, that would be *wunderbar*!" Katie exclaimed.

Jenna grimaced. "If this cat caught a mouse, I'd have to deal with it."

"Maybe not. Maybe we could call Nelson to come over." Turning to him, Katie blurted, "You'd do that, right, Nelson? You'd come right over if we needed ya?"

"Of course I would." Jenna and Katie had no idea how much he meant that. He'd drop anything he was doing if one of them called him in a panic.

Katie smiled. "See, Mamm?"

After meeting Nelson's gaze, Jenna turned back to Katie. "I suppose a kitten might not be a bad addition to our haus." She lowered her voice. "But he is a living, breathing little animal. You would have to help take care of it."

"I will."

"Even if I ask you to help me clean up its litter box?"

Katie nodded solemnly, which was the cutest thing Nelson had ever seen.

"Are you sure, Katie?"

"Oh, yes. I love her!" Katie pronounced before doubt filled her expression all over again. "Or is it a *him*, Nelson?"

"I think it's a *he*, Kitty. He's a little boy cat."

"Does he have a name?"

"Nope. It's up to you and your mom to take care of that. That is, if you want to keep him . . . unless one of you is allergic to cats or something."

"Nee. I'm stunned and surprised . . . but not allergic." Turning to her daughter, Jenna softened her expression. "I don't think I could give this kitten up even if he did make us sneeze. Katie already looks besotted."

"I think so too," he agreed. "I had hoped you'd want him, so I got everything you'd need. I'll be right back."

After he went back out to his truck and retrieved the other items he'd brought, they set up the litter box and left Katie alone in the living room with the kitten.

Nelson carried the other items into the kitchen and then took a seat at the table while he watched Jenna put them away.

As always, Jenna seemed grateful for the gifts, but there was a new shadow in her eyes that hadn't been there before. Nelson feared he'd just crossed a line.

Maybe he'd just made things even more awkward between them. But if he had? If he had, he had no idea how to go about mending the rift without making things worse.

Which was too bad.

The sad thing was that while Jenna thought he was spending too much time and money on her, he knew he was doing a lot of it for himself. Visiting her and Katie was the highlight of his week. Jenna and Katie made him smile. He enjoyed their company. Helping to make their lives a little bit easier made him happy.

Sweeping her barn floor or shoveling a snow-covered driveway made him feel useful.

All of it gave him something to think about besides work.

Being around "his girls" gave him something to dream about, even though he shouldn't.

While Jenna moved around the kitchen, Nelson continued to sit. He sipped his glass of water, tried to look like he was relaxed, and bided his time. He was a patient man and knew if he gave Jenna enough time to gather her thoughts, she'd tell him everything that was on her mind.

When she sat back down at the table ten minutes later, she had a cup of coffee and a plate of scotcheroos in her hands. The chocolatey peanut butter concoction smelled incredible. "Please have one," she murmured.

"Thank you." He placed one on a napkin and put it in front of himself, but he didn't dare take a bite.

He didn't want to do anything until he heard what Jenna had to say. He didn't think it was going to be anything good either. Her expression looked slightly pinched.

At last, she took a deep breath, exhaled, and then turned slightly so that they were facing each other. "Nelson, I think we need to talk."

"All right." He folded his hands in his lap so she wouldn't see them clench. "I'm listening."

And tried to prepare himself for whatever was about to come next.

chapter three

Nelson was staring at her. Waiting for her to speak. Jenna drew in a breath, determined to say what was on her mind. But then, as she so often did these days, she hesitated.

As always, Nelson's unusually colored eyes caught her attention. They were a perfect blend of brown, caramel, and green, framed by thick, dark eyelashes. She was sure he would be mighty embarrassed if she ever told him that she thought his eyes were beautiful. Nelson wasn't one for receiving compliments. Not about his looks and not about his actions.

If he were a different type of man, maybe the topic she was struggling to bring up would be easier.

Instead, she felt like she'd rather have rocks in her mouth. If she did, they'd be far easier to spit out than the words she was trying to say.

But who could blame her?

For the past couple of weeks, Mary and Peter, Jenna's in-laws, had been asking about Nelson. The questions had become more pointed and their confusion about the friendship was becoming more pronounced.

At first, she'd defended Nelson's short visits. Ever since she held the auction for Jimmy's belongings, she'd been struggling. She missed Jimmy and she missed her life with him. Their little house felt too big, and even Katie's needs felt overwhelming. Nelson's visits had been a lifeline for her, especially since he'd gone above and beyond mere kindness time and again. How could anyone ever find fault with that?

But lately she'd been starting to wonder if maybe Mary and Peter had a point. Nelson had been Jimmy's boss. He was English. He was several years older than her. They had nothing in common. And Jenna realized that she was starting to depend on Nelson too much.

Sure, they were friends, but she and Nelson didn't go together.

That notion had cemented itself when she gathered up the boxes of wax paper, foil, plastic bags, and plastic wrap he'd so generously brought for her tonight. The problem wasn't that he was bringing her gifts, it was that her first reaction was gratitude and happiness.

It was almost like she expected him to stop by on Monday nights. She now looked forward to seeing him. Katie did too.

She was becoming too used to his good deeds. Too dependent on him. That wasn't right. After all, she was a grown woman who was raising a child. If she could learn how to pay her bills and manage their piece of land, she should be able to figure out how to stop being so emotionally dependent on him.

Worse, she realized that theirs was a one-sided relationship. Nelson Harper continually gave to her. He gave his time, his gifts, and his patience. She, on the other hand, just took and took. Jenna felt bad about that, but the truth was that she didn't have much to reciprocate.

Nothing besides her gratitude. But that wasn't enough. It wasn't like he needed a quilt or a new shirt or a meal. Compared to the things he brought, she had nothing worthwhile to give to him in return.

Or . . . was he feeling guilty about Jimmy and deciding to do his penance by looking after her for the rest of his life? That wasn't right. Even though Mary and Peter had more than once hinted that they thought Nelson was at fault, Jenna had never thought that. Two workers at the plant had written her notes to say that Jimmy's death had been nothing more than an awful accident. Who was she to argue about that? She would continue to believe that the Lord had a reason for calling Jimmy to heaven so early.

But no matter why Nelson was so kind to her, she realized that it had been a mistake to encourage him so much.

And now he'd brought Katie a kitten. The way her little girl gazed at Nelson was filled with love. She was starting to love Nelson. Jenna knew it wasn't because of his gifts. It was because of his smiles. It was because he listened to her. He kept her company for an hour or so on Monday nights. He made sure Katie knew that she was important to him.

That was all well and good, but what would Katie do when Nelson started a relationship with another woman? When he started courting an English woman and fell in love? No doubt his visits to Jenna and Katie would be over.

Nee, Jenna, she silently told herself. *What will you do when Nelson moves on?*

Even thinking about the possibility made her want to weep, which was a problem in itself. She needed some distance. Maybe they both did.

"Jenna," Nelson prodded, bringing her back to the present. "Whatever you need to tell me is okay. I'll listen and do what you want."

"Pardon me?"

"You don't need to worry about measuring your words around me. I'd rather you were honest instead of polite."

"I am hoping to be both things." But was that even possible? How could she be completely forthright without hurting his feelings?

Nelson leaned forward, resting his elbows on his knees. This evening he was wearing dark jeans, boots, and a bright-white oxford shirt over a white undershirt. The sleeves of the oxford were rolled up on his forearms, revealing an early tan. She wondered how he'd managed that. Of course, neither his clothing nor his tan could compare to his eyes.

Yet again, she felt transfixed. They were the most expressive eyes she'd ever seen. It was as if every single thing he was thinking could be seen from just one look.

So different from Jimmy's dark features, which she'd never been able to easily read. Of course, one didn't need to read his thoughts through an expression anyway. Jimmy had never had a problem with speaking his mind.

"Jenna, just tell me." Impatience tinged every word.

"Okay." She glanced again to make sure Katie wasn't listening. "I'm worried about our relationship."

"What are you worried about?"

"I am afraid that you are doing too much for me and

Katie." When he shook his head, she added, "Nelson, our relationship isn't equal."

"What are you talking about?" His voice had turned clipped. Irritated.

It took her off guard. Feeling a little less sure of herself, Jenna tried to explain. "You are doing all the giving. I don't have anything to give in return."

"I disagree."

He looked so adamant, she made herself mention the thing that Peter and Mary liked to insinuate. The thing that she'd never actually believed yet couldn't completely ignore.

"I am afraid that you, for some reason, feel responsible for Jimmy's accident and have decided to make amends."

Surprise lit his features before he quickly shut it down. "Jenna, you are a widow with a young child. Jimmy died suddenly, and it's not a secret that he didn't leave you much in the way of savings."

He was right. Even though it wasn't her fault, she looked away before forcing herself to remind Nelson about what his company had done. "Alliance Millworks gave me a check, Nelson. A settlement. That was enough. You don't have to keep trying to make things better."

"By doing what? Bringing you a couple of rolls of foil and wax paper? Come on."

"You've done more than that. Why, you brought us a cat today."

"Do you really believe I think a kitten could replace Jimmy?" He lowered his voice. "Is that what you think of me?" Nelson's words dripped with pain. He looked so hurt too.

"Of course not," she said quickly.

"Forgive me, but it sounded like it."

He was so very mad. Ouch. "Nelson, this is why I was so worried about broaching this subject. I think you are a good man. I think you are one of the best men I know."

He stood up. "Then what's the problem?"

"The problem is me, Nelson, not you. I'm taking and taking from you. I'm taking your gifts, and I'm taking your time."

"Everything you are taking, I am giving you willingly."

"But I am getting used to it. I've become used to you being the person we can count on, Nelson." Even though her face was no doubt flaming, she forced herself to continue. "I'm afraid that if we don't take a step back, then I'm going to count on you too much."

"I don't think that's possible."

"Too much means that I will get so used to you, I won't be able to do much of anything without you."

His eyes darkened before he seemed to catch himself. "I'm okay with that."

She laughed, sure he was teasing her.

But he wasn't smiling. He was looking at her pointedly. "I wasn't joking, Jenna. I've never given you anything in order to get something in return. Your company is gift enough for me."

A shiver rushed up Jenna's spine as a new awareness of him settled into her heart. It made her uncomfortable. She never thought she'd think about another man for the rest of her life.

But it seemed she'd been wrong about that.

Desperate, she clung to Doreen Beachy's recent visit.

She hadn't been very excited about attending widows club meetings, but maybe they were exactly what she needed. If she went to those, she would give herself a safety net. She could focus on something besides seeing Nelson once a week.

She could make friends with other women. And maybe those friendships would lessen Nelson's appeal in her life.

If that happened, it would be a good thing. A very good thing. Her heart would be safe.

"Nelson, I'm sorry, but I think I'm going to be a little busier from now on. I've decided to join a women's group."

"What kind of group is that?"

She wasn't sure. "It's just a group for widows who don't want to marry again."

He blinked. "You are twenty-six years old, Jenna."

"I know."

He still looked incredulous. "You have your whole life ahead of you. I know you miss Jimmy, but I can't help but think that he would never have wanted you to spend the rest of your life alone."

"I won't be alone. I have my family. And Katie. And I'll have these women."

"So, what are you saying? That I can't even come over on Monday nights?"

"I think it would be best if you didn't."

He visibly flinched. As if she'd just slapped him.

Suddenly, she felt like maybe she had. She'd just pushed him away, and he'd done nothing but be wonderful to her and Katie.

"That didn't come out the way I intended, Nelson. Of course, I meant that I'll have your friendship too."

"I hope you mean that, Jenna. Because you do, you know. You have me, no matter what. I'm not going to abandon you now."

Something inside her eased, which was wrong. She wasn't supposed to be so clingy.

"Thank you for the kitten. It was very kind of you."

"You're welcome. I'll say bye to Katie, and then I'll leave."

"You don't have to rush away." She'd handled all of this so wrong!

"Yeah, I'm afraid I do. See you later, Jenna."

She stood up slowly but didn't move as she watched him walk over to see Katie.

Her little girl beamed up at him.

His expression tender, Nelson crouched on the floor, pet the kitten, and smiled at what Katie said. Then, after a playful tug on one of her curls, he said goodbye.

Minutes later, Nelson let himself out of her house.

He didn't look back before shutting the door.

She carefully walked to the front window and watched him get into his large, gray truck, sit for a moment, then start the ignition and drive off.

It felt like he'd taken a piece of her heart with him.

Funny.

She hadn't thought she had any pieces of her heart left.

—*chapter* four

"Everything okay, boss?" Fanny, Nelson's personal assistant, asked as he entered the office in the back of Alliance Millworks on Tuesday morning.

He slowed his steps. No, he wasn't doing okay. He was still reeling from Jenna's words the night before. He wasn't going to share that, though. Instead, he hoped and prayed there was a major crisis that he had to deal with.

Okay, maybe he didn't need a major crisis. Something minor would be enough to get his mind off his hurt feelings. "As far as I know, everything's going well. Good enough. Why?"

"Because you look like you either got stung by a bee or missed out on your usual pot of coffee," she replied with a hand on her hip.

Fanny was never one to pull punches. When he first hired her, he was a little shocked about how outspoken she was, but he supposed he should've been prepared for it. After all, Fanny wasn't just his PA, she was his cousin.

Now he kind of looked forward to her banter. She kept him on his toes and made him laugh. In addition, her straight-to-the-point observations were usually right on the money. If something wasn't going right at Alliance, she'd tell him.

Unfortunately, today was no exception. He hadn't thought he looked that bad when he got ready for work that morning. He'd hoped his hurt pride was carefully hidden. Obviously, he was wrong.

"I look that bad, huh?"

"Yep."

"Thanks for letting me know," he called out as he strode across the reception area.

Just as he was about to enter his office, Fanny called out to him again. "What's wrong, boss?"

She might be his cousin and astute about a lot of things, but that didn't mean he was in a hurry to share his personal problems with her. "Nothing you need to worry about. But . . . thanks for asking."

"Thanks for asking?"

Great. Now she was in a snit. "Fan, stop."

She glared at him. "Just for the record, I thought you were going to try to call me by my given name from now on."

"No, I said I'd think about it."

"And?"

"And I did. But I just can't do it. I've been calling you Fanny my entire life."

"Frances sounds much better."

He didn't think so. "I'll try and remember to call you that more often."

"That's what you said last month."

"I know."

"Nelson, come on. You promised."

It was hard, but he was able to not grin. "For the record, I actually never *promised* to call you Frances. Only that I heard your request." The truth was that Nelson didn't like calling her Frances. It was a mouthful and didn't suit her. "I don't know why you hate Fanny. We've all been calling you that for most of your life."

"Stop. You are way too old to pretend that you don't know that 'fanny' is what some people call their . . . backside."

He couldn't help it, he burst out laughing. "Frances, if you're going to find fault with being called Fanny, then you shouldn't be afraid to at least say 'bottom.' Or 'butt.'"

She groaned. "Just stop calling me Fanny so we never have to have this discussion again."

"This means a lot to you, doesn't it?"

"Kind of." She lifted her chin. "I'm twenty-eight, Nelson. I'm not a kid. Plus, I have a very important job being your personal assistant. All that means that I grew up and I need a grown-up name."

"Fine. I can't argue with you there. Now, moving on . . . do I have any messages?"

"Yep. I talked to three people at Welco Trucking about an incoming shipment and a"—she looked down at her notebook—"Mr. Arias about his order."

Nelson frowned. Hank Arias had hired Alliance Millworks to finish out several of the rooms in his mansion with hand-carved custom cabinetry and trim. He was one of their most important clients at the moment. If he loved their work, it was going to open a lot of doors for them throughout the entire Midwest. "Does he have a problem?"

"I don't think so. It was more a matter of him being excited about all the work Big John's going to be doing in his house."

"Okay, good."

"He left you a phone number."

"I'll call him first. Thanks."

She smiled. "You're welcome." She tapped her fingers against her thigh. "I also went into your office and finished unpacking the last of the samples you ordered and put them on the back table with all the cards next to each."

He hated doing stuff like that, and she knew it. He was beyond blessed to have her by his side. "Once again, you've made my life way better. Thanks, Fa—I mean, Frances."

"You're welcome." She looked embarrassed. That was his cousin.

He loved his uncle, but her father had always been too hard on her. He hadn't been there for Fanny when she needed him most and had even gone so far as to ask Nelson not to hire her. Nelson hadn't wanted to start a family argument, but he wasn't willing to hurt Fanny's feelings just because Uncle Darien didn't want to listen to his daughter. "I mean it. I'm really glad I hired you."

"Thanks, but you don't need to say that."

"I think differently."

Taking the messages she'd written down, he was about to enter his office when she called out, "Are you sure you don't want to tell me what's wrong?"

"Yep. It's personal. Not work."

"I know, that's why I'm asking." She leaned against her desk. "I probably know more about how things are going around here than you do . . . and I know that everything here is great." Turning more serious, she added, "Nelson, you've got to talk to someone, right?"

He sighed. As much as he wanted to ignore her words and hide in his office, he was pretty sure she had a point. "Jenna asked me to stop visiting her on Monday evenings."

"Why?" Fanny looked just as surprised as he felt, which gave him some amount of comfort.

"I don't know. She gave me a lot of reasons, but I think it's that I got on her nerves."

A line formed between her brows. "Are you sure?"

"I'm pretty sure. I don't know what I did that bothered her so much." He shrugged. "Maybe I was trying too hard to be her friend?"

"No one gets upset when a friend tries their best to make them happy."

Nelson wasn't all that sure about that. "In any case, she asked me to stop coming over."

"After you got her a kitten?" she asked with a new thread of outrage in her voice.

"I got Katie the kitten, but yeah. Even after that."

"That seems hurtful."

"I don't think she thought it was. I guess I shouldn't have done it."

His cousin stared at him for a long moment. "Do you think she's still missing Jimmy?" she asked in a quiet voice.

"Probably. But I wasn't trying to take his place, Fan. Nothing like that." He drew a breath. "I . . . I was just trying to be her friend. And, you know, make sure she had everything she needed." Okay, maybe he'd been secretly hoping for something more one day. But that was his problem, not Jenna's. He would've never pushed that on her.

After glancing at the door, Frances said, "Do you ever think that Jenna should know exactly what happened the day of Jimmy's accident?"

Glimpses of Jimmy's brash words, his cocky grin, his impatience . . . the way more than one person on the line was always annoyed with his attitude . . . bloomed fresh.

No matter how hard he tried to lock the memories away, he never completely succeeded. Like always, he shut them down as quickly as he could. Remembering faults of the past didn't change how people viewed the present.

"You know, it could be that Jenna is imagining you're partly to blame for Jimmy's accident, but nothing could be further from the truth. He's the one—"

"Stop, Fanny. I'm sorry. I know you mean well, but I think that talking about the accident feels wrong. It's over." Nelson didn't want to relive that awful day.

She folded her arms over her chest. "I'm sorry, but everyone talks about it anyway."

"Really? Who?"

"Don't get yourself in a snit, Nelson. Just because half the workers here are Amish doesn't mean they aren't as human—and as fallible—as you and me. People gossip. Talk about things that bother them."

"They shouldn't, though. Jimmy died."

"Okay, how about this? Everyone also remembers. Not the pretty, clean, easy-to-understand version. But the real one. There's nothing wrong with doing that either . . . except that one day Jimmy's lovely widow is going to discover the truth."

He hoped not. "The truth is that he's dead, Frances. Jimmy is dead, Jenna is a widow, and Katie is going to grow up without a father. That's the plain, unvarnished truth. Talking about that day, dwelling on the details, won't change the facts."

"I'm sorry. You're right."

His cell phone beeped. "I gotta get to work," he said before he hurried into his office, shut the door, and sat down behind his desk.

Only then, when he was completely alone, did he dare face the truth: He was devastated by Jenna's rejection.

He was devastated and he was hurt . . . because he'd been secretly falling in love with her.

Somehow, some way, he was going to have to shut those feelings down. Just like he'd tried to shut down all the talk about Jimmy being mostly at fault for his own demise.

Unfortunately, Nelson feared he wasn't going to be any more successful at removing his infatuation with Jenna than he'd been at removing the talk about her husband's death.

Some things were determined to be out of his control.

chapter five

Three hours had passed since Nelson closed the door to his office with a firm click. Since she was his assistant and he was doing the majority of his calls on the office phone, Fanny knew that he'd been busy. The office phone on her desk had been lit an awful lot.

But still, three hours was a long time for Nelson to be in there without a break. He liked to pace, go get a drink, look for snacks. Ever since Jimmy Graber's accident, he liked to take walks through the large metal garage where a lot of their ready-made pieces were created. Just to make sure everything was going well.

Fanny wondered if he was avoiding her.

"Of course he's avoiding you, girl," she muttered to herself. "You just *had* to give him your opinion about his love life. Loud and clear." Remembering just how many times Nelson had flat-out said that he did not want to talk about the day of Jimmy's accident, she felt even worse. Because not only had she brought it up, she'd also brought up the fact that most of their employees believed Jimmy had been mostly responsible for it.

Why had she done that? No matter what was right or

wrong, it wouldn't change the past. Hadn't her cousin Heidi told her that more than once?

Heidi was her cousin on her mother's side, and they'd been close since birth. Fanny liked to think of herself as rather bold, but her boldness couldn't hold a candle to Heidi's assertiveness.

Even though her mom had told her that Heidi needed to learn to curb her tongue, Fanny trusted Heidi's opinion.

But Heidi wasn't here, and Fanny had already upset Nelson.

"Argh!"

The front door opened when she was mid-growl.

And of course, it had to be a guy who looked like he'd stepped out of one of her favorite Western movies. He wore gorgeous cowboy boots, jeans that fit him just right, a hand-tooled belt, and a pale-blue T-shirt. A tattoo in an intricate black design ran down his right arm.

To top it all off, he had to have black hair and blue eyes too.

Because he was perfect.

He was also currently staring at her with a look that was both confused and amused. "Hey."

"Hey," she replied. Just as if she wasn't paid to be professional and dignified.

"Are you okay? Sorry if I was interrupting something."

"Huh?" Oh yeah. He'd heard her making a stupid noise. And wasn't that just great? Well, there were two choices. Either acknowledge that she often talked to herself or at least try to appear like she had a clue.

"You weren't. I was just, um, irritated about an email," she said. "How may I help you?"

"My name's Hank Arias." He glanced at the digital clock on her desk. "I have a meeting scheduled with Nelson Harper in five minutes."

This meeting wasn't on the schedule. Though she was a little miffed that Nelson had set it up but not added it to the digital calendar she monitored, she pushed her feelings aside. "Please have a seat, Mr. Arias. I'll let him know you're here." She smiled as she stood up and attempted to cross the room in a graceful way.

She didn't usually do things like this. Nelson might run a tight ship, but he didn't stand on formalities. Half the time she simply called out to her cousin that he had a visitor. Or trotted over and opened his door.

Other times it was easiest to text him on his cell since he was almost always on the business line anyway.

But right at this moment, she decided that she needed a few seconds to gather herself together. Maybe even a few more than a few. After a quick rap of her knuckles, she cracked open the door when Nelson told her to enter.

"Yeah, Fan?"

Aware that Nelson's guest was probably watching her, she said, "Mr. Arias is here, Nelson," just like the king of England had entered the office.

Only then did she realize that Nelson was on the phone.

"One sec," he told whoever was on the line before covering the receiver and looking her way. "This call is going to last another ten minutes. Ask him to wait, would you?"

"Um, all right."

Nelson waved a hand. "Or . . . maybe he'd like a tour?"

A tour? "Sure," she said, though Nelson didn't hear

her. He was already staring at the computer screen and clicking his mouse.

Closing the door again, she turned to face Mr. Hank Arias. “I’m sorry, it’s going to be a minute.” Realizing her mistake, she added, “Probably more like ten.”

“I heard.” He stood up. “So, how about that tour?”

The look he sent her way was close to a smirk. Like he was daring her to refuse. She was a lot of things, but cowardly wasn’t one of them. “Of course.”

After glancing at the old-school planner on her desk to make sure that nothing was expected anytime soon, she picked up her cell phone, stuck it in the back pocket of her jeans, and turned back to him. “Would you like a bottle of water or a cup of coffee to sip while we walk?”

“Water would be good.”

“Great. We’ll start in the break room. There are extra bottles of water in there. After that, we’ll take a walk through the various sections of the mill and showroom.”

“Sounds good.”

“It’s right this way.” When they exited the glass doors that separated her desk, Nelson’s office, a pair of restrooms, and two private meeting areas from the mill, the warmer temperatures surrounded them. Turning right, they passed a long wall showcasing a chronological history of Alliance Millworks.

Mr. Arias hardly gave it a second glance.

Instead, he seemed to be completely focused on her. “Are you ever going to tell me your name?”

“It’s Fan—I mean, Frances.”

“Which do you prefer?”

“Prefer?”

"Fan or Frances?"

"Oh, sorry. I meant to say Fanny, not Fan. It's a childhood nickname that stuck. And as you might imagine, I prefer Frances."

"Who calls you Fanny?"

"Pretty much everyone. I've stopped fighting them." Sometimes.

"Funny how that happens, isn't it? My mama said that the only one who ever called me Henry was the nurse at the hospital. She'd always liked Hank better. It stuck to me like glue." He sent her a meaningful glance.

"There's the difference, though."

"What might that be?"

"Hank's a good name and suits you. Fanny, on the other hand, is pretty awful."

He tilted his head to one side. "You sure about that?"

Man, even his gravelly voice was attractive. "Very sure."

The corner of his lips lifted. "I guess we'll agree to disagree, then."

Was he flirting with her? She turned to gape at him as they entered the break room. About half the people inside were Amish, the other half were Mennonite or English. Only a couple of guys near the door acknowledged her. "Hiya, Fanny."

Beside her, Hank grinned.

She pretended she had no idea what he found so amusing. "Hey, guys. This here is one of our customers. Mr. Hank Arias. He wanted to take a peek around, so I'm giving him a tour."

Two of the men exchanged nods with Hank before they returned to their conversations.

"The water is over here." She led him to a commercial-sized refrigerator in the back, opened one of the doors, and took out one of the dozen or so bottles she'd neatly lined up two weeks ago. "Here you go."

"Thanks." He unscrewed the top and drank almost half in one gulp.

She hated that she'd just stared at the muscles in his neck as he swallowed. Almost as much as she hated that she couldn't seem to stop noticing every little thing about him. "Well, um, let's continue on."

She smiled at two younger guys who'd only started a few weeks before as she led the way out. "So far, so good?"

"Jah," one of them said. "Danke, Fan."

"No problem," she said as they walked back down the hall. For the first time in a while, she was glad she was tall and had long legs. Hank didn't dwarf her. But more importantly, she didn't have to trot every couple of steps to keep up with him.

After she showed him the alcove where the bathrooms were and another room where all the office equipment was, they turned left. "The majority of our craftsmen are in this area."

"All right." When they entered the main work area, filled with noise and lots of workspaces that looked a bit like large, rustic cubicles, Hank said, "You seem to know this place real well."

"I guess it's because I do."

"I'm surprised. You don't look old enough to have worked here a long time, but I guess I'm mistaken?"

"Yeah. Nelson, the president, is my cousin. Our grandfather started the mill, and both of his sons—my dad and

Nelson's dad—ran the place after he retired. Nelson and I used to walk around here with our dads on the weekends. We worked here on summer breaks too."

Hank was listening intently. "What did you do? Did you learn any woodworking?"

"No. That wasn't my thing. I just did errands, office stuff. Mailers." She paused. "One summer I worked with the janitor and cleaned bathrooms and mopped floors."

"The daughter of the boss cleaned bathrooms?" Hank raised his eyebrows. "I'm impressed."

"Don't be. Everyone here is taught to help out when it's needed. That includes cleaning toilets." Thinking back to that summer, she wrinkled her nose. "It wasn't my favorite job, but it taught me to respect every job at Alliance Millworks. Every employee here does something important."

"Hmm."

A little embarrassed about her short speech, Fanny felt her cheeks heat. It would be nice if one day she didn't sound quite so down-to-earth. Maybe a bit more classy. She didn't think classy girls discussed toilets.

But who even knew?

Shaking her head, she pushed the wayward thoughts away. "Anyway, when Nelson got promoted and took over the reins, one of his goals was to grow the business. He wanted to double it. When it became apparent that he needed help behind the scenes to keep everything running smoothly, I volunteered to take the job."

"That's pretty impressive. I mean, a lot of people don't want to work with family members. Something can always go wrong, and then the problem seeps over into the rest of the family."

"I don't disagree. But so far, we're a pretty good team. Nelson is good at what he does, and I am too."

"Good to know."

"Yeah," she muttered under her breath. Feeling a little awkward talking more about herself than the business, she gestured to Big John, a master carpenter who was currently making spindles for a staircase. "Hello, John," she called out.

When he saw her, he took off his safety glasses. "Hiya, Fanny."

"This is Mr. Arias. He's meeting with Nelson in a little while, so I'm giving him a tour."

John frowned. "Arias? You the guy with the big house out in Wooster?"

"That's it." Staring at John's workstation, Hank grinned. "And if I'm not mistaken, I'm pretty sure I'm looking at the spindles for the staircase."

Big John chuckled. "Well, you're looking at six of them. I've only got sixty or so more to go."

Fanny couldn't believe it. "Sixty?"

"Jah, Fan." He waved a hand. "Or thereabouts."

She turned to Hank. "That must be some kind of staircase."

Hank chuckled. "I think so. There's going to be these gorgeous hickory spindles, and then some iron ones too. Are you doing those as well, John?"

"Nope. Rudy over at ABC Ironworks is doing those. I saw one of them, though. It's a real good match with mine. I think you're gonna be pleased."

"I'm sure I will." Reaching out to one of the spindles, Hank paused. "May I?"

"Jah. Sure. They're yours, ain't so?"

"I don't want to be a pest."

"You aren't. But remember that I haven't sanded it yet. You'll get something far smoother when they're installed."

"I understand." With a look of true appreciation, Hank ran a hand along the woodwork that John had made. "This hickory looks fantastic."

John nodded. "I said the same thing when they brought in the wood. It's a good, solid piece right here. It'll make a good stairway, I reckon. Strong too. No young'uns should be able to nick it easily."

"I hope not. I wanted something that would last years from now, you know?"

Big John nodded. "I know. These will do the job. One day, your grandchildren will be telling their kinner to watch their step."

"I hope so." As he put it down, Hank reached out a hand and shook John's. "It's a pleasure to meet you."

"Same."

"Do you do other work? I plan to ask Nelson about the progress in the library today."

"I'm working some on that too. Peter is too, I think." He scratched his head. "I could be wrong, but I don't know if all the wood's been delivered for your library yet."

"I'll ask Nelson."

As they continued the tour, Hank took the time to chat with several of the skilled craftsmen. It was obvious that he admired their work. Fanny had always felt the same way, but it had been quite a long time since she'd taken the time to see their skills through fresh eyes. She felt humbled that it took a stranger's tour to do that.

Glancing at one of the large clocks hanging on the wall, she gestured toward the main exit. “I think we better head on back. Nelson is no doubt wondering where we are.”

“No doubt.” There was a hint of humor in his voice. Again. Was he teasing her?

She glanced back at him, hoping to get an answer from his expression, but he was studying the area with interest.

She felt a little silly. They were strangers and would likely not have the opportunity to spend much time together again. Why did she care what he thought of her? It didn’t make sense.

When they approached the glass doors leading into the small office space, Hank stepped forward and opened the door for her. “After you,” he murmured.

She walked through with whispered thanks. And had never been so happy to see Nelson standing outside his office.

“Nelson, as you suggested, I took Mr. Arias on a tour through the mill. We started talking to Big John.”

“I’m sorry to keep you waiting,” Nelson said as he shook Hank’s hand. “I hope Frances was able to show you everything you were interested in.”

“Very much so.” Turning to her, Hank added, “Thank you again for your time.”

“Of course. It was my pleasure.”

Hank grinned.

Nelson cleared his throat. “Hank, I have some preliminary plans drawn for the game room and master suite on the second floor of the house. They’re on the conference table.” Nelson flashed a smile. “I have a feeling that you’ll be pleased.”

"Hope so." Hank followed Nelson to the back, but as he walked by her desk, he winked.

It seemed a little bit cheeky. She was pretty sure she should even be a tad put off by that.

But she couldn't help but replay it in her head again and again the rest of the day.

chapter six

After repeating the directions over and over in her head, Jenna rode her bike to her first meeting of the Amish Widows Club. Luckily, it wasn't too far away, and the road she was on wasn't crowded. No matter how much easier it was to get around Alliance on her electric bike than with a horse and buggy, she still got nervous. Not every car or truck passed her with care.

As she got closer, her stomach began to churn. She still wasn't sure she was making the right decision. Jenna knew that she had to go at least once, though. She was beginning to feel more and more at loose ends when she was home.

Two things had happened to help make up her mind. The first was that her neighbor Hannah Keim asked if Katie could come over one afternoon soon. Hannah's children were a touch younger than Katie, but Hannah was watching her sister's children for the week, who were five and six years old. Hannah had thought Katie might enjoy playing with them for a spell. She'd even mentioned that they'd have a fun picnic in the early evening. They were going to grill hot dogs and s'mores in their backyard.

Though Jenna thought it sounded like a lot of fun for Katie, she was still a little hesitant to accept. She didn't know the cousins, and sometimes Katie still got a little weepy when something reminded her of her father.

However, from the moment she'd mentioned the invitation to Katie, her daughter had spoken of nothing else. Now that school was out for the summer, Katie was restless and missing her friends. Jenna was so happy to see Katie excited about the visit, she didn't dare say no.

The second bit of encouragement came from her pen pal Laura Beth. Laura Beth was New Order Amish and was currently living with her sister in Mexico for a year while they served as missionaries.

In Jenna's last letter to her, she'd shared some of her concerns about her future and had even gone so far as to confide that she spent most of her time alone with Katie. Laura Beth reminded her that Jimmy wouldn't have wanted her to become a recluse. Then Laura Beth had written something that Jenna had taken to heart—that as wonderful-gut as pen pals were, long-distance friends on paper couldn't take the place of real companionship. Everyone, no matter their circumstances, needed friends to share a cup of coffee and conversation with.

Armed with those two things, Jenna had called the number on the back of the card Doreen had given her and received the information about the next meeting. Though she hadn't needed to leave her name on the recording, Jenna had felt as if she'd made a giant step forward and couldn't back out.

Before she could talk herself out of going, she took Katie to Hannah's house for her playdate. She had made arrangements with her in-laws to pick up Katie afterward.

She'd hugged Katie goodbye, said a prayer, and then finally hopped on her bicycle and pedaled the three miles to Anne Yoder's house.

Jenna knew Anne. She was a pleasant woman in her sixties who'd lost her husband during the pandemic. The other thing Jenna knew about Anne was that she loved to go for walks. Anne didn't just walk to go places, she walked for her health—both spiritually and physically. That was something that Jenna admired about her. She hoped that she'd find more of a connection during the evening's meeting.

She parked her bicycle near two others, then tentatively knocked on the back door, as the message on the phone had instructed.

It was immediately opened by a woman who didn't look much older than her, and from the looks of her dress, she was Swartzentruber Amish. "Well, hello there," she said in greeting as she blatantly looked Jenna over from head to toe. "You're new."

"I am. Doreen invited me to attend a meeting."

"What's your name?"

"It's Jenna. Jenna Graber."

"I'm pleased to know you. Mei nohma is Elizabeth."

"That's a pretty name."

Elizabeth inclined her head. "Danke. I've always liked it as well." After closing the door behind Jenna, she waved a hand toward the crowded room just beyond them. "Jenna Graber, welcome to the widows club. I hope and pray that you will find what you are looking for here."

"Danke. Me too." Feeling awkward, she lowered her voice. "What do I do now?"

"Hold on. Let me go check on something." Elizabeth walked over to Anne and another woman who were sipping coffee out of paper cups.

Jenna watched her say something to them, the women looked Jenna's way, and then all three approached.

Anne led the way with both of her hands outstretched. "Jenna Graber, I'm so pleased you are here, dear."

"Me too."

"I trust you found mei haus okay?"

"Oh, yes. I rode my bike."

"Excellent. Come with me and we'll get you something to drink. Do you like coffee or would you prefer water? Or"—her eyes lit up—"I also have Cherry 7-UP."

"That sounds delicious. I'll have the soda."

"Great. Come on, then." After sharing a parting glance with Elizabeth, Jenna followed the women.

"I'm Nina, by the way," Anne's friend said. "I'm kind of new here myself."

"Did Doreen invite you too?"

"She sure did." Leaning close, she whispered, "I have to tell ya, when she first appeared on my doorstep, I didn't know what was going on."

Jenna giggled, feeling the tension that had settled in her shoulders slowly lessen with every smile in her direction. "I felt the same way. I kept offering her coffee."

"I did too! I guess we're two peas in a pod, hmm?"

"Maybe so," she joked. Nina was wearing slacks, a long-sleeved blouse, and a small prayer covering over the bun on her head. It was obvious that she wasn't Amish. Most likely she was Mennonite.

For that reason alone, it was silly to think that they would have much in common. When one considered that Nina was likely in her seventies, it seemed even stranger. Why, Nina was almost fifty years older than Jenna.

However, for all their outward differences, Jenna could immediately tell that Nina was a kindred spirit.

Just as Anne was about to pour Jenna's soda, she was called away by Elizabeth at the front. It seemed another newcomer had arrived.

"Oh dear," Anne said. "Jenna, I'm sorry to leave you alone already."

"I'll help Jenna learn the ropes," Nina said. "Don't worry, Anne."

"Yes. I will be fine," Jenna said.

Anne shot her a smile before hurrying to the door, and Nina picked up an empty plastic cup. "You'll have to get some of the snack mix too, Jenna. It's delicious."

"I wasn't sure if I was supposed to bring anything or not."

"No one expects new members to bring anything besides themselves. Besides, the person who hosts usually takes it upon herself to ask a couple of women to bring in treats. I brought sugar cookies the last time I was here."

"I'll make something next time."

"I'm sure the hostess will appreciate it, but it really doesn't matter if we have a lot of food or not. That's not why all us widows gather, ain't so?" she murmured as she poured Jenna a glass of cherry soda.

Jenna nodded.

After explaining a few more things, such as the general format of the meetings, Nina brightened. "Oh, here are two gals you will be glad you met. Jenna Graber, please meet Fern and Mary Beth."

As introductions were made, Nina greeted another newcomer. Fern playfully curved her hand around Jenna's elbow and led her to a grouping of seats at the end of a long table near the back of the room. "Sit with us. It's the best seat in the house."

With trepidation, Jenna joined them. And even though she had her soda and snack mix at hand, her stomach was in too many knots to enjoy them.

She knew the reason why, of course. This was the time when people she didn't know very well asked about how she was doing. How she was adjusting to widowhood.

Most specifically, they scanned her expression for chinks in her armor and then asked the question that she hated to hear: *How are you?*

She hated that question so much.

Oh, it wasn't the actual question she had a problem with—it was the answer she felt obligated to give. Nothing ever seemed to be the right answer, not for her and not for the person asking the question. People either wanted her to reassure them that she was fine and didn't need a thing from them—that way, they wouldn't be obligated to do it. Or if Jenna did say that she was okay or all right, the listener would silently convey that she shouldn't be, because Jimmy had died and she was now alone.

Of course, the real answer, the one that was in Jenna's heart, was that she didn't know how she felt. She was no longer grief-stricken, but she wasn't always perfectly fine.

She was somewhere in the middle. Her moods lay somewhere in a pool of emptiness that was not altogether uncomfortable but not all that wonderful either.

"Jenna, did you hear me?" Fern asked.

She'd zoned out and ignored these kind women! Frustrated with herself, she shook her head. "I'm sorry, I am afraid that I did not."

"It is noisy in here, isn't it? Anyway, what I asked is if you like blueberry pie."

She had to think about it. "Jah, but it's not my favorite," she said honestly.

Of course, the moment the statement was out of her mouth, she winced. Why in the world had she said all that? All she had to do was say she did like blueberry pie. It wasn't like her preferences mattered.

"Mine either!" The lines around Fern's eyes crinkled as if she was delighted that they'd found some common ground. "I was telling my niece yesterday that I like blueberries, blueberry compote, blueberry muffins, and even blueberry pancakes. But blueberry pie seems like a waste of a good pie crust. Do you know what I mean?"

She looked at the other women at the table. Each was looking at her but not with expectation. It was more like the ladies were sharing her confused amusement with the conversation.

It made her feel good.

"I do know what you mean," she said with a laugh. "I don't believe it's ever occurred to me to bake a blueberry pie."

"Look at that! We only just met but have discovered

that we have something in common. I knew I liked you," Fern teased with a smile.

Jenna returned the smile. Her heart was lifted, and all of her worries seemed to fade into the background. Her pen pal Laura Beth had been right. Jenna needed to spend some time, in person, with other women. She needed to chat and laugh and relax.

She needed to be around other widows too.

Those worries that always seemed to rest on her shoulders would no doubt return soon. They always did. But for now? Well, she was grateful for the small break.

She was starting to realize that everyone needed a break from their life every now and then.

chapter seven

It was strange waking up alone in an empty house. Just before she took Katie to Hannah's the day before, her mother-in-law had stopped by. Mary had offered to pick up Katie at Hannah's and then bring her to their house for the night.

Though Jenna hadn't been all that happy about not having Katie at home, her daughter had liked the idea. With Laura Beth's advice still ringing in her ears, Jenna had agreed to the plan. Katie needed to be surrounded by friends and family too.

Mary had been so pleased, she'd even packed a tote bag with Katie's nightgown, toothbrush, and favorite stuffed animals so everything would be at their house waiting for her.

"We'll bring Katie back to your haus about midday," Mary had said just before she walked out the back door. "Enjoy your evening, dear."

Jenna had thanked her, both for the wishes and for taking care of Katie. But she hadn't been all that excited about leaving Katie with her grandparents.

From time to time, Jenna felt as if she was in a little battle of wills with her in-laws. Sometimes Mary acted a bit as if Katie would be better off with her and Peter than with Jenna.

Jenna was sure this suspicion was all in her mind, but there was still a small part of her that was distrustful of Mary and Peter's continual efforts to get Katie to spend more time with them.

After taking a long, hot shower and enjoying a full hour of silence while she read her devotional and sipped her coffee, Jenna played with Blue—Katie's most recent name for the kitten—and then gave her wooden floors a good sweeping and mopping.

When she heard the clip-clop of hooves outside, she hurried to the door, fully expecting to see Mary and Katie.

Instead, it was her mamm.

"This is a surprise," she said after they hugged hello. "I didn't know you were going to be in Alliance today."

Her parents lived in Walden, which was one town over. They were still in the house she'd grown up in, though they now had a boarder of sorts, a young man doing an apprenticeship with a blacksmith.

To everyone's surprise, her parents loved having the young man there. Jonny was a strapping man in his early twenties who enjoyed helping Jenna's daed in the yard whenever he had time off. He also loved her mother's cooking and was appreciative of her doing his laundry.

He kept her parents just busy enough that they always had something to do. And, of course, now that their children were grown, they had a little bit of money to spend on extras.

"Whose buggy is that?"

"Preacher Eddie's. Eddie needed some help moving around some furniture in his haus, so we got a driver to take us over there. When it became apparent our 'quick' visit was going to take a few hours, Eddie offered me the buggy so I could come see you and Katie." Running a hand along Eddie's gelding, her mother added, "It turns out Eddie's haus and yours are close. Eddie told me about a small trail that practically cuts a direct line from his haus to yours. It was only a twenty-minute buggy ride."

Jenna knew Eddie well. He'd been four years ahead of her in school, but she'd always thought he was nice, though a little bit wild.

She still had a hard time envisioning the boy who'd loved to joke and push his parents' boundaries as a married man and a preacher too.

After they unhitched Eddie's horse, tied him to a post, and gave him a bucket of fresh water, Jenna brought her mother inside for a glass of lemonade and a rest. "I had no idea Eddie and Winnie were so close to me. It was nice of Eddie to let you borrow his buggy."

"It surely was." Looking around, Mamm frowned. "Where is Katie? And who's this?"

Picking up Blue, Jenna cuddled her close before handing her to her mother. "This is Blue, our new kitten."

Her mamm accepted the kitten with a bright smile. Lifting him up to her face, she kissed Blue's cute nose. "He's a beauty. And so adorable."

"Jah. I think so too."

"And Katie?"

"She spent the night with Mary and Peter." Glancing

at the clock on the living room wall, Jenna added, "Mary said she'd have Katie home around midday."

"I didn't know Katie was old enough to have sleepovers yet." Her mother sounded shocked.

"I guess she is. I hadn't planned on it, though. I was invited to go to a meeting with some other women last night, and when Mary heard about it, she asked if Katie could go to their house after she played with some friends."

"What a big night little Katie had!"

"I agree." Jenna smiled. "I'm sure she had a lot of fun."

"What about you?" Mamm asked softly. "Were you happy to have an evening alone?"

"I didn't hate the idea . . . but it feels odd to be here alone. When I heard the horse outside, I thought it was Peter or Mary dropping her off."

Looking down at the kitten she was still holding, her mother said, "Did they give Katie Blue?"

"Nee. Nelson did."

"Nelson, Jimmy's boss?"

"Jah."

Looking a little taken aback, her mother deposited Blue on the floor, then reached for her glass of lemonade and took a sip. "How did that happen?"

Jenna's mom had her same brown eyes and hair. In a great many ways they were alike, which was probably why her mother was visibly attempting to keep her thoughts to herself.

But even though her mamm was attempting to appear curious instead of shocked, Jenna was aware she'd been keeping her friendship with Nelson a secret from her parents. "Well, Nelson has stopped by here on Monday nights."

"He does this often?"

He came like clockwork. She nodded. "He does. He and I have become friends."

"I don't understand. Why is he coming over?"

"Why?"

"Jah." She took a deep breath. "I mean, if you don't mind me asking."

That was her mother. She'd started treating Jenna a little differently after she'd married Jimmy. She'd become a little bit more hesitant to speak her mind, more inclined to listen to Jenna's point of view.

Jenna had always appreciated that.

Just as she was appreciating her mother's quiet questioning now. The only problem was that she didn't know how to explain her complicated feelings for Nelson.

Or the way she'd pushed him away after he gave Katie the kitten.

"When he first started stopping by, I thought it was because he thought he bore some responsibility for Jimmy's death."

Mamm's brow wrinkled. "Nelson shouldn't have. Everyone said it was an accident. There was nothing Nelson—or anyone working nearby—could have done."

"I agree, and I've told Nelson that I don't hold him responsible for Jimmy's death at all. But even after he accepted my words, Nelson continued to stop by." Forcing herself to continue, she said, "I probably encouraged his visits too. He is a nice man, and he never asked a lot of questions. He . . . well, he calmed me. Sometimes his visits were what got me through the week."

"Jenna, Daed and I asked you to move home several times."

"I know you did. And I appreciated that. But I didn't want to leave my haus, Mamm." She took a breath. "He never stayed long. An hour at the very most."

"Oh?"

"Usually, he just dropped something by, checked to make sure that Katie and I didn't need anything done around the yard, and then headed home. It wasn't a big deal."

"I'm sorry, but it sounds a bit different than that. Even taking the time to stop by and check on you is a big deal. In the best way possible, of course."

"Ah, yes."

"I'm so surprised, though. I had no idea that you were seeing so much of Nelson. I can't believe he's been visiting you weekly for . . . for almost a year?"

It was more like almost a year and a half. But admitting that was more than she was willing to do.

Plus, her mother's usually vague way of responding to her questions had gone out the window. She was currently staring at Jenna.

It was like her mother was accusing her of keeping a big secret from her.

But . . . maybe she was?

Jenna felt her cheeks heat. "I don't know why I didn't tell you about it." Though, she kind of did know why—she hadn't wanted anyone to tell her that she shouldn't accept Nelson's friendship. There had been more than one occasion when only his visit had lightened her mood. She hadn't wanted to give him up.

Not until she started to wonder if her feelings for him had veered away from gratitude and headed into far different territory.

"I think that was very kind of him. Plus, I got the feeling when I spoke to him at Jimmy's funeral that he doesn't have a lot of family to fuss over."

"I don't know." Guilt flowed through her. She'd taken and taken from Nelson. His gifts, his attention, his kindness. She'd never even asked him about his family.

"Perhaps. What does Katie think of him?"

"She loves when he comes over. Sometimes he reads her a book or plays a game with her."

"Hmm. Maybe there's something else that might be going on, Jenna."

"Like . . . ?"

She smiled and inclined her head. "Like . . . you know."

"Mamm, I really don't know." That wasn't exactly true, though. She had almost felt something new toward Nelson. Almost. But it wasn't right. She wasn't supposed to have romantic feelings for another man ever again, was she? At least not so soon.

"I never thought you were the type to pretend ignorance, child. But if you want me to say it, I will. I have a feeling that Nelson has developed feelings for you."

"I hope not."

Mamm studied her face. "I hope you are telling me the truth, Jenna. Because even though he is a good man and it's obvious that he cares for you and Katie, nothing can become of your relationship."

"I know. He's just a friend." Looking away, she added, "It doesn't matter now, anyway. I've asked him not to stop by anymore. Even though he gets along so well with Katie."

"I reckon Katie is missing a male figure in her life. A dawdi just isn't the same."

"No."

"I'm glad you've stopped his visits. I'm sure a future with Nelson is tempting. He would be a good provider. You wouldn't have to worry about bills or getting something for Katie that she really needed."

"I would never marry someone for financial reasons." Plus, Nelson was more than his bank account. He was a lot more.

"Perhaps not, but some women would take that into account. Having food to eat and a safe place to sleep is important. You could do much worse than relying on a man like Nelson to make sure everything you need is taken care of."

Jenna was taken off guard. What in the world was her mother saying? She'd gone from being confused about Nelson's friendship to promoting him as a possible suitor. "Mother, you're making me so confused. I thought you loved Jimmy."

"Of course I did. Jimmy was a gut husband to you, and he was a gut father to Katie. He made you happy." She lowered her voice. "But he's not here, dear, and you are still so young. All I'm saying is that I don't necessarily hate the idea of a man like Nelson Harper wanting to look after you and Katie. He always seemed like a steady sort . . . but he is not Amish."

"I know he isn't."

Folding her hands in her lap, she said, "I can't help but wonder if there's a reason that God has been encouraging Nelson to visit so much. Maybe He's wanted Nelson to be your good friend . . . until you found a man more suitable to call on you."

Jenna wasn't sure that the Lord was all that worried about her friendship with Nelson or her single state. All she did know for certain was that He wouldn't be okay with her breaking her baptismal vows.

Which sometimes made her a little sad.

"We're just friends, Mamm," Jenna said again, though she wasn't sure if she was attempting to convince her mother or herself.

After taking another sip of lemonade, her mother nodded. "I understand." She took a deep breath. "Now tell me who you saw last night. What was this meeting you went to?"

"It was a group of widows."

"All widows?"

She couldn't help but smile. "Jah. Every one of them."

Her mother's eyebrows rose. "That's . . . interesting."

"Jah. I guess it's a secret group that's not so secret. They call themselves the Amish Widows Club. They meet fairly often, sometimes once a month. Sometimes twice. Women attend when they can."

"It's all Amish widows?"

Remembering Nina, Jenna said, "Almost. I guess maybe ninety percent of them are Amish? I'm still not quite sure about that." Remembering the snack mix and Elizabeth checking her in, she added, "It's all very organized."

Her mother still looked puzzled. "And what happens when you get there? Do you have grief counseling?"

The truth was so far from that, she almost smiled. "Oh, nee. Nothing like that. Instead, everyone just visits and talks."

"About what? Your husbands?"

"Oh, nee. We just chat about simple things. At least, that's how it was last night."

"That's it?" Her mother couldn't seem to understand Jenna's need to be around other women who'd lost their husbands. It made Jenna realize that she really was part of a club that was exclusive. No matter how much a woman might think she understood what it was like to be widowed, it wasn't really possible until it happened to her. "It's enough. Believe it or not, I talked about the pros and cons of blueberry pie with one lady."

"I never was a fan of blueberry pie," her mother admitted with a wrinkled nose. "Plus, it stains my teeth. I hate that."

Jenna couldn't help it, she started laughing. "See, Mamm? The talk was like that. Talking about blueberry pie is like talking about nothing . . . but yet . . ."

"But yet it's the kind of conversation that everyone needs every once in a while. It makes you feel happy inside," Mamm finished.

Glad that her mamm was finally understanding, she nodded. "Jah. That. I'm still not sure why I was invited or why the Lord decided to encourage me to attend, but I'm glad I did. Simple conversation with other women who have gone through what I'm going through has been really helpful."

Her mother stared at her for a few seconds. Seemed to study her face, looking for something hidden.

Or maybe it was a spark of happiness that had been absent for far too long?

"I think I better start coming over here a lot more often, darling," she said at last. "You've had a lot going on."

Everything inside of her melted. Even after all this time—and even after being a mother herself, Jenna still wanted that reassurance. Wanted her mother's approval. It looked like she had it once again. "I don't know if I've had a whole lot going on, but I'm always happy to see you, Mamm. I'd like it if we visited each other more often."

"I feel the same way, child." Reaching out, her mother took her hand. "Let's plan on it."

–*chapter* eight

Nelson had managed to stay away from Jenna for two entire weeks. It had been hard to do, though. When Monday afternoon faded into evening and he was still at home, staring at his empty backyard, his skin felt as if it were on fire.

It was like every part of him was fighting against his decision. Not only did he crave time with her and Katie, but he liked taking care of her. He knew how much money Jimmy had made a week—and that he hadn't been much of a saver.

Maybe her family and Jimmy's were looking out for her now. He hoped so. But even if they were, it was obvious to him that she was living on a very tight budget. That would be a challenge with a growing daughter, and he thought Jenna was the type of woman to put Katie's needs before her own. He hated to think of Jenna going without something she needed.

So, yes . . . he felt protective of her. He enjoyed making sure she was taken care of. Maybe he felt a tiny bit obligated too.

And guilty.

Jenna didn't know it, but Nelson had been the one who'd passed over Jimmy for a raise. It was a few months before his death, and Jimmy's supervisor had brought up his name more than once as someone who was becoming increasingly careless.

When Jimmy had knocked on his office door the day after he learned that he hadn't received his raise, he was very angry.

"I can't believe you listened to Paul's gossip," he'd said, all attitude and bluster.

Jimmy's words rubbed Nelson the wrong way. He was the president of the entire company. Not only was Jimmy complaining, but he'd gone over Paul's head too.

Nelson didn't like Jimmy's blatant insubordination. He liked Jimmy's attitude even less.

"It wasn't gossip," Nelson replied, irritation seeping into each word. "Paul is your direct supervisor. He's done a good job for years." Pulling out a file folder, he showed Jimmy the three reports Paul had completed about Jimmy's performance. "I know you've seen these." Leveling his gaze at Jimmy, he added, "Curtis's initials are here as well."

"Curtis didn't talk to me. All he did was listen to Paul's report."

"That is Curtis's job. He's in charge of the entire shop where you work."

When Jimmy folded his arms over his chest, Nelson felt like rolling his eyes. Jimmy was acting as if no one was giving him a chance to succeed, when everyone in that building had been giving him multiple opportunities.

Jimmy had ignored them, and he was under the mistaken impression that Nelson would override Paul and Curtis's decisions.

"Jimmy, you and I both know everything I'm telling you isn't a surprise. Your signature is at the bottom of these reports."

"I had no choice but to sign them."

"Did you not agree?"

"Of course I didn't agree." He picked up the sheets and shook them. "This was only Paul's opinion. He doesn't like me, Nelson. He never has. And because of that, I'm not getting either the recognition or the pay that I deserve."

Jimmy was so angry, his cheeks were flushed and his hands were shaking. Nelson was taken aback. He'd never been all that fond of the formal evaluations and the paperwork they entailed, but he believed in them. His father and grandfather had told him that doing such things helped both their workers and the supervisors from being caught off guard.

Nelson had always agreed, though he'd usually only agreed because they had such a solid, high-performing staff. And Jimmy could have been that way as well. It was just that he seemed to let his temper get the best of him from time to time, which had affected his productivity.

He remembered scanning the reports again. "Jimmy, I'm looking, but I don't see any notes about you wanting to dispute these evaluations."

Jimmy folded his arms across his chest again. "Of course I wasn't going to dispute them. I need this job. If I complained too much, I'd get fired, and then what would I tell Jenna?"

Nelson didn't appreciate Jimmy making it sound like the company was run that way, but he didn't think there was any reason to dwell on that at the moment.

"Ah, yes. You are married and have a little girl, don't you?"

Jimmy nodded.

For the first time, Nelson saw something else in his expression. Was it worry? Stress? Whatever it was, it made Nelson take a deep breath and find some patience for the young man. He obviously had a family to support and didn't want to let them down. "Listen, I'm sorry that you were caught off guard about the pay raise, but this doesn't mean you're in danger of getting fired."

"It means I'm going to have to tell Jenna to make do on my meager salary until I'm able to somehow convince Paul to stop misconstruing everything I do." He shifted. "Or you allow me to switch departments."

"Which department are you hoping to move to?" Paul's group prepared lumber basics and simple ready-made pieces for people's homes. Other divisions were made up of master craftsmen, which Jimmy wasn't qualified for, and shipping and deliveries, which involved a lot of odd hours and lots of manual labor and attention to details.

Even if Jimmy did want to count, recount, check, and double-check items, Nelson couldn't see how coming in on Saturday mornings or staying late on a Thursday because a delivery truck was late would be an improvement to his life. Nelson had never been married, but he would imagine Jimmy wouldn't want to be away from his wife and daughter more often.

"I don't know."

"I see. Well, if you'd like to discuss this further, let me know."

"That's it?"

"I'm afraid so, Jimmy. My hands are tied."

Jimmy's light-blue eyes looked almost empty. "Jah. I feel the same way," he uttered as he walked out.

And then, of course, two weeks later, he got mad, yelled at Paul, and fed wood into the planer incorrectly without a partner. When it jammed, he ignored everyone's advice and tried to fix it himself.

The "accident" that had taken place hadn't actually been a true accident. It had been user error compounded by Jimmy's mistakes and Paul's inability to take control of the situation.

Paul was so upset by what happened, he wanted to quit a month after Jimmy's death. Curtis got involved, refusing to let Paul take complete responsibility for Jimmy's mistakes.

Nelson ended up bringing all thirty men in the department to a meeting off-site and even hired an outside consultant to help guide the conversation.

He learned that all the men felt partly responsible for Jimmy's accident because they hadn't wanted to cause any trouble.

The day had been eye-opening for everyone. When more than one man said he didn't want Jenna and Katie to have more to deal with than they already had, Nelson suggested that they would accept the truth as a company but wouldn't discuss it openly.

No good could come of laying that burden on Jimmy's parents or on a widow and her daughter.

But there was a collective agreement that Jimmy had been at fault, and his coworkers, his managers, and Nelson weren't to blame. Along with that decision was the belief that Jimmy's wife never needed to know the complete, unvarnished truth.

It had sounded like a good idea too. After all, Jimmy had died. He'd already paid the ultimate price.

But now Nelson was beginning to wonder if knowingly keeping a secret like that had been a bad idea from the start. He hadn't counted on having real feelings for Jenna. He hadn't counted on his wish of one day having a relationship with Jenna. A marriage and vows. But was it ever possible to begin a strong and steady marriage when the basis of it was a lie?

He didn't think so.

All of that was rattling around in his head as he drove up Jenna's driveway. When he reached the crest, he couldn't help but tap his brakes for a moment. Because there, right in front of him, were Katie and Jenna next to their vegetable garden. Katie was wearing a pale-purple dress and no shoes. Jenna was wearing a bright-yellow dress, slip-on white tennis shoes, and a light tan. Both of their kapps looked crisp and white, and the tails were fluttering in the breeze.

It was the prettiest sight he'd seen in two weeks.

And, if he wasn't mistaken, little Katie was squealing at something on the ground. Not in fright but doing what he supposed all little girls instinctively knew to do from the youngest of ages.

He couldn't wait to learn what she was squealing at.

As he drove forward, Nelson braced himself for Jenna's

reaction. Maybe she'd be mad at him for going against her wishes. Maybe she'd be hurt that he hadn't listened to her.

Maybe she'd pretend everything was fine. He had no idea.

All Nelson did know was that he couldn't take another week of not seeing this woman and her little girl.

There were moments when he felt that Jenna and Katie were as necessary to his life as bread and milk. He could do without them, but life wouldn't be near as good or sweet.

chapter nine

Katie was happy that school was out for the summer. Jenna was too. She loved these lazy days with her daughter, especially since her five-year-old was such a busy girl. Each morning, she jumped out of bed when the sun rose and hurried into the living room to play with the kitten.

After Jenna got up with her the first morning of summer vacation, she realized that Katie preferred having some time to herself. Her little girl had her own routine. After waking up Blue, she would go to the cookie jar, grab an oatmeal cookie, and then play in the living room with that silly cat.

When the kitten was ready for a break, she'd eat her cookie and look at her library books or color pictures.

After spending the last year rushing to make sure Katie's lunch pail was full and her schoolwork was done before walking her to school, Jenna appreciated these lazy mornings very much. She would have a cup of coffee, get dressed, and make them both a good breakfast. After that, they did a few chores in the house.

And after that?

Well, Katie wanted to run and play outside, go exploring, help water plants, and generally be a busy little girl. She was a joy. A muddy, dirty joy, but a joy, without a doubt. She was also interested in everything. Which, at the moment, was a toad that had been happily resting in a patch of mud on the edge of the garden before Katie spied it.

"Mamm! It hopped!"

Indeed it had. Its big eyes were actively looking for an escape route. "Goodness, child. It's just a toad, and it's likely its suppertime. Let the poor thing get on its way to its family." Sure, she was making up a whole life for this toad, but since it was almost their suppertime as well, Jenna figured the storytelling was warranted.

"But it's ginormous!" Katie started jumping up and down, her little hands grasping the skirt of her dress and lifting it high over her ankles.

The poor toad looked petrified. It was obvious that it didn't know where to go but that it would do most anything to escape as soon as possible. When it hopped, Katie squealed, scaring the poor creature half to death.

Jenna couldn't help it. She started laughing. And then she couldn't stop. Not even as she watched Nelson park his truck and hurry over to join them.

"What's going on?" he called out. "Are you two okay?"

"We're fine," Jenna said as she continued to try to stop laughing. "It's a toad you should be worried about."

"A what?"

"That!" Katie pointed to the now rather disgruntled-looking toad sitting in the middle of all of them.

Nelson tilted his head to one side, then looked down. "Katie Graber, are you squealing at this toad?"

"Jah!" She jumped up and down, then shrieked again when the poor thing attempted to hop toward freedom. "He was in our garden and now he wants to hop on me!"

Shaking her head, Jenna said, "I'm afraid all he's trying to do is escape. My darling daughter is making poor Mr. Toad's efforts mighty difficult."

"Nee, Mamm, he's trying to hop on my foot."

"If he is, it's because your foot is a muddy mess, child."

Nelson bent closer to the toad. "I think Mr. Toad regrets his decision to hop in your garden, Kitty. What do you think, Jenna?"

"I think so too," she replied as she attempted to catch her breath. "Kitty is being so silly, though. I don't know if I've ever heard her raise such a fuss about a frog."

"It's slimy and ugly and huge, Mamm." She lifted her chin. "It's also a toad, not a frog. Right, Nelson?"

"Well, now, I can't say that I agree with your description," he said slowly as he bent down to look at the toad more closely. "He is a toad, but he's not slimy or ugly. I think he is a very handsome toad."

Katie wrinkled her nose. "Toads canna be handsome."

"Of course they can. Otherwise they'd never find themselves a toad wife, true?" He lowered his voice. "You see, I reckon he's a right good-looking toad to all the female toads around here."

"He was trying to get the zucchini." Katie pointed to the zucchini patch in the garden.

"I don't know about that. I reckon he'd rather have a fly than a zucchini, don't you think?" When Katie shrugged, Nelson smiled. "I agree with your mamm—he's trying to escape." Nelson looked around, found a sturdy twig, and picked it up. "How about we help him move along?"

Katie's eyes widened. "Are you going to kill him?"

"Not at all. Just give him a nudge." Nelson glanced at her. "Is that okay with you, Jenna?"

"It's more than okay. I agree that Mr. Toad would like nothing better than to move on." She reached for Katie. "Step over here, child, so Nelson can help our visitor hop away."

Carefully, Nelson nudged the toad. To everyone's surprise, the toad didn't budge.

Katie frowned. "Is he hurt?"

"I don't think so." Nelson bent down, scooped up the toad in his hands, walked a few feet, and then deposited it on the edge of the neighbor's yard. "Here you go, buddy. Have a good evening."

Katie scurried over to Nelson's side and grabbed his leg as they watched the toad sit for a second, then hop away. Thirty seconds later, he was out of sight.

"Danke, Nelson," Jenna murmured with a small smile. "You surely came to our rescue today."

"Are your hands yucky?" Katie asked. "Do you have toad slime on them?"

He held up his hands. "Not at all. Obviously, you need to hold a toad one day soon. Just because he's not a cute furball like your kitten doesn't mean he's an awful creature." Leaning down, he added, "Not all of God's creatures are beautiful, but that doesn't mean that they are bad."

"Mamm?"

"I must agree with Nelson, dear."

"Next time he comes to the garden, I'll try not to scream at him," Katie pronounced.

"I could be wrong, but I don't think he'll ever venture this way again," Jenna said. Pointing to the four zucchini that she'd picked and laid on the ground, she said to Katie, "Go rinse off your feet in the hose, then put these zucchini on the kitchen counter."

"I'm gonna take a shower too."

Thankful that her daughter had been taking showers on her own for several months, Jenna nodded. "I think that's a gut idea. Be sure you put on a fresh dress. I'll be in soon."

"Are you coming inside too, Nelson?"

"It depends on your mamm. She might have something else planned for the evening."

"Do we, Mamm?"

She knew Nelson had given her a way out on purpose. Katie might think that they had plans, but what Nelson was really asking was if she was going to allow him to visit.

She had pushed him away but regretted that decision almost immediately, and she realized that she didn't want to push him away again.

"We have time for a visit," she answered at last. "Nelson, would you like to stay for supper?"

"Thank you. I would." He smiled over at Katie, who was rinsing her feet with the hose. "I mean, I would as long as Katie isn't covered in mud."

"I'm going into the shower now!" she called out, completely forgetting the vegetables on the ground as she shut off the hose and hurried inside.

Nelson laughed. "I'm afraid the hose didn't clean her

feet too well. You're going to have footprints on your floor."

Jenna shrugged. "There are worse things to worry about."

As she hoped, his gaze warmed. "Jenna, the truth now. I came over because I didn't want another week to go by without checking on you two. But are you sure you want me to stay for supper?"

"You'd be doing me a favor if you did. I made meatballs. With it, we're having buttered noodles and pan-fried zucchini."

He blinked. "All that?"

"It's nothing too special, though I did make fresh bread and some shortbread cookies. The cookies are delicious."

"It all sounds delicious."

"So you'll stay?"

"You forget that I'm a bachelor, right? You had me at supper. I would've said yes to a sandwich."

"Sometimes I think you are too easy to please," she chided as she led the way inside.

Nelson hurried forward, scooped up the zucchini, and reached for the door. "Funny, I've thought the same thing about you from time to time."

Jenna was taken aback by his words. She was eager to ask him what he meant, but she also didn't want to press him for an explanation. It would surely seem as if she was begging for compliments, and Jimmy had never liked her to do that.

The random thought caught her off guard. At least a week had passed since the last time she'd thought of Jimmy. It was far longer than that since she'd recalled something so specific. Most of the time, whenever she thought of him now, it was in vague, general terms, such as how long it had been since he'd passed, or how he loved warm summer days so very much.

Hardly ever did she allow herself to think anything negative about him. But the truth was that sometimes he had gotten impatient with her or would blurt something that she would take the wrong way.

She walked through the open doorway, hurried to the kitchen sink, and washed her hands. If Nelson hadn't been following, she would have splashed some cold water on her cheeks as well.

"Hey, are you having second thoughts?"

She turned off the faucet. "Nee. Why do you ask?"

"Because you look like you've just seen a ghost. If the thought of me sharing a meal with you makes you uncomfortable, then I will leave. No hard feelings."

She noticed then that Nelson was still standing near the door, like he was prepared to exit immediately the second she told him to.

"I don't want you to leave. I'm not uncomfortable."

Realizing that he was still staring at her, waiting for her to give him an inkling of what was on her mind, she met his gaze. "I had just thought of something that Jimmy would have said to me. It took me by surprise."

"Ah. Does that happen often?"

She shook her head, wondering if she should feel guilty about that. "Not really. I mean, sometimes I'll remember something about Jimmy, but it's nothing specific. Just now, I was reacting to something that he would've said." She opened a cabinet, pulled out a plate, and carried it to the table.

"How can I help?"

"You are our guest. Katie usually . . ." She'd been so taken aback by her confusing thoughts about Jimmy, she'd completely forgotten about her daughter. What was wrong with her? "I should go check on Katie." Hurrying up the stairs, she called out, "Katie, are you in the shower?" She opened the bathroom door and discovered that Katie was doing exactly what she'd said, getting clean.

"Mamm, I can do this by myself!"

"You're right. I'm sorry," she said before she closed the door and walked back down the stairs.

"Everything okay?" Nelson asked.

"Jah. She's fine." Feeling foolish, she said, "She practically told me to leave."

Holding up a zucchini, Nelson said, "How about I help you with supper?"

"Thank you."

They spent the next fifteen minutes slicing and sautéing vegetables, boiling noodles, and warming up meatballs.

"I'm all done!" Katie exclaimed, looking fresh and clean as she stood in the doorway with Blue hanging from her arms. "Blue wants me to cuddle him."

"Careful with him, Kitty," Nelson cautioned as he gently rearranged the kitten in her arms. "Blue is still a baby cat. They like to feel secure."

"This is better?"

"I think so." He put his head toward her. "Do you hear him purring now?"

"Uh-huh."

"I think that means he's happy."

"I love Blue, Mamm."

"I know you do, but you need to put him down and help me set the table."

Katie smiled. "I'm glad that you're gonna stay awhile longer."

"Me too. And guess what? I'm being useful too. I've even been helping to get supper ready."

Sheer delight brightened Katie's sweet face, reminding Jenna that she wasn't the only one who'd become attached to Nelson. It had been wrong of her to push him away.

Bending down, her daughter let go of Blue and then hurried to the silverware drawer. "We need everything for three," she said in an important tone.

"That's right. Get busy and set the table, child."

"What would you like me to do now?" Nelson asked.

"You've done enough. You may sit in the living room."

"How about I go get the things I brought for you and Katie first?"

"All right."

When he walked out, Jenna realized that she had a small burst of excitement inside her. She was glad that he was here. Glad that he was sharing a meal with them.

They all enjoyed their dinner, and Nelson insisted on helping her clear the table and wash all the dinner dishes. Now she was making a pot of coffee for the two of them.

Katie was in her room, changing into her pajamas and looking at her books, while Nelson sat at the table, a plate of cookies in front of him.

When Jenna brought over their coffee—both of them

liked it black—she said, "You didn't have to wait for me, you know."

"I did." When she lifted an eyebrow, he added, "There's no way I would ever eat without you."

She picked up a cookie and took a bite. "Now you may eat too."

After he took two bites, he said, "You are an incredible cook, Jenna. I'm starting to feel silly for bringing you so many meals and store-bought treats."

"I enjoy cooking, but I enjoy taking breaks from dishes too. Everything you've done for me has been appreciated."

He grinned at her.

She was worried she liked it too much. Reminding herself that he was English and she was not, she blurted, "When do you date?"

Nelson froze. "Pardon me?"

"Um, I was just thinking about how you've spent a lot of time with us, but our conversation is always about Katie and me. I wondered if you are going steady with someone."

"Going steady?"

She looked away. "I guess you have a better name for it. Do you have a girlfriend, Nelson?"

"No. I'm not dating anyone at the moment."

"Why not?"

"It's not all that easy to date in one's mid-thirties, I guess." He winked. "All the good ones have already been snatched up."

"Surely not."

He laughed. "'Surely not' is right. I'm sure there are a lot of very nice women out there, but I'm not interested in dating right now."

"Because of work?"

"Work does keep me busy," he agreed. "But, well, there are other things that are important to me. And those things take up a lot of my time."

Nelson seemed to be speaking very cryptically. Jenna wondered what or whom he was talking about. Perhaps someone in his family was sick? If so, she would hate that she never asked him about it. That she never lifted a finger to try to help.

Why, at the very least, she could pray for the person. Before she cautioned herself not to be so nosy, she asked, "Is it your family that has taken up your time? Is someone sick?"

"My family?"

"Jah." She waved a hand because he was staring at her like she was speaking Pennsylvania Dutch. "One of your parents? Or, um, your cousin, perhaps?" She did recall that he'd mentioned a cousin who worked closely by his side.

"No." He smiled, but it didn't reach his eyes. "No one in my family is sick."

"Oh. Perhaps one of them is going through a difficult time." She'd once had an aunt who'd been involved in an accident and couldn't sleep for months afterward.

Nelson looked flummoxed. Seemed to be debating how to answer. Then he finally shrugged. "There are a lot of reasons I'm not too interested in dating right now, Jenna. But don't worry about me. I'm not doing anything that I don't want to do."

"All right. If you're sure."

"I'm sure. And I'll see you next Monday, yes?"

Jenna nodded before she could stop herself.

"Good. And now I better get on my way."

"All right."

He was smiling. She was certain that he was meaning something by that. Something important.

But she decided it would be better to leave it alone.

After all, Nelson had been at their house for almost three hours. He was probably eager to go home.

chapter ten

Fanny wasn't nervous. Nope. Not even a little bit. She wasn't nervous at all.

There was no reason to be. All she was doing was delivering a bunch of samples for Hank Arias and his "team" to look at for his library and office. She probably wouldn't even see him. And if she did? Well, big deal. It wasn't like he'd remember her.

She'd learned that Hank Arias was from Texas, that he'd married a woman whose family had made it big in the oil business, and that he'd then made a bunch more money all on his own. He'd started a company that made some kind of piece or part used in oil rigs. Or maybe it was used in large steel structures, like bridges? Whatever it was, people all around the world had really liked it. They were also pleased that the facility was located in the Midwest. He'd sold his multibillion-dollar company right about the time his wife was diagnosed with stage 3 breast cancer. She'd died after a yearlong battle a few years ago.

Then he'd traveled a bit and finally decided to settle down, sit on the boards of a couple of companies, and build his dream house—in the middle of Amish country, of all places.

Fanny shook her head. Nope, she hadn't been too interested in his life at all.

"You need to get your head together, girl," she told herself. "This strange fascination you have with the county's wealthiest citizen isn't good for you or your company. Plus, if Hank Arias ever found out about your crush, it would be beyond embarrassing."

She knew she wasn't wrong. Fixations on clients' private lives weren't a good thing. Plus, it would be the type of thing that Nelson would tease her about for the rest of their lives.

"Think about something else," she muttered.

She should be looking forward to getting off work an hour early and beating the traffic home. Not that there actually ever was all that much traffic between her house and Wooster. But there could be. Sometimes the Mt. Hope auction had a lot of people there. Buggies everywhere. One time, a goat had gotten free and gone rogue. If something like that happened, it could be a big problem.

But as Fanny carefully drove down Hank's very long driveway lined with pear trees and blue spruces in an odd way that completely worked, she knew she had to admit the truth to herself at the very least.

And the truth was that she'd practically jumped at the chance to drop the items by. Because she had a crush on him. It didn't make sense and it wasn't a good idea, but she couldn't do much about that. It was what it was.

When she parked at the end of the drive, which just

happened to be a circular drive in front of a very, very big house, she realized that her hands were kind of clammy.

"You've got to get ahold of yourself, girl," she whispered. "If not, you're not only going to embarrass yourself, but Nelson is going to hear about it and he'll call you into his office to have a heart-to-heart, which would be a whole new low."

That thought got her back on track. So much so, she even decided *not* to look in the mirror again. Or put on lipstick.

Because that would just be silly.

She got out of the vehicle, popped the hatch open, grabbed her purse, and strode up the steps to a pair of gorgeous front doors that Jude Troyer, one of the mill's most treasured craftsmen, had built. The doors were a dark-stained hickory and opened together in a way that made her think of the movies. Back in Alliance, she'd chuckled with a couple of the other workers, wondering just how big a house had to be to need a set of doors like them. Now she knew.

You needed a really big one.

She rang the doorbell and prepared herself not to get flustered when she told Hank that she had his samples.

When she heard the door unlock, her foot kind of tapped—a long-forgotten nervous habit that had decided to return. She pasted a smile on her face.

And then gaped.

Because it wasn't Mr. Tall, Dark, and Handsome Hank Arias. It was someone blond, slim, and gorgeous. She had dark-brown eyes and was staring at Fanny like she'd never seen a girl like her before.

"May I help you?"

"Yes. I have some samples from Alliance Millworks for Hank."

She tilted her head to one side. "Hank?"

Why had she asked for him by his first name? "I'm sorry. Mr. Arias."

"Oh." She looked her over. "So . . . you're from the lumber mill?"

"Yes."

Her expression cleared. "Ah . . . now it makes sense." She flashed a small smile. "Sorry, I was expecting a man."

Fanny had been expecting one too. "My cousin Nelson—he's the head of Alliance Millworks—he was going to drive out here, but he was swamped with work. I told him that I didn't mind delivering these samples instead. My apologies, we should've let you know."

The woman shrugged as if to say that whoever came from the mill made no difference to her. Looking at Fanny's empty hands, she added, "Where are they?"

"They?"

"Yes. The samples?"

"Sorry. They're out in my vehicle. I'll bring them in."

"Thank you." She looked more than ready to get Fanny on her way.

But unfortunately, the awkward conversation was going to continue. "I'm sorry, where would you like me to put them?"

The blond pursed her lips. "Would it be too much trouble to place them in each room?"

"Not at all." She smiled. "I'd be happy to."

"Okay . . . thanks."

Fanny realized that the woman was not going to offer to help her. She shouldn't either. She was in a bright floral sundress that looked as if it belonged in a country club.

"I'll be right back." More aware than ever of her casual outfit of baggy jeans, tennis shoes, and a short-sleeved cotton blouse that looked like it needed to be ironed, Fanny walked out to her SUV, reached inside the open hatch, and pulled out the first two of five samples. Each was the size of a kitchen cabinet door. Not terribly heavy but not all that easy for a woman of her size to carry.

Just as she was carefully walking up the wide front steps, the object of her affection called out to her. "Hey, let me get that for you!"

Fanny stilled as he strode forward and pulled them out of her hands.

And then, there he was. Holding those two cabinet doors like they were two pieces of mail. And scowling at her.

"What's wrong?" she asked.

"You should've asked for help, Fan. Why didn't you ask for me?"

She had. But though she might be younger than him, she sure wasn't so young that she didn't know to keep some things to herself. That blond wasn't going to appreciate her tattling.

So she shrugged. "Would you like me to get the others while you take these inside?"

"No. Wait here a sec." She did exactly as he asked, standing where she was while he carried the two pieces inside, murmured something to the blond, then walked back out again. "Are the others in your vehicle?"

"Yes, sir." She followed him back down the walkway and stood while he reached in and retrieved the last three cabinet doors.

Then she closed the hatchback and followed him back to the front door.

"Close that, would you?" he asked after they passed through. "Janine went to the kitchen to get you something to drink." He flashed a smile her way. "Then we'll see what these samples look like."

"Okay," she said hesitantly, "but there was no need for Janine to wait on me."

"It's warm out. It's no trouble."

Janine came out then, a glass in her hand. "I was going to pour you an iced tea, but some people don't care for that. So it's just water."

"Water is just fine. Thank you." The glass was filled with ice and had a lemon wedge in it.

"Janine, we're going to look at these samples. Want to see them now?"

"Yeah, no thanks." She smiled at Fanny. "I've learned that nothing about this house gets decided on easily," she added as she turned back to the kitchen.

Still holding one of the cabinet doors, Hank led the way down the hall. "Here's the living room."

The walls were white, but there were color samples swiped on one of them. There was also a basic fireplace with terra-cotta tile. "Wow. It's really pretty in here."

"I like it too. I was thinking of this wood to make the mantel and the bookshelves out of. What do you think?"

"I'm not sure."

"No?"

"I've learned that everyone usually has some specific ideas and wishes. It's better not to get involved."

Hank set the door down. "I wouldn't ask if I didn't want your opinion."

"Maybe we should let your, ah . . . Janine decide when she's ready?"

His eyebrows rose. "Janine?"

A weird, uncomfortable feeling settled in her stomach. "Yes, um, maybe she has some fabric or something planned for a sofa or the curtains?" Fanny let her voice trail off.

"Uh, Fanny . . . Frances, Janine is one of my assistants. She works for me."

She felt like she'd just made the stupidest mistake ever. "Oh. I'm sorry. I thought Janine was your girlfriend."

Lines around his eyes crinkled—the only evidence that he was amused. "Janine's engaged. She also started working for me when she was in college. A summer internship turned into a receptionist job, and it went from there."

"Oh."

He lowered his voice. "Whatever you do, don't tell her that you thought she was my girlfriend."

"No, sir." She would also start praying that she never saw him again for the rest of her life. How could she mess something up so badly with so little effort? "I'm so sorry. I'm really embarrassed." She also really hoped Mr. Arias didn't call Nelson about it. She couldn't imagine why he would, but she'd also learned over the years that customers complained about far littler things.

Still staring at Fanny with an expression that was both amused and confused, he murmured, "For the record, I'm not dating anyone. My wife . . . my wife died a few years ago."

"I'm sorry about your loss."

"It was a long time ago." He raised an eyebrow. "I guess Janine didn't introduce herself?"

"No. But it wasn't like there was time. All I said before you found us was that I was here to deliver samples for Nelson." Plus, she'd been just planning to drop off the samples and get on her way.

"Gotcha." He folded his arms over his chest. "Well, now that you know I don't have a girlfriend to confer with, what do you think?"

Fanny was anxious about telling him that she had no preference. But honestly, she could hardly be able to trust herself buying clothes.

But . . . she kind of did have an opinion. "I think a darker stain would look better than this one."

"Why?"

"This is cherry. I think it's too fancy of a hardwood for a rustic home like this."

He slowly nodded. "I can see your point. Let's go see about the other rooms."

"Yes, sir."

Fanny would later not know how she did it, but for the rest of their time together, she'd quietly shared her thoughts for the library and his office.

And then it was time for her to leave.

"Please tell Nelson that I'll email him with my choices tomorrow."

"I'll do that." She reached for the door handle.

"Here. I'll walk you out."

As they walked toward her SUV, he said, "How old are you, Fanny?" Before she could answer, he added, "Sorry, I just realized that's inappropriate."

"I don't mind you asking. It's not a secret. Twenty-eight." Just to tease him, she said, "What about you?"

"I'm forty-two."

"Fourteen years older."

Still staring at her, he nodded. "I've been a widower for quite a while."

"It must be really hard going through that."

He waved a hand. "This isn't going to come out right, but in a lot of ways, I've come to peace with it."

"I don't think that came out wrong at all. I've always felt that the Lord doesn't give a burden that He won't help you through."

"Years ago, I might have argued that, but I think you might be right."

She reached for the door handle of her vehicle. "Have a good night. I'll tell Nelson that you'll be in touch."

"Thanks. Oh, Fanny?"

"Yes?"

He looked down at his feet. Almost smiled before he lifted his head again. "You'll be the one who will be coming back to check on the progress, right?"

"Yes. I mean, I will be if that's okay with you."

"It is. I want you to come back." When her eyes widened, he groaned. "I mean, it would be best if I didn't have to talk to a bunch of other people, right? A detail could slip through the cracks."

"Right. Of course."

"Great. I'll give you a call soon."

"Okay! Can't wait!" she called out before she realized just how idiotic she sounded.

And because she felt like she'd just walked into a scene in one of her favorite rom-coms, she smiled.

She got back into her vehicle in a daze. Actually, she was probably in a daze the entire drive home.

Wondering if he actually would call . . .

And if he did . . . she should tell her boss.

Eager to tell someone, she called her cousin Heidi and put her on speaker.

"Fanny?"

"Hey, can you talk?"

"Um, sure. Hold on a sec." Fanny heard Heidi say something to one of the dogs she watched, then open and close a cabinet. "Sorry. Just getting settled. Now, what's going on? Are you not home yet?"

"Nope. I'm on my way from Hank Arias's house."

"Who's he?"

"Oh, just about the dreamiest guy I've ever met."

As she'd hoped, Heidi giggled. "Well, come on. Tell me all about him." She snapped her fingers. "Hey, wasn't he the quarterback at Berlin High School?"

"Nope. He's from Texas, and he's much older."

"Wait . . . what? How did you meet him?"

Pretty sure she was smiling hugely, Fanny started at the beginning as she headed back to her apartment. She still kind of doubted that Hank would ever really want to take her out . . . but it sure was fun to think about.

At the very least, it was a nice change from work.

chapter eleven

Katie had been churlish from the moment they started walking to Jimmy's parents' house on Saturday evening. That surprised Jenna—usually Katie seemed to like going to Mary and Peter's. It had been a long day, and Jenna was ready for a break. Breaks were good for them both. Katie was used to going to school and seeing her friends, and Jenna was used to having a few hours a day to herself. As much as she loved summer, there were some drawbacks.

That said, she wasn't all that excited to be seeing Mary and Peter either. The biweekly visits always seemed to come too quickly, and the two hours in the Grabers' large homestead always seemed to feel much longer.

To make matters worse, the air was hot and thick with humidity. It would be a miracle if they didn't get stuck walking home in the rain.

But first, they had to get there on time.

"Katie, dear, you must stop dragging your feet. Come along, now."

Instead of picking up the pace, her daughter stuck out her lip. "It's so hot."

"I know, but it's summer. It's supposed to be hot."

"I hate walking over to Mammi and Dawdi's haus."

"You mustn't say that."

"How come? It's the truth."

Feeling her patience slowly ebbing away, she took a deep breath. It didn't really help. Focusing on the uncomfortable way her new pink dress was sticking to her skin, Jenna tried to rustle the hem a little bit. Anything to give her a bit of a breeze.

Or to calm her temper.

Because Katie had once again fallen a good yardstick's measure behind her. "Katie, catch up, if you please. I don't want to be late."

"Because Mammi will get upset with you?"

Yes. "Because it is rude to show up late."

"I want to show up late. I'm tired of going over there."

"Katie, what's wrong? This isn't like you."

When her darling daughter turned her way, Jenna noticed tears in her eyes. It surprised her enough to stop walking. "Why are you crying? Do you have a blister?"

"Nee! I'm crying because I don't want to go."

"Why? I thought you liked going to their house. You know how much they love you."

"They never seem happy."

"I've told you that they are upset about your father dying."

"So?"

"So? Katie Graber, you are being mighty awful. Don't say such things."

"It was mei daed who died, Mamm. How come they never say that? They should be nicer."

She was so taken aback by Katie's words, she felt frozen. Katie was only five years old. Jenna wouldn't have thought that she was capable of thinking such things. But maybe all this time, Jenna had been the one in the wrong. Mary and Peter had been so devastated that she acted as if their feelings counted more than hers.

Or, at the very least, more than Katie's. Katie had barely been four when Jimmy passed away. So young. Jenna had begun to imagine that she'd probably already forgotten how different her life had been when her father was there.

She'd been so very wrong. Grief and loss were felt by everyone, regardless of one's age.

Now here they were, standing on the side of the road in the hot sun, her daughter in tears, and Jenna couldn't think of a single comforting word to say. But she thought it may be best if she responded with honesty. "I agree with you, Katie," she said softly.

"You do?"

The wonder in her daughter's eyes broke her heart. "I do. I also agree that it can be difficult to be around people who are sad all the time. I'm sorry for that, and I wish that they didn't act as if their heartache mattered the most. Love and loss aren't like that. It all matters."

"I miss my daed too."

"I know you do." Jenna sighed, hoping to think of the right words that would make everything better, but she just wasn't sure that was possible. "I keep hoping that one day they will be back to their old selves."

"Me too."

Holding out her hand, Jenna said, "Who knows? Maybe today will be that day."

"I don't think it's gonna be, Mamm."

Jenna didn't even try to stop her chuckle. Out of the mouths of babes! "Since there's nothing we can do about their moods, let's get through tonight. I'll also see if we can just visit them a little less for a while."

"Do you promise?"

Some children expected promises for everything. From a scoop of ice cream for dessert to staying up past bedtime. But Katie took promises seriously. Which meant that Jenna didn't dare promise anything she didn't feel she could deliver. "I promise," she said at last. "Now, I'm sorry, but we really do need to get to Mammi and Dawdi's haus. We're already late."

"They're gonna be mad," she mumbled as they increased their pace.

"Probably. That can't be helped, darling. It is their way."

Katie didn't say anything the rest of the way. Maybe she was too hot, or maybe she knew better than to complain anymore.

When they did arrive at Jimmy's parents' door, all Jenna wanted to do was drink a large glass of cold water and close her eyes for five minutes. Maybe say a prayer. Anything to give her a moment's respite.

That wasn't going to happen, though.

"You are late," Peter said when they walked in. "You should have been here fifteen minutes ago."

"I know. I'm sorry."

"Hmmph," Peter mumbled before giving Katie a hug.

Jenna smiled at him. At least he was kind to his granddaughter.

"I was worried about you, Jenna," Mary chided as she

led the way into the kitchen. "I wish you wouldn't have gotten rid of Jimmy's horse and buggy."

"It was too much for me to take care of. You know that."

"It would've gotten you here on time, though. Ain't so?"

"Perhaps." Instead of continuing to apologize, she walked to the cupboards, pulled out two glasses, and poured herself and Katie some water. "Here, dear. Sit down and relax for a moment."

"Nee, Katie. You must wash up and get ready to sit at the table. The food is ready."

When Katie glanced her way, Jenna spoke up. "I know it's ready, but she needs to sit for a moment. I do too. It was a long, hot walk." Pulling out the kitchen chairs, she motioned for Katie to join her.

Mary's expression pinched, but she didn't say a word. Instead, she started bustling around the kitchen as if she was expecting a crowd of twenty instead of just Jenna and Katie.

When Peter walked in, he stared at them in confusion. "What is going on? I thought we were about to eat."

Jenna stood up. "We are. I'm sorry, but Katie and I needed to cool off for a moment after the walk."

"Oh. Well, Mary, are you ready now?"

"I've been ready."

"Go sit down with Dawdi, Katie," Jenna said. "I'm going to help Mammi carry the serving dishes to the table."

"Okay."

Standing up, Jenna reached for the platter that Mary was about to pick up. "I'll take this in."

"Danke." Mary's tone was like ice. Jenna couldn't help

but wish that it would cool the temperature of the room as well.

After everything was at the table and they bowed their heads in silent prayer, Jenna served Katie the baked meatballs, noodles, broccoli salad, and fruit with Cool Whip before filling her plate as well.

Maybe Mary wasn't always the easiest to get along with, but she was certainly a good cook. After Jenna took a few bites, she said, "This is as delicious as always, Mary. Thank you for having us over tonight."

"You are welcome. Peter and I were anxious to see you."

"Oh?" She smiled softly, ready to hear how Katie's presence brightened their day.

"We heard some distressing news yesterday, and it kept me up all night."

"I'm sorry."

"I am hoping you will be able to tell us that the story we heard was only a rumor."

Jenna put down her fork. "What news are you referring to?"

After Mary and Peter exchanged looks, Peter answered, "We have heard that Nelson Harper is stopping by your haus from time to time. Is that true?"

"It is."

Mary inhaled sharply.

Peter frowned. "This is most irregular. I never understood why he had the nerve to visit you in the first place. But what I really don't understand is why he is still visiting you."

"Why are you allowing him on Jimmy's property?" Mary asked.

Jimmy's property? It was hers now. Wasn't it?

Before Jenna could think of a civil reply, Katie exclaimed, "Nelson is our friend! He gave us Blue."

"Who is Blue?" Mary asked.

The tension between her and Jimmy's parents was almost unbearable. She would give anything to simply stand up and walk away. But these people were Katie's grandparents. For her sake, Jenna knew she needed to be civil. "Blue is a kitten. One of the workers at the mill was giving away free kittens. Nelson brought him over for Katie."

"And you accepted it?"

"Indeed, we did."

"Blue is so cute, Mammi."

"I don't understand why Nelson Harper brought a gift to our granddaughter," Peter said in a low voice. "It is unseemly."

"It wasn't unseemly. Katie loves it." This conversation was getting stranger and stranger. Why were they now acting as if she didn't count?

"Nelson gave me a kitten because he calls me Kitty." Katie took a bite and announced, "I love him."

And . . . things just managed to get worse.

Peter's expression turned thunderous. "Nelson is the reason Jimmy died, Jenna. It is his fault that he's dead."

It took everything she had not to run to Katie when she cried out. But she was too angry to do anything but speak her mind. "That is old news that was never true in the first place. Everyone knows that Jimmy had an accident."

"That's what everyone at the mill wants us to think," he whispered. "But it is not the truth."

"The truth is that the police and all sorts of people investigated Jimmy's accident. Everyone in the building was interviewed, and the machine was even examined by the company who made it. In addition, I spoke to the police officers who were on the scene. I also spoke to the EMTs, and the doctors and nurses who attended to him in the hospital. Jimmy was in an awful accident. It wasn't anyone's fault. But if you do want to blame someone besides Jimmy, Nelson isn't the right man. He was nowhere near Jimmy when it happened."

"It was his company," Mary said. "It's because of him that we no longer have a son. And why Katie won't ever have a daed."

Tears were now streaming down Katie's face. Jenna felt herself shaking as she realized that Peter and Mary's words were likely to never be completely forgotten. They were scarring her poor daughter.

It wasn't right. It wasn't right at all.

She got to her feet. "Come along, Katie. We are leaving." When Katie hurried to her side with a grateful look, any traces of doubt that remained inside of her vanished.

"You can't go, Jenna. You just got here," Peter said as he stood up.

"We cannot stay. Not now." She put an arm around Katie's shoulders.

"But what would Jimmy want?" Mary asked. She sounded on the edge of tears.

That was the last straw. "I don't know what Jimmy would want, Mary. He has been gone for almost two years. All I do know is that he treated me and Katie like we were precious to him. He loved me and he adored Katie, and there is nothing you can say that would convince me that he would be okay with you making Katie cry."

"Your friendship with Nelson is the problem."

"Nee, it is your refusal to admit that it is no one's fault that Jimmy died. And your refusal to see how much harm your cruel words about Nelson and my acceptance of his friendship have caused."

Jenna hurried to the front door, grabbing her purse. "Come on, Katie. We don't need to be here anymore." As the door closed behind them, she felt as if she was talking about more than just this one meal. It felt as if she was talking about their future.

It was painful to acknowledge.

Katie gripped her hand as they walked back through the yard and eventually got to the road.

When thunder roared overhead, Katie didn't even flinch. She simply kept clinging to Jenna's hand and walking in a straight line.

Jenna was thankful for the silence. Honestly, she had nothing of worth to say.

Nothing that would change their reality, anyway.

chapter twelve

Nelson had hoped to beat the storm on his way home, but it looked as if that wasn't going to happen. As he turned the windshield wipers to a higher setting, he tapped his brakes with a sigh. He'd driven down to Cincinnati that morning, stopped to have lunch with one of his suppliers in Columbus, and then got stuck on I-71 when an accident shut down one of the lanes.

Now that he was only a few minutes away from home, the heavens had decided to work against him. He slowed down further and turned on his lights. One had to be careful on these narrow, winding roads all the time because of the number of Amish buggies, bicycles, and scooters that frequented it.

In a torrential rainstorm, it was a white-knuckle situation. All he wanted to do was get out of his vehicle, quickly answer the pile of emails that were sure to be in his inbox, and take a hot shower.

Shifting in his seat as the muscles in his back protested, Nelson gritted his teeth. Ever since he'd gotten hurt playing softball a couple of years ago, his body hated sitting for long periods of time. "Almost there," he muttered to himself as he moved to turn up the radio dial.

Then he saw them.

An Amish woman and her little girl walking under the worst umbrella ever. The thing was small and didn't seem to be any match for the rain pouring down.

He hoped they'd accept a ride from him. After checking that there wasn't anyone right behind him, he slowed down even more. Nelson was about to lower his window to offer them a lift when he realized it was Jenna and Katie.

Glad there was still no one behind them for miles, he quickly pulled to the side of the road just ahead of them and hopped out. "Jenna! Katie!"

"Nelson?" Jenna said.

"Yeah. It's me. Come here," he added as he strode toward them. The closer he got, the more worried he became about them. Each of them was soaked to the skin, and visible goose bumps were on Katie's arms. Why were they out in this storm?

"I'm so glad to see you!" Jenna exclaimed. "This rain has been awful."

"You're right about that." Fighting the urge to pull her against him, Nelson grabbed hold of her useless umbrella instead. "Are you okay?"

"I think so. We're just wet."

After he closed the umbrella, Nelson bent down for Katie.

"I'm gonna pick you up, Kitty," he said as he scooped her up against his chest. With his free hand, he wrapped his arm around Jenna's shoulders. "Come on. Let's get you inside the truck."

To his surprise, Jenna didn't utter a word of protest as she leaned toward him.

Sure, it was pouring down rain and he was worried about Katie, but there was something inside him that felt as if he was finally doing something for Jenna that she appreciated. No, that she needed.

And that made every protective instinct he'd ever possessed come to life.

Opening the passenger-side door, he helped Jenna get in and then handed Katie to her. "Buckle her up in the middle, Jenna," he murmured before trotting back to his side.

He was soaked to the skin, and he'd only been outside a few minutes.

Anger lit inside him as he wondered where they'd been. Who would have encouraged them to walk home when it had been so obvious that it was about to storm?

Nelson pushed those thoughts aside and forced himself to focus on the present. There would be plenty of time to discuss their situation later.

"Katie, are you all buckled in?" he asked as he turned the ignition back on.

"Uh-huh." She tapped the seat-belt buckle to show him.

"And Jenna?"

"I am too, Nelson." She touched the strap across her chest with a smile at her daughter. "But it's time you buckled in as well, jah?"

He gave her a small smile. "Yes, it is," he added while he quickly buckled his own seat belt. Glad he'd turned on his hazards when a car zipped by, splashing water from the road's surface, Nelson fiddled with the air, turning it to a warmer temperature. "We're close to my house. I'm going to take you both there so we can get you dry."

Jenna looked like she was about to argue but seemed to notice the way Katie was shivering too. "Thank you," she said.

"I've never been to your house, Nelson," Katie said as he pulled back onto the road.

"I know, and I can't wait to show it to you."

"I'm cold."

"I know, baby. I'll help your mom get you wrapped up in some warm blankets."

She giggled. "I'm not a baby."

He couldn't believe that word had slipped out, but maybe it wasn't much of a surprise after all. Honestly, there were even moments when he'd wanted to call Jenna a bunch of endearments, but he'd bitten them back. It seemed that all he'd needed was for them both to be soaking wet and cold for one to finally see the light of day. "You are right," he said. "You are a big girl. Not a baby at all. It was my mistake." He glanced at Jenna, ready to apologize for the slip, but she didn't seem upset by it. Though, no doubt, she was likely trying her best to keep calm for Katie's sake.

They drove in silence for the next few minutes, only the heat blasting from the vents disturbing the quiet. When he turned into his driveway at last, he breathed a sigh of relief. "We made it."

Katie's eyes widened. "We're at your house?"

"Yep."

"Are we gonna get wet again when we get out?" Katie asked.

"Nope. I have a garage." He slowed to a stop and pointed to the opener. "Press the button for me, Kitty."

Reaching up, she pressed the garage door opener and then beamed when the door started going up in front of them.

After he pulled in, he and Jenna exited. Just as Jenna was about to reach for Katie, the little girl turned to him. "Will you carry me again?"

"Of course. Come here."

When he wrapped his arms around the five-year-old, Nelson was struck again by just how soaked her pink dress was. Her arms were still cool to the touch as well. "We need to get you warm, Katie."

"I know."

Jenna chuckled under her breath as she followed him into the house.

Nelson was glad that she was still not protesting his decision to bring them to his house. In fact, she looked as chilled as her daughter.

He walked them through the sprawling ranch to the master suite. "Jenna, I'm starting to think that you girls might need to take a warm shower. How about I pull out some of my sweats for you and an old T-shirt for Katie?" he asked as he gently put Katie down. "You two can get warm while I put your clothes in the dryer."

It was obvious that Jenna was ready to protest that idea—until she caught sight of herself and Katie in the mirror. They really did look like wet rats. Plus, more important than that was the fact that they were both chilled. "Danke."

He strode to one of the walk-in closets nearby, then

opened a couple of drawers, pulled out sweats, two T-shirts, and a zip-up hoodie, and set them on the counter. "There are extra towels in the cabinet next to the shower and shampoo and conditioner in the shower if you want to wash your hair."

"We won't be doing that."

"Use whatever you need, Jenna. When you're all done, bring me your wet clothes, okay?" When she nodded, he smiled. "I'll leave you alone, then. Please, take your time."

"Thank you."

Not wanting to make her any more uncomfortable than she already was, he walked out and headed down the hall.

After stepping into the guest bath and towel-drying his own damp hair, he frowned. He could use a change of shirt too. Glad that he still had a pile of clothes on top of his dryer from his housekeeper's last visit, Nelson switched to a dry one.

Feeling better already, he padded down the hall in bare feet to the kitchen. He knew Jenna well enough to know that a cup of fresh coffee was in order.

Digging in the back of a cabinet, he found a packet of hot chocolate mix too. Pleased to have something else to do to help Jenna out, he got to work.

It was amazing how taking care of Jenna and Katie felt like second nature to him.

No, more than that. It was as if he'd been waiting years to have the chance. Now that it was here, he needed to concentrate on the moment. Not worry about what was going to happen next with them.

Because he was pretty sure that as soon as he served Jenna and Katie hot drinks, gave them a couple of Oreos, and handed them back their dry clothes, the two of them would be more than ready to leave.

And after he dropped them off, would Jenna still let him visit? Or would things be awkward once again, especially after Jenna reminded him that she had no interest in ever marrying. It went without saying that she certainly didn't want to marry an Englisher.

Or her husband's old boss.

Regret filled him as he realized that this would probably be the only time Jenna and Katie were in his house. One of the master suite's closets would never be Jenna's, and neither of his two guest rooms would ever be filled with Katie's laughter.

The best thing he could hope for was that he and Jenna would still be friends.

Then later, when she decided to eventually marry again, their relationship would grow even more distant. She'd have no reason to see him anymore.

After all, anything more would be next to impossible.

chapter thirteen

Jenna knew she shouldn't be surprised by the number of questions Katie was able to ask while they were in Nelson's very plush and fancy bathroom, but she was. From the moment Nelson left his bedroom suite, Katie had become a magpie.

She was curious about everything. Nelson's big, bright, sprawling house. The carpet in the bedroom, the large, stand-alone bathtub that looked as if it had never been used. The wide, glass-enclosed shower that held not one but three showerheads. Katie had been so confused by that, she'd even asked Jenna who Nelson took showers with. Jenna didn't know if her face had ever been so red.

Instead of answering, Jenna concentrated on getting them both warm. It was a blessing when she figured out the temperature controls and got into the shower with Katie. She practically moaned when the warm spray soaked into their skin.

Before she knew it, Jenna was breaking her vow to get in and out of his shower in five minutes. The hot water felt too good, and the coconut-lime-scented bath soap, shampoo, and conditioner felt too wonderful to ignore.

Katie was happy to let her finish showering on her own. She got out, successfully wrapped herself in a towel that was as big as she was, and sat on a bath mat, playing with a collection of small soaps she'd found in a basket under one of the two sinks.

Jenna thought it was a strange collection for a man like Nelson to have, but perhaps there was a story there. Maybe he had once shared this house with a woman. He was a handsome Englisher man in his mid-thirties. Perhaps he'd built this house for her. Jenna had no idea, but she had a feeling that Katie would ask Nelson soon.

Maybe later in the evening or tomorrow Jenna would be embarrassed about the direction of her thoughts. Not now, though. It would be wrong to focus on such things when she felt so relaxed and relieved.

That walk home had gotten so bad, so quickly. She'd been afraid for Katie and felt guilty for not taking better care of her.

Reminding herself that they were both all right, Jenna leaned against the shower wall, closed her eyes, and gave thanks. Before Nelson had picked them up, she'd started to wonder if they should turn back. It would have been difficult to do. Not only would they have been backtracking, but she would've had to listen to Mary fuss over Katie in a way that would somehow put the blame for the sudden storm on Jenna's shoulders. Her daughter would've been safe and warm, though. Putting up with a few more hours of discomfort would have been worth it.

Now Katie was safe and warm, and Jenna was enjoying the best shower of her life. The Lord had surely been looking out for them today.

"Mamm?"

She opened her eyes. "Jah, Katie?"

"Nelson has seven soaps in this basket. That's a lot."

"Jah, I suppose it is."

"Four of them are blue. Do you think he likes blue soap?"

"I have no idea."

"One of the soaps is pink, and another is white."

"It's quite a collection." She smiled. No doubt Katie would soon let Jenna know what color the seventh soap was.

"Mm-hmm. Are you gonna get out soon?"

"Hmm? Oh yes. I should probably do that." Realizing she was probably using all of Nelson's hot water, Jenna turned the knob to the right.

Instantly the luxurious spray ceased, leaving her in a cloud of fragrant, warm steam. Jenna paused for another lovely minute before reaching for the second large, fluffy bath towel.

After securing it around her body, she opened a drawer, found a comb, and went about combing both Katie's and her wet hair, then got them both dressed in Nelson's clothes.

"Nelson's shirt is almost as long as a dress on me!" Katie giggled.

"That is true," she said with a smile. Looking at herself in the mirror, Jenna noticed that she was swimming in Nelson's clothes too. But his T-shirt, sweatpants, and zip-up felt cozy and comfortable after being soaked to the skin.

"Do we have to put back on our kapps now?"

Both of their kapps were resting on the marble bathroom countertop. Despite the fact that she'd attempted to pat them dry, they still looked rather soggy and flat. "Not yet," she decided. "After our clothes are dry, we'll pin up our hair and put them back on. That will be soon enough."

"Oh, gut. I don't like tying up my hair when it's all wet."

"It's not my favorite thing to do either, child. But that reminds me, we need to give Nelson our clothes so he can put them in the dryer. You hold your towel."

Nelson was waiting for them in the living room when they walked out. He'd also changed and looked as handsome as ever in a pair of jeans and a long-sleeved light-blue T-shirt. Jenna stopped in surprise. Since when had she ever thought such a thing? He was Nelson. Her friend.

You are a widow, yes, but you still have eyes, a silly, nagging voice in her head reminded her. She blinked. She was tempted to be ashamed but then realized that it would be silly to be embarrassed by nothing more than a passing thought.

She should have no problem recognizing Nelson's good looks. It was the same as appreciating a beautiful flower or admiring the scent of fresh-baked bread. She simply had a friend who was exceptionally handsome. And kind. And good with Katie. And who made her smile. Why, she should be grateful to have such a person in her life.

And she was. She was grateful for Nelson. Nee, she was glad to have him as a friend.

There was nothing wrong with their friendship or her feelings for him. Was there?

"Jenna, did you hear me?"

Things were getting worse and worse! She shook her head. "I'm sorry, what did you say?"

He frowned. "I was telling you where the laundry room is, but maybe you don't have one in an Amish home?"

"We do."

"So . . ."

Katie giggled. "Nelson already took my towel."

"Of course. I mean, yes, please let me know . . ."

"I'll take you there."

To her surprise, the laundry room was near the bedroom off the hall. The door had been closed when they'd walked by. She'd supposed it was a closet. When he opened it, she was shocked to see a sizable room with not only a washer and dryer but also a small refrigerator, a countertop, and lots of cabinets.

"This is a big room for laundry, Nelson." And so very fancy.

He smirked. "Yeah, I guess it is. When I first went over the plans with the architect, I told him that I'd never need anything like this. But he reminded me that a wife and two or three children would take up a whole lot more laundry space than I could imagine. But as you can see, I've put it to good use."

She tossed her clothes in the dryer and put the used towels in the washing machine. "I've always thought that one cannot have too much storage space."

"I agree." He turned a knob, pushed a button, and the dryer set to work. "I bet everything will be dry in fifteen minutes or so."

She hadn't thought it would be so fast. "I guess I should now ask if you happen to have a hair dryer?"

"I'm sorry, I don't. As a bachelor, there aren't a lot of feminine touches around here, I'm afraid." Looking sheepish, he added, "The only thing I have for women is a basket of soaps someone from work gave me three Christmases ago. His wife made them, and I've been afraid to give them away."

Well, there was the answer to Katie's question. And hers. "That's all right. Katie and I can pin up our hair before we leave." She noticed then that he was gazing at her hair. For a second, she considered apologizing, but there was nothing to apologize for. He'd invited her to use his shower, and she had long hair. "I guess it must be strange for you to see my head uncovered."

"Um, yes. But really, I was just thinking that I hadn't realized how long your hair was."

Feeling self-conscious, she smiled at him. "When one doesn't ever cut one's hair, it grows and grows."

"It's beautiful."

"Thank you," she whispered before she realized that she probably shouldn't have acknowledged the compliment.

Nelson met her gaze. Inhaled. Then, seeming to collect himself, he smiled at her daughter. "Yours is too, Katie."

"I like when I don't have to wear my kapp. It feels gut not to have any pins in my head."

"I bet." His gaze warmed when he glanced Jenna's way. After a second, Nelson looked away again. "How about some coffee and hot chocolate?"

Katie's eyes widened. "You have hot chocolate here?"

"I do. Plus, I brewed a fresh pot of coffee."

Just as aware of the new tension that seemed to be flowing between the two of them, Jenna cleared her throat. "That would be nice, Nelson. Danke."

After noticing how nice his living room furniture was, Jenna suggested that they sit at the kitchen table. Nelson had tried to encourage them to relax, but Jenna knew better. "Little hands and hot chocolate cups are practically begging to have accidents, Nelson. Your ivory couches won't appreciate the messes."

"Understood."

After Katie sipped about half her drink, she asked Nelson if she could lie down on the couch and use the blanket that was tossed over it. When Nelson agreed, she crawled around on the couch, made a little nest, and then promptly fell asleep.

Jenna was surprised but knew that she shouldn't be. It had been a long evening, and now Katie was warm and clean and felt safe and relaxed. It was no wonder she didn't want to leave.

She felt very much the same way. Which wasn't good. "Nelson, if you give me a few minutes, I can gather our things together while Katie is sleeping."

"No reason to do that yet, is there? I mean, your clothes are still in the dryer."

"Yes, but—"

Nelson stood up. "How about we go into the hearth room off the kitchen? We can have another cup of coffee and chat while your clothes are drying."

"All right." Following him into the other room, Jenna attempted to get a grip on herself. Sure, she felt awkward, but she told herself not to be so foolish. She was a grown, independent woman, and Nelson was her friend. Friends relaxed over a cup of coffee in the evening all the time. No one would ever have to know that she was sitting alone with him with her hair down and her clothes in a dryer.

After topping off their coffee, Nelson flicked a switch next to the fireplace. Orange flames appeared, warming her skin. "This is nice," she said.

"I agree. Every time I'm in here, I realize that I should use it more often."

"You don't relax in here in the evenings after work?"

"Not usually."

Jenna realized then that she didn't actually know what Nelson did in his spare time. "How come?"

He frowned. "I usually bring work home. By the time I finish, all I want to do is take a shower and collapse in bed."

"When do you eat?"

He shrugged. "While I'm working. It's usually just a sandwich or something."

"Nelson, that isn't good."

He chuckled. "I suppose you're right. I can't help it, though. I feel obligated to make sure Alliance Millworks continues to grow and prosper."

"Because it's your family's company."

"Yeah. My dad and uncle are retired, but they're still emotionally invested." He shrugged. "I am too."

"Nelson, I think you should think about doing less work at home. Everyone needs some time to relax. Even you."

He chuckled. "I bet you're right."

"I know I am."

"Hey, I have gotten better," he teased. "On Monday nights, I visit a friend of mine and her little girl."

Meeting his gaze, Jenna realized that she'd been looking at their relationship all wrong. She'd been thinking only of what he did for her, but now she realized that he'd been needing her and Katie in his life too. They were giving him a reason not to work all night.

They visited with him, joked, and chatted about all kinds of things that had nothing to do with his company. And that was so true. She wasn't Nelson's friend because he was successful. She was his friend because he was kind and easy to be with.

"I'm sorry I pushed you away. I won't do that again."

His gaze softened, pulling her closer. For a brief moment, Jenna allowed herself to study his face. She loved his eyes. Loved the way there were faint lines around them when he smiled. She liked his clean-shaven jaw . . . and the way it looked now, with the faint scruff from a day's growth.

"Jenna, why were you and Katie walking home in the rain?"

The question felt like ice water splashing against her skin. Spurring her back to reality.

"I got upset with my in-laws," she said. "I didn't like the way they were speaking to me."

He leaned forward. "What were they saying?"

It was so tempting to say that it was nothing important. To gloss over Mary and Peter's comments as foolish talk. Or maybe put the blame on herself and proclaim that she'd been too sensitive.

But she couldn't.

"They . . . well, they haven't gotten over Jimmy's death. Sometimes they act as if I should still be wearing black and constantly crying."

"Jenna, can you imagine what Jimmy would say to that?"

"Jah, I can," she replied with a faint smile. "He would have a lot to say about that." Jimmy had been full of life and would have expected her to be the same way.

"Is that all they were upset about?"

"Nee." She swallowed but forced herself to look him in the eye. "They don't like our friendship, Nelson."

"They blame me for Jimmy's accident."

She nodded because agreeing out loud would feel too awful.

"I'm sorry," he said after a moment passed.

His words hung in the air, but they eased her. The truth was that she was sorry that Jimmy's parents were still angry too. She was sorry that they seemed to put his memory above her very human needs.

But most of all she was sorry that Nelson was aware of how angry they were at him . . . and she had no idea how to make that situation better.

chapter fourteen

When Jenna opened her eyes the next morning, she thought of two things. The first was that she was glad it was Sunday and there was no church that week. The second was that she was alone in her bed once again.

Last night, about two hours after Katie had fallen asleep on Nelson's couch and she and Nelson had traded some secrets, Jenna woke her daughter up. Nelson gave them the option of sleeping in his guest room, but Jenna had refused. He'd looked disappointed but didn't argue. Instead, he nodded, helped them get their things together, and drove them to their house.

After making sure they got inside okay and didn't need anything, he'd driven away. From the front window, Katie had watched his truck's taillights fade from view. Only then would she accept that it was time to go to sleep in her own bed.

Sleep had come much later for Jenna. She'd been bothered by warring emotions and the feeling of emptiness when she finally got between the cool cotton sheets of her bed.

Now, as she stared at her blank walls, reality set in again. Like a sledgehammer to her heart, the reminder of all she'd lost was crushing. Her husband was forever gone. No matter how much she prayed or wished things would be different, they weren't going to be. She'd never see Jimmy's smile again. She'd never playfully kick his foot when he started snoring in the middle of the night.

He'd never hold her until she fell asleep.

"I miss you, Jimmy," she whispered. Pretending that she could almost hear her words floating in the air, she closed her eyes. And wished she could hear a reply. It would sure be nice if she could.

Sitting up, she moved to the side of the bed but hesitated to hop down and start her day. Instead, Jenna allowed herself to remember how things used to be. To think of what she used to take for granted just two years ago.

Every morning, long before the sun rose, Jimmy would arise before she did. While she tried to catch a few more minutes of rest, he would quietly pad into the bathroom, turn on the flashlight, and get dressed.

Then, still in bare feet, he would check on Katie, then walk down the hall to the kitchen and light the gas stove so the percolator would start making coffee. While it was brewing, he'd open a drawer in the mudroom and pull out a pair of socks, slip on his boots, and then head out to the barn.

When they had a cow, he'd milk her. After he finished that chore, he would tend to the horses and hens as well. If it had snowed in the night, he'd clear off their front porch and steps, then shovel a path from the house to the barn.

Only after all of that was done would he go back to

the house. Then, after taking care of the milk, he would finally slip off his boots and pour himself a cup of coffee.

That was about the time when she would wander into the kitchen at last.

"You look pretty today, Jen," he'd say just before he kissed her.

She'd feel warm and pleased when she'd rest her hands on his chest. Then not think about much at all when their lips met. Well, nothing much beyond the fact that Jimmy tasted like coffee and fresh air and Jimmy. She'd been sure there wasn't a better moment on earth.

Unless it was on the rare days when she'd accidentally sleep late and he would bring her a cup of coffee in bed. That was when he'd kiss her awake and murmur sweet, romantic things in her ear.

In the days before Katie . . . well, sometimes he'd climb right back in bed, and her coffee would be ignored until it had grown cold.

She'd been so blessed. And once, when she shared with a girlfriend just how much Jimmy doted on her every morning, she'd blushed. Even back then she knew that most husbands didn't spoil their wives in such a way.

"Did I ever tell you how much I adored those mornings, Jim?" she whispered.

This time, the silence broke her heart. Mainly because she knew that answer.

No, she'd never actually told him that. She'd been too embarrassed. She'd thought it was unseemly to mention how much he'd always seemed to desire her. She'd been sure no one ever spoke about such things in the light of day.

That had been a mistake.

"You should have said the words, Jenna," she said out loud, even though the tears that were threatening to fall seemed to be clogging her throat. "You should have told Jimmy how much you loved feeling so wanted. He should have known how you felt before he died."

"Mamm, who are ya talking to?"

Jenna turned her head. Katie was standing in the doorway in her nightgown. One of her hands was gripping the fabric around her thighs. Almost as if it would provide her security.

"No one," she murmured. "I was just . . . well, I was just thinking about your father."

"Daed?"

"Jah." She stood up and held out her arms. "Come here and give me a hug."

Katie hurried over and wrapped her arms around Jenna's waist. "When you think about Daed, do you always talk out loud?"

"Nee. Usually, it's just in my head. But sometimes, when I'm sleepy or really missing him, I do talk to him out loud." Katie looked surprised, and Jenna ran a hand down her daughter's hair. "What about you? Do you ever talk to Daed when you're in your room?"

She shook her head. "Nee. I didn't think I was supposed to. Would God be mad if I did?"

"I don't think He'd mind," she said as they drew apart.

"Mammi said I should only talk to Daed when I'm standing next to his headstone." She paused, seemed to consider her words, then blurted, "Do you talk to Daed there too?"

"I have, but I think you can talk to him anywhere." Hoping her words would help and not give the child more to worry about, she added, "When I talk to Daed, I know God is listening. And I know that your father loved us so much."

"Oh." She swallowed. "I'm glad. I don't really like talking to him in the graveyard."

Jenna frowned. She could only remember walking Katie to Jimmy's headstone once, and that was on the anniversary of his death. Katie had looked so sad afterward, she promised herself not to take her there again until she asked. "When did you do that?"

She shrugged. "I don't know. We go to see Daed's grave a lot."

Jenna was shocked, both about what Mary had told Katie about talking to Jimmy . . . and that Mary had taken Katie to Jimmy's grave. "I didn't know that."

"I know." Katie looked sad.

And Jenna was feeling even more confused than ever. "Katie, dear, do you want to visit your father's grave more often?"

She shook her head.

"Are you sure?"

"Jah." Lowering her voice, she whispered, "I miss Daed, but I don't always remember everything about him. I don't like going to the graveyard either." Her eyes widened. "Is that bad?"

"Nee. Not at all."

"Are you sure? Because Mammi and Dawdi say I should always be thinking about Daed."

Jenna felt her temper rise. How could her in-laws say such things to a little girl? She wanted to yell at them. Or, at the very least, tell Katie that Mary and Peter were wrong.

Neither was a good choice, though. No, what she needed to do was say something reassuring without making Jimmy's parents sound terrible.

Pulling herself together, she carefully sat back down on the side of the bed and held out an arm. "Hop up here by me."

When Katie climbed up, she cuddled close to her side. Inhaling, Jenna smelled her little-girl goodness, and that eased her temper. And helped her find the right words too. "Katie, your father was in a terrible accident. One moment he was okay, and the next he was badly injured and didn't know what was happening. He didn't have time to get his thoughts together and tell us what we should do when he died."

She took a deep breath. "But, if he had, I am certain that your father would tell us to trust God, and if we ever needed to talk to him, God would understand."

"Even if we're not standing at his grave?"

Gathering her thoughts, Jenna whispered, "Katie, I promise that your father did not want you to go stand in a graveyard to talk to him. You don't have to go there all the time. He knows you loved him. And . . ." She took a deep breath. "Honey, Daed wouldn't want us to be sad for the rest of our days. He'd be upset if we were."

"Really?"

"Really. He loved us. Do you want people you love to always be sad?"

"Nee." She shook her head as if to emphasize her point.

"I don't either. I want people I love to be happy. Or, if they're not really happy, I want them to be okay. Not sad and angry or crying."

"I don't want that either."

"Okay, then. I'm going to speak to Mammi and Dawdi and tell them how we feel."

Her eyes widened. "They might get mad at you."

"If they do, I'll explain how I feel and how I think your daed would feel. I'm sure they'll listen and understand." Jenna felt a little pinch of unease as Katie seemed to process her words. The truth was that she wasn't all that sure that Mary or Peter would appreciate her point of view. She was actually pretty sure that they'd argue with her.

"I hope so."

"Me too." Standing up, she held out a hand. "Now, let's go downstairs and have some breakfast."

"Even if we're still in our nightgowns?"

"Yep. Today's a special day. I'm calling it 'Eat Breakfast in Nightgown Day.'"

Katie clapped her hands. "I like this day!"

Her heart full, Jenna looked down at her sweet daughter. She imagined that years from now, when Katie was a grown woman with a family of her own, she might tell Jenna how talks like this got her through such a dark period in their lives.

Jenna would be so pleased to share that she felt the same way. She wasn't sure how she would've been able to get through some of her darkest days if she'd been alone.

Not only had Katie given her a reason to wake up every morning, but she'd also given her a reason to smile. She thought that was just as important.

"Me too, child," she said at last. "I like this day too. I like it a lot."

chapter fifteen

"Hey, Nelson?" Fanny called out. "Do you have a minute?"

Nelson looked up from the pile of invoices and neatly written notes on his desk. Once a week, each of his division managers was required to give him a summary of the orders taken, work that had gone out, and a listing of any jobs that still needed to be fulfilled.

He knew the managers detested the practice, especially since most of it was already online. More than one had grumbled that compiling everything in a paper clip with handwritten notes was antiquated and a waste of valuable time. Nelson would've agreed if the practice hadn't proved to be beneficial to the business. The simple practice of organizing numbers and jobs had highlighted all sorts of problems—and ways they could be remedied. Employees had been overlooked for bonuses or raises when it was obvious that they went above and beyond. The opposite had been true too. Some employees consistently were behind schedule or continually made mistakes that had to be corrected.

Then there were the vendors who consistently ran late

with deliveries and customers who did the same with their payments. If his area managers didn't flag the problems and mark them in a specific folder, Nelson had no doubt that it would take twice as long to investigate where the gaps were in production—or in the anticipated earnings for each quarter.

But although all these things were very good and important for Alliance Millworks' well-being, Nelson privately hated the paperwork as much as everyone else did.

Because of that, he happily pushed aside the papers and put down the reading glasses he'd recently had to start wearing. That's when he noticed that Fanny's usually chipper manner was absent. "What's going on, Fan?"

She held up a letter. "You got another one."

Surprise followed by its new buddy dread filled him as he stood up. "Are you sure it's from the Grabers?" he asked, making sure to keep his voice low as he approached her desk.

"I'm afraid so. It's the same handwriting on the same stationery. Just to make sure, I pulled out the file where I kept the others and compared them."

"Thank you for doing that."

"What would you like me to do?"

"Nothing. Well, nothing besides hand it over." Taking the unwanted note, he sighed. "I keep thinking that Peter and Mary are going to move on with their lives and stop, but I don't know. Maybe they can't let their grief go."

Fanny shook her head. "There's grief, and then there's what they've been doing. Mr. and Mrs. Graber seem to be determined to hurt you."

Even a year ago, Nelson would have disagreed with

Fanny's statement. Everyone at the company had been shaken by Jimmy's accident and death. Nelson might have wanted Jimmy to be more focused while he was doing his job, but that didn't mean he had ever thought Jimmy deserved to get hurt.

Plus, Jimmy had been a friendly sort. Most everyone had liked him, and his loss was a tragedy.

"Yeah. I think you're probably right," he said at last. That acknowledgment didn't make him feel any better, though. Especially not after Jenna quietly relayed the things Peter and Mary had told her when she'd been at his house.

Relief filled Fanny's expression. "I'm so glad you feel that way." She took a deep breath. "Listen, I've been thinking about this situation, boss, and I think that it's time you got some help with it."

"From whom?"

"The police."

She looked so earnest, he didn't want to crack a smile, but it was hard not to. "Fanny, Peter and Mary Graber aren't doing anything illegal. All they're doing is sharing their thoughts. They're entitled."

"They're doing more than that, and we both know it. At first, yes, they were just sharing their pain and their opinions."

"That was their right."

"Yes . . ." She grimaced. "But they were also voicing their thoughts about an accident they didn't see and that they don't know the whole story about."

"For them to know that Jimmy had once again decided

to operate the machine without a partner was unnecessary."

She waved a hand. "Allowing them to think that he was simply a victim in a bad accident is not okay. Especially now, because the tone of their letters is a lot more threatening and mean than it used to be."

"How do you know what's in this letter? You didn't read it, did you?" he teased, since it was obvious that the envelope was still sealed.

"You know I didn't, but what else do they ever write?" With a sigh, she leaned back in her chair. "I feel sorry for their loss, but everyone here knows that Jimmy was—at the very least—partly to blame for the accident. It wasn't your fault. Not at all."

"I hear what you're saying."

"Are you sure, Nelson?" Getting to her feet, she walked around her desk. "Because sometimes it feels like you might *know* you aren't responsible for his death but you still feel guilty."

"I don't feel guilty," he said quickly. Because he didn't. It was more a vague feeling that someone had to be ultimately responsible for the accident and he was the last stop. As the head of the company, there was no one else to blame.

"If you don't feel guilty, then why are you still bringing food to his widow?"

He was still bringing her things because he was still half in love with her. "We're not going to talk about Jenna. She's off-limits."

"Why? Is it because you don't care about her at all . . . or because you care too much?"

"Fanny, I wasn't joking. I don't want to discuss Jenna."

"Okay, fine. But I hope you'll eventually remember that you've got a lot of people in your support system."

He had to smirk. "Support system?"

"Don't make fun of me. I'm being serious. You've got plenty of people here at the mill and in your family to discuss your feelings with. Jimmy's death and his parents' fixation on hurting you because they're hurting isn't nice or fair." Folding her arms over her chest, Fanny smiled softly. "There's no reason to keep everything all inside, cousin."

"I'm not. We're talking about it, don't you think?"

"No. I think we're not even scratching the surface. I'm really worried that one of these days something with the Grabers and Jenna and you is going to blow up. And when that happens, it's going to be really tough, not only because you haven't been open and honest with what you've been dealing with but because by the time that happens, you'll have isolated yourself so much that you won't even know where to turn."

"I hear you. Thanks for letting me know about the letter."

"You're welcome."

Just as he was going back to his pile of paperwork, he remembered a text he'd received on his cell phone from Hank Arias. "Hey, I just remembered that I never double-checked with you about the visit to the Arias house. Did it go okay?"

"I think so. Why?"

"No reason, other than the fact that Hank texted this

morning, asking if we could talk this afternoon. I wanted to be prepared in case there was a problem."

"There didn't seem to be a problem," she said quickly.

There was something off about her tone. "You sure?"

"Positive." She looked around the room. "All I did was drop off samples."

"But you did go inside the house, right?"

"I did."

"And?" He waved a hand.

"And . . . it was gorgeous. The house is like something out of a Hollywood movie. I put the samples in the different rooms."

"Did you see Hank?"

"I did. I saw his PA too. Her name's Janine. Have you met her?"

"No." Looking at her more closely, he asked, "Did you have a problem with her?"

"A problem? No. Not at all."

Something about Fanny's answer didn't ring true, but he let it slide. "Okay . . . what did Hank think about the samples?"

"Oh. I think he liked everything just fine."

Yep, something was definitely off. Fanny kept averting her eyes, and he could be wrong, but he was kind of, sort of seeing a new shade of pink in her cheeks. Why was that? Was she embarrassed?

Or . . . had Hank done something inappropriate? He seemed like a good guy, but he could've misjudged him. Feeling protective, Nelson leaned forward. "He didn't bother you, did he?"

"Bother me?"

"You know what I mean." He cleared his throat. "Hank wasn't disrespectful or anything, was he? Was he rude to you?"

"No. He wasn't any of those things," she added, sounding more flustered. "Not at all."

"Okay, but, um, piggybacking on our earlier conversation . . . you aren't alone either. If a customer ever gives you problems, you don't have to deal with it on your own, because you've got a pretty good support system too."

"I hear you, boss, but I'm fine. Hank has never done anything to make me uncomfortable."

"All right, then." He walked into his office, closing the door. As he sat down, he stared at the envelope that was addressed to him, each letter of the cursive looking as if a penmanship teacher had written it. It was that perfect.

Fanny was right. There was only one person who wrote like that: Mary Graber.

Knowing that it wasn't going to get any easier if he delayed the inevitable, he opened the envelope and pulled out the note.

And then read the three paragraphs over and over again. Dismay filled him, followed by a burst of anger, followed by frustration and an overwhelming sense of helplessness.

The letter informed him that Peter and Mary had recently hired a lawyer because they intended to sue both Nelson and Alliance Millworks. For a million dollars. Because someone needed to be held responsible for the loss of their beloved son.

Nelson felt like throwing something against the wall. Not because he feared what the lawyers would find. He knew neither the company nor the other men Jimmy had been working with were to blame.

It was because all the secrets about just how difficult Jimmy could be were going to be brought to the surface and his reputation would be sullied.

And when that happened, both Jenna and Katie were going to have to live with the consequences.

And the fallout would likely follow them for the rest of their lives.

chapter sixteen

Fanny considered it her job to fix things for Nelson. He would probably disagree, since her job title was officially administrative assistant and not fix-it girl. But that didn't matter to her. Over the years, she'd taken on a lot of other jobs at the mill that Nelson Harper was likely not even aware existed.

She was often Nelson's gatekeeper, counselor, errand runner, and dietician. She made sure nobody wandered into his office to talk about things that didn't matter and that he didn't drink coffee or energy drinks all afternoon.

Half the time Nelson was both a little bemused and frightened about how much she knew about the company and his personal habits.

Fanny didn't care what he thought. All that mattered to her was that she was his cousin and she was good at the many jobs she did for him. Besides, she owed him.

She owed him everything.

What most people outside of the family didn't know was that she'd briefly been married when she was just a teenager. Kevin had been the bad boy in her high school class and the opposite of her studious, student-council-member self. Against her parents' wishes, she'd started dating him.

And then against her better judgment, she'd married him one weekend in Vegas. She was so sure that she could fix him, that they were wildly in love, and that everything was going to be wonderful.

It wasn't.

It was actually very far from that. Her parents refused to see her, and Kevin had no money, no goals, and a giant chip on his shoulder. She soon learned that he didn't want her to have anything to do with her family.

Within the year, it was apparent that he also didn't want to have anything to do with her. Eventually, she snuck over to see Nelson and shared her whole embarrassing story. Instead of pointing out how foolish she'd been, he gave her a hug, sat her down on his living room couch, and asked how he could help.

When she tearfully admitted that she wanted either an annulment or a divorce, he nodded and called a lawyer.

When Kevin lashed out, Nelson moved her in with him, contacted the police, and made sure she got that divorce as quickly as possible.

At nineteen, she was divorced, working at a grocery store, and living in a little loft apartment in Wooster.

Her parents eventually came around. She appreciated it, but to her, the damage had been done. As far as Fanny was concerned, if they hadn't been there for her during her lowest point, she didn't want to depend on them now.

Nelson used to look annoyed whenever she mentioned that she was saving up to get a new pair of tennis shoes or something. She'd tease him, saying not everyone ran a successful lumber mill like he did. His response was always that if she ever needed something, she could call him. No matter what.

Fanny had shrugged that off, thinking he was merely being kind and said it to everyone. Usually, she'd even forget about it because they would only see each other once or twice a year.

A year after that, she received word that Kevin had died while swimming in Lake Erie. He'd ignored the red flag warnings, gone out, got caught in the riptide, and drowned. Around that time, Nelson asked if she'd consider becoming his new PA since his current assistant was moving to Florida. Fanny had stepped into that position with as much hope in her heart as nervousness.

It turned out to be the best decision she'd ever made.

Unfortunately, at the moment, Fanny had no idea how she was ever going to help Nelson. He looked really torn up by the latest letter from Jimmy's parents. Usually, she tried to add a little bit of levity when mentioning them, even going so far as to refer to Peter and Mary Graber as *the parents who shall not be named.*

Unfortunately, an hour after he'd taken the envelope, new stress lines seemed to be etched around his eyes.

Whatever was in that letter had been bad. Maybe worse than usual.

Sitting across from his desk now, she crossed her legs and tried to think of a way that she could broach the subject without making things worse.

She couldn't think of a single way to do that.

"I didn't hear your answer, Fan. I know you were there

last week, but would you have time to stop by Hank's house again on your way home? Big John's been out there working hard, and I think he's got two other guys there too. John told me that he's pleased, but I want to make sure Hank feels the same way."

Hank Arias's house was in the opposite direction of her apartment. Nelson knew that. "Of course," she said.

"Okay, thanks." He glanced at his phone. "Since it's already after five, I better walk around the plant and make sure things are good. You can take off now if you want."

"Will do." She took a deep breath and stood. "Look, I'm just going to ask this. What was in that letter?"

"Nothing you need to worry about."

"Stop saying that. I am going to worry." She propped her hands on her hips. "Nelson, I'm not just your PA, I'm your cousin. And . . . I'm not just your cousin, I'm your PA."

His lips twitched. "Is that right?"

"Oh, stop. What I'm trying to say is that you couldn't get rid of me if you tried because I'm intertwined in almost every bit of your life."

"I wouldn't go that far."

"Whatever. What did that letter say?"

He studied her face. Took a sip of coffee from a mug that had been likely sitting on his desk for the last hour. "You're not going to let this go, are you?"

"Nope."

"Fine. It was bad news, Fan. Mary and Peter have hired a lawyer."

She couldn't believe it. "For real?"

He chuckled, but it wasn't a happy sound. Instead, it

was filled with bitterness. "They're unhappy with how the accident was handled."

She threw up her hands. "How would Mary or Peter have handled it? What would they have done that no one here did?"

"I . . . I could be wrong, but I'm starting to think that maybe they are wanting some money."

A ball of ice formed in her belly. Money. Of course it was about money. She should have guessed. "For whom? Jenna and Katie?"

As always, Nelson's expression tightened every time one of their names was mentioned. He never said how protective he was over the pair, but he didn't need to. She was both his PA and his cousin. And she cared about him. She already knew how important they were to him.

"I don't know," he finally answered. "Like I said, I don't know for sure about the money thing. I could be wrong."

"Or you could be right. And let me guess, you don't think that, *if* they are after money, it's for Jimmy's widow and daughter."

His lips pursed but he stayed silent.

As far as Fanny was concerned, that was answer enough. She also knew that she wasn't going to get any more information than that. She picked up both her cell phone and her tablet, which she usually wrote her to-do list on. "Okay, I'm going to take off and visit Mr. Arias. I'll see you tomorrow."

"Call me if he's got a problem."

"Will do." She smiled at him before exiting his office and shutting down her computer. But she was still thinking about him. No, still thinking about his situation with the parents who shall not be named.

While she drove, she stewed on the possibility of the Grabers suing Nelson and the mill. Unable to stop herself, Fanny allowed her imagination to get the best of her and started playing a variety of worst-case scenarios in her head.

By the time she pulled into Hank's driveway, she'd gotten herself into a bit of a frenzy.

So much so, when Fanny climbed out of her SUV, she'd almost forgotten what she was supposed to be doing at Hank's house. When she rang the doorbell, the answer hit her hard. Oh yeah! She was supposed to make sure their most important client was happy. She needed to put on a smile and push aside her worries for the next fifteen minutes.

"Fanny, hey," Hank said when he answered the door.

"You look surprised. Did Nelson not warn you that I was stopping by?"

"He texted that he or someone would. I thought it would be him or Big John."

"Sorry, but it's just me again," she joked. "Okay if I come in and see how everything looks?"

"Of course." Hank stepped back, looking his usual handsome, Western self in Wrangler jeans and boots. When he closed the door behind her, he touched her arm. "It is good to see you. Thanks for stopping by."

"It's not a problem. Where would you like to start?"

"The library?"

"Lead the way." Remembering this wasn't a date and they weren't even friends, she felt herself blush. "Or, if you don't mind, I could head there on my own. You know, if you have something else to do."

"I'm good. Besides, I wanted to ask your opinion about something."

"Oh! I'm sorry. I forgot my tablet. Let me go get it so I can take notes."

"I don't think you'll need it. It's more like I was just wondering how you felt about something." He flashed a smile. "I'm seeking your opinion, not pointing out a problem."

"Understood." When his blue eyes warmed, she pretended not to notice. When they entered the library, she noticed that Big John had been busy. "Oh, wow. It's really coming together in here."

"I agree. John does amazing work."

She smiled at him. "He always does."

Hank folded his arms across his chest. "Has he worked for Alliance for a while? Every time I've tried to talk with him, he looks uncomfortable."

She laughed, totally able to picture how the interaction between the two would go. "He's not one for small talk."

"Or any talk," he said with a grin. "I offered to take him out to lunch the other day. He refused, saying he preferred to eat the food he brought from home."

"That's John, without a doubt. Don't take it personally. I think he's such a good craftsman because he focuses on one thing at a time. Whenever he is working on a project in the shop, everyone knows to leave him alone. He won't thank anyone for interrupting his concentration."

"That's a relief. I was starting to worry that he hated working here." Looking more unsure, he added, "Or that maybe it was an Amish thing."

"It's not as much an Amish thing as a Big John thing. We're all pretty used to it. I imagine you'll get used to his ways too." She ran a hand along one of the bookshelves. "All that matters is that you're satisfied with his work."

"I am. More than satisfied."

"That's great. I'll pass that on to Nelson."

"Ready to see the next room?"

"Yep. That's why I'm here."

He nodded. "Of course."

Something flickered in Hank's eyes. Almost as if he was disappointed that she had only been happy to see him because he was a client.

Which was ridiculous. He was so handsome. Plus, he was wealthy and had an air about him that was mesmerizing. He probably was used to women flirting with him all the time.

They walked down the hall to the next room. One of John's apprentices had already nailed in the framework. It was waiting for Big John's finishing touches.

"You'll see real progress in here when the library is done," she added, mainly for something to say.

Hank nodded. "I understand."

The last room was much the same. A skeleton framework had been put in. This one, however, would likely take John a day or two to complete. "Everything looks like I'd hoped. Thanks for letting me stop by."

"I'm glad I was home. Would you like something to drink? Iced tea? Lemonade? A Sprite or something?"

"I'd love a glass of water."

"Come on in the kitchen and I'll get it for you." He

poured two glasses and sat at a barstool. She sat next to him. "Do you have another house to visit tonight?"

"Nope. I get to go home after this."

"Who's there waiting for you?"

"Excuse me?" That question had come out of the blue . . . hadn't it?

He lifted a hand in mock surrender. "Is that too personal?"

"It's not too personal. I was just surprised by the question." She swallowed. "There's no one at home waiting on me."

"I'm surprised nobody's snapped you up."

"Oh, I've been snapped." Her mouth felt dry as she forced herself to continue. "I was married. But, ah, it didn't work out. We got divorced. It all happened a while ago." She averted her eyes, not wanting to meet Hank's. Sure, she could blame her brief love affair and marriage to Kevin on being young and dumb, but the memories still stung.

"Wow. You're so young."

"I know." Used to people saying that, she shrugged. "I'm the poster child for going crazy in Vegas."

His blue eyes lit up. "You got married in Vegas?"

"Unfortunately, yes."

"Hey, I'm sorry."

"Thanks. I'm not going to lie, there were some really bad moments, but the whole thing only lasted about a year."

"I feel terrible for bringing it up." He paused, then added, "Do you ever see him now?"

"No. He died when I was twenty."

Hank's eyes widened before he seemed to get a grip on

himself. It was obvious he wanted to ask her more but didn't want to impose. "All I can say is that I'm really sorry. Both for your loss and for bringing it up. Usually, I am better than that."

"There's nothing to apologize about. You didn't know." She exhaled. "And, like I said, it was a long time ago."

"Let me walk you out."

"All right." Feeling grateful, she shot him a smile. "Thanks."

Hank not only walked her to the front door, he opened it and stayed by her side until they reached her vehicle. "Fanny, is there any chance I could have your number?"

"Why?"

"I thought . . . well, maybe we could text."

"You want to text me about the job?"

"Yeah. But maybe because we're becoming friends." He looked down at the floor, as if he was embarrassed about how awkward things were between them.

Fanny blinked, clumsily attempting to process what he was saying.

"I think the two of us being text buddies would be good. I mean, I'd like that."

"Great." He held out his phone. They exchanged numbers, and he looked pleased. "When I text you later, don't get freaked out."

"I won't."

"If you get freaked out and don't tell me, I'm going to be pretty bummed."

"I won't get freaked out." Opening the driver's side door, she climbed in. "I'll tell Nelson and John that everything looks good and that you're pleased."

"I'd appreciate that. Thanks."

"Night."

"Yeah. Good night, Fanny."

When she was driving home, for the first time in a long while, Fanny realized that she wasn't looking forward to a quiet night in front of the TV. She had something new to expect.

She couldn't wait to see what he had to say.

chapter seventeen

This time, the widows club meeting was taking place in the backyard of someone's home. It looked like a picture postcard. There were five square card tables decorated with white tablecloths with a wicker basket positioned in the center of each. Inside of each basket was an assortment of cloth napkins and silverware, all in order to enjoy the apple pie that the hostess had made.

Jenna thought the decorations and setting were all very lovely. She was surprised too. She hadn't imagined that their semisecret club would meet out in the open like this.

Of course, she had a feeling there were a great many things about the club that she still needed to discover.

"Your name, please?" a dark-haired woman asked when it was Jenna's turn to check in.

"Jenna Graber."

While the woman scanned the guest list neatly written on a sheet of paper, Jenna held her breath. She'd only been to one other meeting. She hoped no one expected her to come every single time.

At last, the woman looked up. "Ah. I finally found your

name right near the end. That's the way it always goes, right?"

"I suppose?"

"Don't mind me," she said with a laugh. "Sometimes I start talking to myself." She winked. "I haven't answered my own questions, but I think it's only a matter of time."

"I've found myself doing the same thing," Jenna said.

"I'm glad I'm in good company." She held out her hand. "Wilcom! Mei name is Sally."

"It's nice to meet you."

"Go enjoy yourself. There's a nice group of women here tonight."

"Danke," she replied shyly. As she turned around, she took a fortifying breath. She needed to be here. She needed to be around other women who were walking in her shoes. Being alone with only Katie wasn't enough for her well-being.

But still, as she scanned the area, she felt as shy as she had the last time. Deciding to go get a cup of coffee, she smiled awkwardly around the yard.

Several women looked up and smiled back as she passed them.

Just as she was about to reach for a cup, Doreen hurried over to her side. "Jenna! Welcome back. I was just telling Anne here that I hope we didn't scare you away."

"You didn't scare me at all. I'm sorry. I didn't mean to stay away so long, but I have a little girl at home. It isn't easy to get away."

"Of course it isn't. She needs to be your priority. I hope she's doing well?"

"Katie is. Thank you."

"And how are you doing?"

She shrugged. "I have good and bad days, if I'm being honest."

"I love when women are being honest." Doreen's eyes were soft as she seemed to take in every inch of Jenna's face. "Tell me, what was today for you? Good or bad?"

Jenna had to think about it. "Neither," she said in a wry tone. "In all ways, it was rather unmemorable."

Doreen nodded. "Those days have their own challenges, I think."

"Yes. That's why I decided to come out tonight. I think I needed a change from my own company."

"Since you're here at Courtney's haus, I think you'll feel like you have definitely experienced a nice change of pace. It's lovely out here, don't you think?"

"Oh, yes. Very much so."

"I hope you enjoy this evening's get-together." Lowering her voice, Doreen added, "One thing I've learned is to not worry too much. There is no right or wrong way to do anything, especially grief."

"I hope you are right."

"I believe I am." Doreen winked before leaving to greet another newcomer.

"Courtney made Dutch apple pies," Elizabeth said to Jenna when she went to the coffee bar. "It don't matter if you've already had dessert or not. You'll want to have a slice."

Jenna chuckled. "Is that because the pie is that good?"

"It is gut, but it's also because Courtney is a worrier. She'll decide that her pie must not have been good if someone doesn't have a slice."

"Gotcha." She was amused but could relate. "Luckily for me, I came hungry."

"That's the spirit," Elizabeth joked. "Go enjoy yourself now."

"Danke."

"Oh! If you need to find a place to sit, go over with Violet and Mary Beth." She pointed to a nearby table that had one space available.

Since Jenna had no idea where else to go, she went right over. "May I join you?"

"We'd be upset if you didn't," Violet said. "You are one of the youngest women here. Please tell me that you have something to talk about besides your feet or knees."

"Pardon me?"

"Do you have issues with your joints or bunions?" The woman's clear blue eyes were piercing.

"Nee," Jenna said quickly. "I have no trouble walking. Does someone need a helping hand?"

"Not at all. What I need is knee surgery, and I fear it's all I can talk about," the lady across from her said with a sheepish smile. "Mary Beth here has been very patient with me while I've listed my ailments."

"At least I'm not talking about Snout."

"Pardon me . . . did you say Snout?"

"Oh, jah." Mary Beth looked like she was trying not to laugh. "He's my pet pig."

"Your pig? That's a pet?" Had she heard that right?

"He's very smart and good company," Mary Beth said.

Jenna wasn't sure what to say. Was she speaking the truth or was she pulling her leg because she was still new to the group? "Oh," she said after a moment's pause.

"Do you have pets?"

"Um, yes. I recently got a kitten."

"Well, that is very fun. Is it good company for you, dear?"

"So far, all he's done is look for things to sharpen his tiny claws on. But my daughter, Katie, has enjoyed him very much."

Mary Beth's playful expression faded into one of concern. "How old is your daughter?"

"She is five."

"And when did your husband pass away?"

"Almost two years ago now. Katie was four, and she'll be six soon."

"You're raising her on your own. That must be mighty hard."

A lump formed in her throat. "It is." She picked up her cup and took a fortifying sip. On one hand, she appreciated how direct all these ladies were. On the other hand, it made her feel like she should have her guard up and be ready for anything.

"So, what are you doing to heal?"

"I'm not sure what you are asking."

Mary Beth set down her coffee cup. "When I lost my husband, I didn't do anything at first. I think I was numb. And then I tried to be grateful that he was no longer suffering. I was grateful for that. After all, he'd been sick for a very long time." She took a deep breath. "But grief is a difficult thing to describe, ain't so? Some days I was almost as right as rain. On others? Well, on others it felt hard to get out of bed." Frowning slightly, she whispered,

"But then some of my relatives and friends told me that I had mourned long enough."

Another woman nodded. "Even though they still had their spouses."

Mary Beth picked up her cup again. "It was all very hard."

"What did you end up doing?" Jenna asked.

After taking another sip of coffee, Mary Beth smiled. "I joined this group, which helped. And then I started shelving books at the library."

"Oh?"

"Mary Beth is Alliance Library's best volunteer," Violet said. "She goes in two times a week, rain or shine."

Mary Beth laughed. "Rain or shine are the easy days. It's the January snow and ice days that are the hardest."

"I'm not sure if I have time to volunteer at the library." Or, truth be told, the interest.

"Some women go to work. Others are older, so they help with their grandchildren and such," Violet said. "A few women here have started traveling. The important thing is to do something to get yourself out and about."

"I'll think about it."

"Gut." Violet lowered her voice. "But here's the most important thing . . . don't think that you have to do everything all by yourself. Or only with other members of your family. Sometimes the people closest to you aren't the ones who understand the most."

"That is how I feel! Sometimes even my parents act as if I should be okay now."

"I know." Mary Beth nodded. "That's why I befriended my pig. Sometimes you have to give yourself permission to not be okay." She winked. "Snout has no problem letting me know that he's okay with how I am, even if it's not fit for human company."

Jenna chuckled. "Jah. Sometimes I think I'm only fit for a pig's company."

"Well, now you know that you are fit for more than a pig. You can come over to my haus, and I'll be pleased for company—no matter what your mood. Come as you are, Jenna."

Jenna was so touched, she realized that she was struggling not to cry. *Thank you, Gott*, she silently prayed. *Thank you for bringing me here to these women again.* "I just might take you up on that invitation."

As the meeting continued, Doreen encouraged everyone to move between groups so they could get to know each other. Jenna felt more and more at ease. She'd never been anywhere else where she wouldn't have resented being told to move around again and again. Even at church, she had her favorite places to sit and favorite people to spend time with.

Here, though, she found herself eager to get to know more women. By the time she left, she realized that she'd made several more friends. Some of the women had even asked if she'd like to join them for coffee sometime soon. Jenna was looking forward to having an hour or two to visit with them before the next meeting.

When she got home, her mother was sitting at her kitchen table cutting out fabric for a new dress for Katie. Blue was at her feet, happily playing with a few of the bright-pink scraps of fabric.

"Ah, Jenna. You came at the perfect time."

She eyed the fabric warily. "Please don't tell me that you want me to help you stitch this together tonight."

She set down the scissors in her hand. "No?"

"No."

She chuckled. "That was a joke, child. Sometimes I think you lost all of your humor when Jimmy died."

"Mamm, that isn't fair. I still have my sense of humor. I just don't want to sew . . . and you are a night owl."

"I have made a dress in the evening before, but I'm ready to stop." She folded the various parts of the dress over each other, then finally placed them all in a canvas tote bag resting on one of the chairs. "I'm gonna leave in a few minutes, but first tell me how your meeting went."

"It went well. Better than the first meeting, I think."

"I'm afraid I still don't understand what kind of group this is."

Jenna knew the Amish Widows Club was an unsecret secret. No one was hiding their membership, but every member preferred that no one talked about it.

Now that she was slowly getting to know the other women, she understood their reasoning. Some women shared some vulnerable things about themselves that other women—married women—would never understand.

Everyone thought the hardest part of widowhood was the grief and sense of loss. And that was hard. But sometimes, Jenna thought it was more overwhelming to have everything in her life fall on her slim shoulders. Every decision for Katie. The bills. Even something as simple as shoveling the walkway to the barn or weeding a flower bed. Sometimes she was just plain tired.

And, yes, sometimes she was angry with Jimmy too. It

wasn't fair and it wasn't right, but she resented that he was gone while she was still here, doing her best to get through each day.

But she couldn't tell her mother any of that.

"Like I told you, Mamm, it's a group of Amish widows. We get together occasionally, eat some snacks, sip coffee, and catch up on our news."

"Well, I suppose I could understand how you might enjoy their company."

"Danke," she said in a dry tone.

Walking to the sink to rinse out her coffee cup, her mother added, "Of course, I bet your participation in the group will run its course."

"Why do you say that?"

"Well, those other women are much older than you, for one. Thank the good Lord that not too many women your age suffer the tragedy that you have."

Jenna bit her lip.

"Then, of course, there is the obvious reason."

"What is that?"

Looking slightly uncomfortable that she was being forced to say it, she added, "Well, soon you'll be accepting callers."

"You mean men?"

Her mother chuckled softly. "Well, of course I mean men. What other kind of callers could you be entertaining?"

"I don't know," she blurted quickly. Though that was a lie. She had Nelson. Kind, handsome, oh-so-capable Nelson, who seemed to know her needs before she did.

Who never irritated her or pushed too hard for her to be different. She loved that about him.

Wait. Did she really *love* things about him?

"I don't think I'll be ready to have any callers anytime soon, Mamm."

"Darling, you must. After all, you have Katie to think about."

"It is Katie who I am thinking about. Whatever man I choose, he's going to be a father to Katie. I must choose carefully."

"Of course, it will take some time for your new husband to accept Katie, but he will in time."

"I don't want a man to merely accept her. I want someone to love her. Mamm, it's Katie."

"Jah, I understand. But not every man is going to have an easy time of that." She clucked her tongue. "You should be prepared for anything, Jenna. Why, Katie might even have to stay with Daed and me for a spell while you and your new husband get used to living together. Most men want time alone with their new brides."

"I would never agree to such a thing." She was shocked that her mother had suggested it.

"You might have to, honey."

"Mamm, stop."

Her mother looked completely taken aback. "Have you really not thought about getting married again?"

"No."

"Jenna, you are going to need someone."

"We have Nelson," she blurted. "Nelson is my friend, and Katie loves him. He's kind to her. I'm in no hurry to put someone else in our lives."

"But Nelson is only visiting you because he feels guilty, right? Plus, when he finds his own wife, she's not going to want him visiting you and Katie."

"I don't think he's looking for a wife."

"If he isn't today, he probably will be tomorrow."

"Mother, you don't know him. Nelson isn't like that."

Lowering her voice, her mother stared at her intently. "Jenna, you need to pull your head out of the clouds. Whatever you and Nelson have is not sustainable. It's going to end. And then one day, this odd relationship the two of you have will be just a memory."

The prospect of losing Nelson was painful. Tears filled her eyes.

If this was her new reality, then it pinched something awful.

Almost as bad as losing Jimmy had.

chapter eighteen

Another three weeks had passed in a blur. After much debate, Nelson called Peter Graber and told him the real, no-holds-barred account of Jimmy's accident. He shared that several employees had been interviewed by the police and their statements were on record. Finally, he relayed that he'd been trying to save Jimmy's reputation for both him and Jenna. If Peter and Mary moved forward and actually sued Alliance Millworks, he'd have no choice but to bring all the statements to light. He couldn't let Peter or Mary ruin the company's reputation. Peter had almost immediately backed off. When Nelson hung up the phone, he felt relief but no pleasure. He realized he would always mourn Jimmy and would always wish that he could have helped him in some way.

A few days later, he'd started visiting Jenna again. Each visit was very brief.

Worse, she seemed okay with that.

It was just as well because a prospective customer he'd been meeting with for the last year had finally made a decision. Gibson Logistics gave them a huge contract. His little family-owned company was not only going to be doing all the built-in cabinetry, workspaces, and flooring, but they had been hired to work on the president's house as well. George Gibson lived in a hundred-year-old sprawling estate on the banks of Lake Erie in Bratenahl. The opportunity would showcase their work to a whole new audience.

Nelson had planned to tell everyone about the news in their company's newsletter. Fanny had shaken her head and planned a party instead.

And that was why the front lobby of Alliance Millworks was packed with people, and any space that wasn't filled with men and women was filled with streamers, balloons, plates of food, and stations of soda, coffee, tea, and water.

"Wow," Nelson said when they got out of the elevator in the back of the lobby.

Standing beside him, Fanny smirked. "Wow? Come on, boss. You better start thinking of some better words in your vocabulary, because *wow* isn't going to cut it."

"Yeah, it probably isn't." Fanny had put this shindig together in a thoughtful and pleasing way. The food looked amazing, and the decorations looked fancy. It was a far cry from someone ordering a couple of deli plates from the grocery store and taping up a couple of streamers.

She cast a side-eyed glance his way. "Are you nervous?" Before he could answer, she continued in a rush, "I mean, it's okay if you are because this isn't really your thing, but I hadn't expected you to be tongue-tied."

"I'm not."

"Not nervous or tongue-tied?"

"Either." Frustrated with how his cousin could make

even the most simple conversation seem convoluted, he added, "I'm fine."

"Oh. Good." She smiled. "Because pretty much all two hundred employees are staring at you, boss. It's time to get your game on."

Fearing she was right, he turned. And yep. Fanny wasn't exaggerating. It was like he was Santa Claus and it was Christmas morning. He needed to do this.

Stepping forward, he cleared his throat. "Hi, everyone." Uh-oh. Only a couple of people had stopped talking.

"Here." Fanny thrust a microphone into his hand.

Where she'd gotten it, Nelson had no idea. But that was supposedly why he kept her around. Well, that and a million other reasons. Fanny could work small miracles in five minutes. She was also always prepared and seemingly unflappable.

"Thanks."

When he heard his voice echo through the vast lobby, a couple of people chuckled.

He chuckled too. "Well, I guess it's obvious that speaking to all of you with a microphone isn't my forte. But I'm glad Fanny handed it to me because I want to make sure every person in this room hears what I have to say." He took a deep breath. "Congratulations, everyone. We did it. Because of your hard work, we just earned the Gibson Logistics account. We're now a multimillion-dollar company. In addition, our employees' accomplishments are so strong, it's time to expand. I'm pleased to share that within one year's time, we will be starting a new branch in Wooster."

"Woo-hoo!" Fanny called out and started clapping.

Little by little, everyone in the room cautiously began clapping with her, their confused expressions giving way to bright, honest smiles.

"When my grandfather started Alliance Millworks, he had one goal in mind, and that was to provide quality construction and locally made materials to the area for an affordable price. My father and uncle improved upon that goal, and I've spent the last ten years of my life making sure that everything our company does will both be lasting but also appreciated for years to come."

Looking at all the faces staring up at him, Nelson felt a lump form in his throat. "I know all of you by name. For some of you, I even know your families. It's been my honor to have you work here and my honor to call you friends. Thank you for making this company everything my grandfather could only dream of. Thank you for everything you do."

Taking another breath, he said, "When we got the news about the Gibson account, Fanny and I knew that we should mark the occasion, so we immediately got busy with ordering everything we could get our hands on—well, Fanny did!"

"Obviously I went a little overboard!" Fanny called out.

He grinned. "Please enjoy yourselves, have some cake, eat some sandwiches, and please take the envelope with your name on it before you leave. Everyone is receiving a small bonus today. One hundred dollars for every year you've been part of the Alliance family."

A gasp from Big John made everyone grin, especially himself. Big John had been there twenty years. He was going to be bringing home a nice check to Tam, his wife.

"What about you?" Big John asked. "Are you gonna be giving yourself a bonus too, boss?"

"Not at this time."

"You might be needing it, Nelson," Big John teased. "It's about time you got yourself a wife and started a family like the rest of us."

He felt his cheeks flush, but he knew the ribbing was all in good fun. "When I find the right woman, I'll act on your advice," he joked. After everyone's laughter died down, he said, "Enjoy yourselves, thank you for always going above and beyond, and get ready to hear more information as things get organized."

"Here's to Nelson!" Victor Hershberger called out from the floor.

"To Nelson!" everyone cheered.

Pleased that his speechmaking was done for the day, Nelson handed the microphone to Fanny. "Here you go." Wordlessly he scanned her expression, looking for the telltale signs of either her acceptance or displeasure with his talk.

She patted his arm. "You did good, boss. Now go on down and get something to eat and drink."

"If I'm doing this, you are too."

"I know." Her cell phone rang. "After I take this call."

He shook his head. That was Fanny. She encouraged him to take breaks without ever doing the same thing. But maybe that was why they were a good team. They continually pushed each other to excel and to concentrate on what really mattered the most.

When he got to the floor, he walked over to Big John first. Not only because he was one of their most senior employees but because he was one of the few people in the room he felt completely at ease with.

"Ah, Mr. Harper. You sure have outdone yourself today."

"Not so much."

John waved a hand around the room. "I think differently. This was a good thing, boss. Your father's gonna be proud." He winked. "He'll probably question the whole party and bonus thing, but he'll be pleased with ya."

"I dare say you are right. I hope you know how grateful I am that you've stayed with us, John. You're a master craftsman and one of the main reasons for our company's good reputation."

"Danke."

"How are things going at the Arias house?"

"It's gut. I've been bringing Tim with me, and he's taken over the majority of the woodwork in the master bedroom. He's also been talking to Hank."

"Oh?"

John nodded. "It seems that the two of them have taken a shine to each other."

Nelson grinned. "That's good."

"That's what I said." Waving a hand around the room, Big John continued, "I think all this is a good thing too."

"I hope so. I wasn't sure how it would go over."

"Look around ya. Everyone's eating and smiling and calling their families to tell them about their checks. Even if you weren't handing out money, this recognition is good for everyone's souls. Especially after the last two years."

After Jimmy's accident. "You're right."

"I know I am. They're real glad about this party. But

don't get me wrong, my bonus is gonna be much appreciated by my wife."

"Good. Changes are going to be coming, and I want everyone to feel as energized and hopeful as I do."

"I reckon they will."

"Don't forget to take a piece of cake home for Tam. She's likely going to appreciate that as much as your envelope," he teased.

"I reckon so."

Before Nelson knew what was what, Big John enveloped him in a hug.

A few men surrounding them laughed at Nelson's awkwardness, but he didn't care as he hugged Big John back.

It was a good moment. No, it was more than that. This was an afternoon to treasure.

He supposed he'd needed this party as much as the rest of the employees did. Taking some time to rest and recharge was a good thing.

chapter nineteen

Jenna was walking down the driveway to the mailbox when Nelson pulled in. Pleased to see him since it was a Friday and not a Monday, she stopped where she was and gave him a little wave.

"Hey," he called out as he rolled down the window. "Are you going for a walk?"

"Just to the mailbox." She held up the three letters in her hand.

He waited until she'd deposited the letters in her mailbox and put up the flag before calling out again. "I have something for you. Want a ride to your door?"

She didn't need one. After all, it wasn't like her driveway was all that long. But it seemed rude to refuse his offer. "All right." She opened up the passenger side door and climbed into his very large, gray pickup truck.

Even though she'd ridden in it when he picked her up in the rain, she'd been too upset to notice a thing. Now, with clear eyes, she was able to take note of everything. Nelson's truck was as fancy inside as an expensive sports car. It smelled good too. Like Nelson's cologne and some kind of leather cleaner. The combination was lovely. Even though she hadn't seen the need for the ride, it was a nice break. Leaning back with a happy sigh, she smiled at him. "This is a mighty comfortable truck, Nelson."

He grinned. "I've always thought so. When I first bought it, I was a little embarrassed. It seemed like it was too fancy just to drive to work and such, but it's turned out to be a good thing." He parked in his usual spot at the top of the drive. "I've driven several clients and customers to different buildings and houses to see work. No one wants to ride in a smelly old truck."

"I reckon not."

"Stay there. I'll come around and help you down."

Help her down? The request seemed odd, but Jenna stayed where she was.

Then, of course, she got all flustered when Nelson opened the door and held out a hand for her to take.

After she took it, he placed a hand on her waist and practically lifted her out.

She gripped his arms as she let out a girlish squeal.

He laughed. "I guess you didn't expect me to do that?"

"Not at all."

"Sorry, but I couldn't help myself. It's a pretty big jump and you aren't all that tall." He winked. "Hearing you squeal was an added bonus."

"No doubt." She'd squealed like she was on a carnival ride. "I shouldn't have screamed in your ear."

He laughed. "You're lucky I didn't twirl you in a circle. For a second I was considering it. Maybe next time."

She'd be lying if she said she didn't want there to be

a next time. The idea of being twirled in Nelson's arms would be memorable.

But probably nothing she should ever think about.

Feeling the beginnings of a blush on her cheeks, she tried to pull herself together. "So . . . what did you bring me today?"

He was still smiling at her. "Hmm? Oh. Here. Let me get it. It's in the back." He strode to the back of the truck, jumped on the tailgate, pulled up a tarp, and then lifted a large, carpeted item. "What do you think?" he asked as he lowered it to the ground and then jumped down after it.

It was a monstrosity of a thing. It was several feet high and was covered entirely with tan carpet. Honestly, it looked like an ugly carpeted tree. "I don't know what to think," she said slowly. Really hoping that Nelson didn't think it was an interesting piece of art or a clothes hanger, she asked, "What is it?"

"It's a cat tree."

"A what?"

His smile widened. "It's a cat tree for your kitten, Jenna." Touching one of the tree's carpeted limbs, he said, "See? Blue can climb all over it instead of on your couch. Cats like things to do, such as sharpen their claws."

She supposed cats did, but did she need this in her cozy house? She walked over to inspect it more closely. "It's mighty big, Nelson."

"It is. The guy who sold it to me said it's sturdy enough to hold two cats at a time. What do you think?"

"I'm not quite sure."

Little by little, some of the enthusiasm in his expression faded. "Uh-oh. Do you hate it?"

Hate was a strong word to describe how she felt. But . . . "I don't know where it could go."

"How about in the living room? I'll carry it in, and we'll see what he thinks." He lifted it right up and headed toward the door. Just as if he were carrying in a Christmas tree or some such item.

"Oh, Nelson."

"If you hate it, I'll take it back. I promise," he called out.

He was so good to her . . . and he sounded so excited. Just as if it was Christmas in July. Hurrying to keep up, she said, "I don't *hate* this, ah, cat tree. It's very kind of you to get it for Blue."

"And for you."

"And me," she said weakly as she followed him up the front steps. She opened the door, stepped to the side to let Nelson and the giant cat playground inside, and then led the way into the living room.

As she'd suspected, the cat tree looked sorely out of place. Her living area was small, and she already had a couch, a coffee table, and an easy chair in the space. "See, Nelson? There's just not much room in here." She exhaled. Surely he would see how inappropriate the . . . the furry tree thing was and take it right back out to his truck.

But he didn't.

"How about if I moved everything over a couple of feet and then we put Blue's tree over against the window?"

"The window?"

"That way Blue could look out the window when you're busy and Katie is at school. He'll love it. What do you think?"

He was making it sound as if she truly did sit around

and think about activities for a kitten to do. She did nothing of the sort. But instead of correcting him, Jenna bit her lip and nodded.

"Okay, can you lift that side of your coffee table?"

"Sure." Together they moved it several inches to the side. Then Nelson scooted the couch and Jimmy's chair over. Finally, after everything was arranged to his liking, Nelson picked up the cat tree and carefully set it down in front of the window.

She bit her lip again in dismay. The kitten now had the best view in the house. Plus, he would probably never use it. Katie would think it was a jungle gym for herself.

Still looking pleased, he said, "I think it looks pretty good in here. What do you think?"

"I'm not sure, Nelson." And now she was a liar, because she was very sure she did not like it.

"Blue? Blue, where are you?"

This man! This silly, incorrigible man. "Nelson, Blue doesn't really come when you call—"

"Hi, kitty," he said gently as Blue strode right to his side and stretched his paws on a calf. "Look what we got for you."

"We?" Jenna rolled her eyes.

Neither the cat nor Nelson paid her any mind. Instead, Blue gazed up at Nelson adoringly, then practically went limp when Nelson picked him up and carried him over to the climbing tree.

Blue meowed when Nelson put him down on one of the little resting nooks among the branches. The kitten's sweet little body was tense.

"I think he's afraid, Nelson. Get him down."

"Hold on. We've just got to give him a second." Lowering his voice, he scratched the top of Blue's head, right between his ears. "What do you think, kitty?"

Blue stretched, ran his kitten claws along a carpet-covered branch, then seemed to suddenly notice the window. He meowed again.

Next thing she knew, Blue climbed to another branch, batted a section of it playfully, then became completely obsessed with his view. He froze, then resituated himself a bit . . . all before contentedly perching on the branch and gazing out the window. Seconds later, his tail was resting limply at his side.

"Look at him now, Jenna!" Nelson grinned. "I think my gift is a hit. What do you think?"

"I think Blue likes it very much." And she, unfortunately, now had a very large cat playground in her living room.

"You don't seem very thrilled about it."

That was because she wasn't. She was starting to feel a little bit out of sorts too. Nelson had a lot of nerve to act hurt because he'd gotten her something huge for a kitten she'd never asked for in the first place.

"You took me by surprise, Nelson. This tree is very big. Plus, I didn't even know you were going to stop by today."

He stuffed his hands in his pockets. "Okay, I get it. You don't want this at all."

"It's not that I don't want it, it's that you should've asked me first. Don't you see the difference?"

"Yeah. Yeah, I do. I'm sorry." He ran a hand through his hair. "You're exactly right. I shouldn't have decided to bring you something for your house without checking with you first."

He was listening to her. Really listening. It seemed as if he understood her point too. She was so pleased that she'd spoken her mind and had been honest with how she felt. She'd never done that with Jimmy and was often frustrated with him. She was getting stronger.

But . . . Nelson wasn't Jimmy. He wasn't anything like Jimmy. He never lost his temper. He was always calm and caring and gentle with her and Katie. He was even gentle with kittens.

"Nel—" She stopped mid-word because he was now holding Blue in his arms and obviously attempting to remove his new favorite spot in the living room. "Wait."

He looked at her from over his shoulder. "What's wrong?"

"You can't pick it up and take it out of here."

Nelson still wasn't meeting her eyes. He was acting like it was because he was busy trying to navigate the toy, but she knew better. He was upset.

"I said I would abide by your wishes. I meant it. You are right."

"But—"

"No, it's not a problem," he continued. "As soon as I put this on the front porch, I'll come back in and move all of your furniture back. I'll be out of here in five minutes."

He was going to leave in a hurry because she was being ungrateful.

She felt terrible.

"You don't need to do that," she said in a rush. "I can keep it."

"No, that's not what I told you," he reminded her again. "I told you that if you didn't like it, I'd take it back. I meant what I said."

"I know you did."

He lifted it up. "Could you get the door for me, please?"

She felt kind of sick.

Then Blue went and made everything worse by leaping back onto the cat tree.

"Blue, no!" Nelson called out. He set the kitten's toy on the ground, reached in, and pulled him off the contraption. And then he gently petted him before finally placing him in her arms.

Blue didn't try to leap away, but he was very far from relaxing contentedly against her.

Actually, the cat was staring at her. Blue mewed quietly.

"Oh, Blue." She wouldn't have thought it was possible, but she was sure Blue was now looking at her with disappointment. Jenna felt even worse. She had taken away the kitten's toy and he was sad.

When Blue mewed one more time before turning his head away from her, reality set in.

She had gotten so intent on making sure that she kept her pride, Jenna realized, that she was ignoring all the signs in front of her.

Nelson was a good friend and had gone out of his way to give her a gift. It wasn't all that different from the times she'd spent the morning making a pie or cake for a friend and stopped by unannounced. If someone had refused her gift, saying it wasn't appropriate—or worse, that she should've waited to be invited over—she would've been hurt.

She was being churlish and rude. Why, she was worse than . . . than . . . than the Grinch at Christmas!

Feeling as if she was going to forever regret it if she didn't make things better, Jenna rushed over to Nelson's side. "Put this thing down. I'm keeping it."

"Jenna, stop. I promise, it's okay."

She reached out and grabbed hold of his arm. "Nee. You stop. I was wrong. Please, put it down."

"All right." Bending, Nelson put it on the floor at his feet. When he straightened, he seemed to gather his thoughts and then said, "Jenna, listen, I feel really stupid. You are—"

"I am being foolish and ungrateful. Would you please accept my apology?"

"You don't have anything to apologize for."

"We know that's not true. Thank you for bringing this cat tree for Blue. He's going to love it, and I know Katie will too. It was very kind of you to think of us."

"Your words are sweet but unnecessary."

"I disagree."

She stared at him. Noticed that there was a new tension in his shoulders. He was upset about this. She knew that he was heaping everything that had gone wrong on his own shoulders, which wasn't right at all. "Nelson, even though this is going to make all the wives in the world no doubt cringe, I have to tell you that sometimes women get in a snit for no reason."

His hazel eyes brightened. "Is that right?"

"Oh, for sure and for certain." She waved a hand, as if she were an expert on hormones and marital relations.

"Sometimes we say and do things that make no sense. Why, I used to even lie to Jimmy from time to time."

"You lied?" His lips twitched.

She lifted her chin. "I did indeed. Every now and then I would tell him I was fine when he and I both knew I wasn't."

"I see."

"Do you? Because he rarely did. You are going to have your hands full when you go about learning the ways of wives and women one day."

"One day?"

"Oh, yes. When you finally take a bride." She smiled, though she was starting to not like the idea of Nelson fussing over another woman. Of him lifting another girl out of his truck and twirling her around.

No, she didn't like that idea at all.

"At least I'll know who to come to for advice," he teased. "It seems you will have all the answers."

"I will. Why, I might even have to ask the bishop for a cell phone so you can put me on speed dial." She smiled, though she still was trying to fight off her unwanted burst of jealousy.

He chuckled. "You, Jenna, are something else."

When she smiled up at him, something new exploded in the air between them. Was it an awareness? Or was it something more like tension? No, this was something better. Sweeter. Her mouth went dry as a burst of longing filled her heart. She felt a little bit warm. A little bit unsteady—as if everything she knew and thought was slowly sliding away. And in its place was simply Nelson. Before she knew it, she was leaning toward him.

Gathering herself together, she stopped just in time.

"Come here, Jenna," he murmured.

As if she had no control over her body, Jenna stepped closer. He moved toward her too, until there was nothing left between them. And then, just as if they did this all the time, he pulled her toward him.

She lifted her hands around his neck. He wrapped his hands around her waist. And then pulled her close.

He was hugging her. A sweet, loving, protective, warm hug. The kind she hadn't experienced since Jimmy died. Unable to stop herself, she rested her head on his chest. Felt one of his hands flatten against the center of her back.

Holding her securely.

And then she was pretty sure that he pressed his lips against her temple.

She closed her eyes, lost in the moment. She was surrounded by Nelson's clean, masculine scent. It was almost as if nothing and no one could get to her. No stress, no strangers, no worries. All she could feel was comfort.

She hoped this moment would last forever.

And it might have . . . if the door hadn't opened.

chapter twenty

Nelson was starting to wonder how a day that had started so well ended so badly.

After the party, he'd messed up a phone call. When he was so irritated with himself he snapped at Fanny, he knew it was time to take a break.

He'd gone to downtown Alliance, gotten a Coke, and looked in the store windows. When he noticed that one of them was Fanny's favorite place to shop, he went inside and bought her a card and a gift certificate. Hopefully the gesture would ease his cousin's hurt feelings.

It was the specialty store's fault that it had to be right next to a pet store. And that they had a cute tiny kitten practically posing in the window on its fancy cat tree. The sight—and the fact that he was in no hurry to return to the mill—had been enough to lure him inside to see what cat trees were all about.

Kurt, the pet shop clerk, had a lot to say about cat trees. So much, Nelson had given in to impulse and bought one for Jenna. And Katie and Blue, of course.

But really for Jenna, because he was learning that few

things made him happier than seeing Jenna Graber smile. Instead of returning to the office and handing Fanny her card and gift, he'd driven directly to Jenna's farm. All the while, he'd been daydreaming about her reaction.

Yes, to his shame, the fantasy reaction had included a beaming smile, profuse thanks, and a really good hug. He was so full of good intentions and obliviousness that the moment he'd seen her, he'd gotten all goofy.

Then, of course, he'd completely messed it up. Jenna was caught off guard, the thing had taken up a good slice of her compact living room, and then she'd somehow been almost on the verge of tears when he tried to carry it out.

And, well . . . as far as he was concerned, Jenna Graber had already cried too many tears in her short life. He hated to see her upset, and he really hated that he was the reason she was upset in the first place.

So he hugged her.

And it wasn't one-sided. She hugged him back. When she rested her head on his chest and seemed to relax when he pressed his palm on her back, he went and did the unthinkable—he gave in to impulse and kissed her.

Oh, sure. He kissed her brow. But that was enough, wasn't it? Wasn't there something written somewhere that said a hug between friends didn't involve lips?

If there wasn't, there should be.

But just as he was regretting that . . . she relaxed against him. And he did too. And he began to think of all sorts of reasons why hugging should now be part of his visits. Because holding her made him feel good. She felt perfect in his arms.

And, of course, imagining future hugs might very well include a whole different sort of kiss.

Not that he should ever imagine that would be possible. She was Amish. She'd professed her faith when she was baptized. He knew enough about that to realize that she could never turn her back on those vows easily.

But what if her heart was involved? What if one day she would be willing to risk everything in order to let him love her?

He had no idea if she'd ever be willing to do that. He could only hope . . . and settle for hugging his "friend" in the meantime.

She fit him perfectly. So much so, he didn't want to let her go.

It was just too bad that he didn't.

"What is going on in here?" Mary Graber said as she stood in the doorway.

Jenna jumped away from him like her skin was on fire. "Nothing," she mumbled.

"It doesn't look like that. It looks like you were carousing with a man who isn't your husband."

Nelson was so irritated by her tone—and her words—he raised an eyebrow. It was either that or attempt to push Jenna's mother-in-law right back out the door. "Carousing?" he asked.

"You know what I meant."

"No, I know what you insinuated, and it was wrong. Jenna was not carousing with anyone. And, for the record, as painful as this is to remind you, Jenna's husband is no longer living. She's no longer able to do anything with him."

"Nelson, stop," Jenna whispered.

He didn't want to. He didn't want to do anything besides wrap her in his arms again and hold her close. He wanted to whisper that she had nothing to be embarrassed about. He wanted to whisper all sorts of things to get her to relax and smile again.

"Nelson," she said again.

He tried to relax his stance. "Only for you," he whispered.

Jenna's cheeks bloomed, but she remained quiet.

Which seemed to give Mary the idea that she could continue throwing out her verbal bombs. Her eyes narrowed as she fastened her attention on him. "I can't believe that you have the nerve to step foot in this house, Nelson Harper."

Every word she said seemed to be infused with venom. He didn't appreciate it. Just as he was about to tell her exactly what he thought about her words, he noticed that Katie was standing in the doorway. She was staring at all three of them with wide eyes.

Shame filled him. How could he have not seen her earlier? Furthermore, how could he defend himself with Katie peeking out from the doorway? "Come on in, Katie," he said in a gentle tone. "I'm sorry you heard me speak so crossly."

Just as Katie stepped forward, Mary put out her arm, essentially preventing Katie from entering. As if she thought Nelson would ever hurt that little girl.

Everything inside of him was fuming as he debated how to proceed next. Luckily for everyone involved, Jenna spoke. "Nelson did nothing wrong, Mary, and neither did

I," she said. "Now stop standing in the doorway and let Katie in. You're letting in flies. Plus, we canna have Blue escaping."

Jenna's orders seemed to register because Mary did just that. Katie ducked under her arm and hurried to the cat tree. Mary walked inside and closed the door behind her.

Now all of them were standing in the very small entryway. Crammed in tight against the stupid cat tree. Which, by the way, Blue had climbed on again.

"What's this?" Katie asked as she ran a hand along one of the carpeted branches.

"It's a climbing toy for Blue," Jenna said. "Isn't it something?"

Katie nodded. "I think Blue likes it."

"It's unnecessary," Mary said. "You have no room for such nonsense, Jenna. Besides, cats should live in the barn."

"Nee, Mammi!" Katie called out. "Blue lives inside with us."

"Mind your manners, child," Mary said.

Nelson was tempted to remind Mary to mind her manners when he saw that Jenna was not shying away from her mother-in-law at all.

"Katie is right, Mary. Blue is an indoor cat. And as far as this cat tree goes, I think differently," Jenna said. "Our new kitten is rather rambunctious and likes to explore. Plus, Katie and I were reading in a library book that tiny kittens enjoy sharpening their claws. I'd rather he not ruin the couch. We need it."

"What you don't need is a cat. It's going to ruin your house. Besides, Jimmy wouldn't have wanted a cat. You should get rid of it." Looking out at the field, she said, "If you don't want to make it live in the barn, then go take it to the field. It can live there."

Nelson was shocked. He couldn't believe that Mary would suggest such things to Jenna. But for a grandmother to say such things to her little granddaughter? It was both unthinkable and cruel.

"Nee!" Katie cried out before he could intervene. As tears filled her eyes, she grabbed Blue and held him tight in her arms. "No, you can't do anything to him. He's mine! He's my kitten!"

"Mary, what in the world has gotten into you?" Jenna asked as she reached for Katie.

But Katie ran to him. "Nelson, don't let them do it!" she cried out as she reached for him.

She was crying hard now. Awful, heavy tears.

He knelt on the floor and pulled her into his arms. "Shh, Kitty. It's okay." He gently ran a hand down her back as her little arms tightened around his neck. "Shh . . . shh, shh. Your mommy would never let anything happen to Blue."

Katie started crying harder. "I love him."

"I know, sweetheart. I know you do. He loves you too," he whispered as he carefully patted her back. Raising his eyes to Jenna, he silently asked what she wanted him to do. He was pretty proud of himself for doing that too, because he was more than ready to kick Mary out of the house and refuse to ever let her see Katie again.

Visibly shaken, Jenna stepped in front of him and her daughter. "Mary, I don't know what has gotten into you, but I think we both know that you are saying things that don't make sense. It's time you left. Come back when you are thinking more clearly."

"This was my son's house, Jenna. I have every right to be here whenever I want."

"We know that isn't true. This is my house. Jimmy bought it for us. For our family. He loved me, and he loved Katie, just as we loved him. Jimmy would've never been all right with you behaving like this. I know it and you know it."

Mary closed her eyes. From his position on the floor, Nelson was sure that the woman was about to apologize. But instead, she fisted her hands. "Jenna, every time we converse, I'm taken aback by how much you've changed. My son thought he'd married a dutiful wife. But now you're going out, accepting gifts, and behaving improperly with the man who killed your husband." Her mouth pinched. "If you aren't careful, I'm going to speak to the bishop about your negligence and wanton behavior."

Katie cried harder. Nelson was pretty sure she didn't understand Mary's words but was upset with her tone of voice. "Hush, honey. Don't worry. Everything's going to be all right," he whispered into her ear, adding a string of nonsense words and phrases. Anything to try to replace the awful things Katie was hearing her grandmother say.

"Speak to the bishop as much as you want," Jenna said, her voice as cold as ice. "Invite him over here for coffee. If he stops by, I'll be pleased to see him." After a pause, she added, "But Mary, make no mistake, I will defend myself and Jimmy's memory. I will also always, *always* put Katie's needs first." She lowered her voice. "Right now, my daughter needs some peace and comforting. You need to go."

Her mother-in-law remained motionless. It was obvious that she was stunned by what Jenna was saying.

Jenna strode the few steps to the door, threw it open, and pointed outside. "Mary, please leave."

Mary shook her head slowly. "You are misconstruing everything. It's you who isn't thinking clearly."

"Please leave, or I will have Nelson escort you out."

"You canna mean that." Mary's expression was as incredulous as her tone.

But Jenna didn't budge. "I think we both know I do. Leave. Now."

Mary turned toward the door. "You will regret this."

"I am sure I will regret a great many things one day. But this won't be one of them," Jenna bit out before closing the door behind Mary.

The three of them stayed silent as they listened to Mary climb into her buggy and eventually guide it down the driveway.

Katie hiccupped. "Why was Mammi being so mean?"

"I don't know," Nelson whispered. "But are you ready to help me move the cat tree over near the window?"

When she nodded, he released his hold on her, got to his feet, and picked up the tree. Blue meowed and hopped onto the couch when Nelson passed by it.

After he set the tree back where it had originally been, Katie smiled. "I like it here. Do you, Nelson?"

"Yep."

"Mamm? Do you like it too?"

"I do, Katie."

The little girl laughed as Blue leapt back onto the cat tree, appearing very put out that he was having to climb onto it one more time. In less than a minute, he situated himself in front of the window.

"He likes it!"

"He sure does, sweetheart." Concerned about Jenna, Nelson turned to her. "Are you okay?"

"Nee," she said.

"What can I do?"

She seemed to gather herself together. "Nelson, I think I need some time. Thank you for your gift . . . and your help, but I'd like to be alone now."

Nelson wished Jenna was clinging to him. Not because she was weak but because he wanted her to want him near. To trust him to take care of her. To care for her and Katie.

But they weren't there yet. They might not ever be.

"I understand." Bending down to where Katie was standing next to the cat tree, he said, "I'll see you later, Kitty."

Her eyes, still so damp from her tears, widened. She didn't protest, though. She didn't say a word.

As he walked out the door and climbed into his truck, he felt as if the weight of the entire world was both falling on his shoulders and crumbling around him.

Maybe that was because it was.

In just a few short months, Jenna and Katie had become his whole world. And now, in the span of a few minutes, he was alone again.

chapter twenty-one

Jenna feared that it was going to take days to undo the damage that Mary's awful words had done. Katie loved her grandmother, but she loved her new little kitten too. Plus, she was pretty sure that her sweet daughter was falling in love with Nelson.

Jenna didn't blame her for that. Nelson was easy to love.

Why, in some of her weakest moments, she was starting to feel as if she was falling in love with Nelson as well. How could she not? He was attentive and kind and had been looking after her and Katie for over a year.

Unfortunately, he was also everything she shouldn't want or have.

After wrestling with her emotions for most of the night, she was grateful to spend much of her early morning at her desk, writing letters. She needed her pen-pal friends.

Though each held a special place in her life, Jenna decided to ask her friend Beatrice for advice. Bea was a teacher in England and just about her age. Bea's most recent letter had been all about her new boyfriend, Thomas.

Jenna thought that Bea might be the best person to understand what she was going through. She continued writing.

So that is my problem in a nutshell, Bea. I've secretly fallen in love with a man who is not only a bit older than me but Jimmy's former boss . . . and an Englisher! I have no idea what I should do.

As you might remember me telling you years ago, no one in my faith gets baptized as a baby. We wait until we become adults and have a few years to prayerfully consider living both Amish and English. These vows are meant to be as devout as one's marriage vows. I professed my faith, and I should stay Amish.

But even though my brain is telling me that is how it is, the rest of me feels differently.

After all, I am a gut Amish woman. When I got baptized, I intended to be Amish for the rest of my life. But I also had intended to be married to Jimmy for the rest of my life.

Now Nelson is the only man I think I could exchange marriage vows with. But if I did that, I'd risk being pushed away by my family and friends. That would hurt me, but it would hurt Katie too.

But I can't marry an Amish man that I don't love.

Plus, do you really think the Lord would be happy if I did that?

Bea, do you have any advice? I know you love Thomas. What would you do if loving him could hurt your relationship with your parents?

This is one of those times when I wish we were

next-door friends instead of pen pals. I could sure use your advice as soon as possible.

Wishing you a good day.

Love,
Jenna

After she walked the letter to the mailbox at the end of her driveway, she felt much better about everything. No, she still didn't know what to do, but reaching out to one of her dear pen pals reminded her that it was possible to have much in common with someone who had a very different life.

She walked into Katie's room. Her little girl was curled on her side under her sheets and blankets. She was holding a stuffed animal, and Blue was curled up against her back.

Tears pricked her eyes as she sat down next to her daughter. Sure, everything felt confusing and difficult right now, but that didn't mean that she and Katie wouldn't get through it.

"Katie, it's time to wake up," she said as she rubbed her back.

"I'm still sleepy, Mamm."

"I know, but the sun is up and you need to get up too."

"Why?"

"Because I want to take you to Brenneman's for breakfast."

As expected, Katie sat up with a jolt. "Really?"

"Of course, really. I wouldn't joke about that. What do you say? Would you like to go out to breakfast?"

"Jah."

Bending down, she pressed her lips to Katie's brow. "Gut. I'll lay out your dress. Go brush your teeth and wash your face."

For once, Katie didn't have to be told twice. When the bathroom door clicked shut, Jenna straightened Katie's sheets and placed her daughter's favorite pink dress on top. If only everything in life were this easy.

When they got to Brenneman's, they didn't have to wait long to be seated. "What would you like to get, Katie?" Jenna asked as they scanned the menu together. Katie knew only a few words by sight, but Jenna thought it was a good idea to encourage her to at least go through the motions of reading. Besides, Katie already knew what breakfast foods she liked.

"Can I have waffles?"

"Of course."

"Can I have strawberries on them?"

"You may."

Looking mischievous, she chirped, "And whipped cream too?"

Jenna pretended to act shocked. "Whipped cream on waffles? Are you sure about that?"

Eyes bright, Katie bobbed her head up and down. "Jah, Mamm. It's gut."

"Then I suppose I'd better say yes to that too."

Katie clapped her hands together. "Yay."

"Yay, indeed." Just as she was returning her attention to her own order, she noticed Fanny Harper sitting by herself at a table next to them. She was smiling at Katie. When Jenna caught her eye, she smiled. "Good morning, Fanny."

"Hi, Jenna. And good morning to you too, Miss Katie," Fanny added when Katie turned her head to look at her.

Katie just stared.

"Katie, this is Fanny Harper. She's Nelson's cousin, and they work together. Remember when she came by last year and brought you that stuffed bunny?"

Katie slowly nodded. "I remember now."

"It's good to see you again," Fanny said.

"Guess what? Nelson brought Blue a cat tree."

Fanny's eyebrows rose. "A what?"

Realizing how it must sound, Jenna translated. "Blue is Katie's kitten, and a cat tree is a jungle gym of sorts for a cat."

Looking very important, Katie said, "Kittens need trees on account of them not listening too good."

"Is that right?" Fanny asked.

"Uh-huh. Sometimes Blue forgets that his nails can hurt the furniture."

Fanny covered up her mouth, obviously in an effort to hide her laughter.

"Don't worry about laughing," Jenna said. "I think it's all quite humorous too."

After Fanny went back to looking at her menu and Jenna was looking around for the server, Katie tapped on her arm. "Mamm?"

"Jah, Katie?"

"Is Fanny sitting alone?"

"I don't know. I think so," she whispered.

"Maybe she'd like to sit with us?"

"You'd like that?" she asked in Pennsylvania Dutch.

"Jah."

Jenna nodded her head. "Why don't you ask her, then?"

Brightening, Katie called out, "Fanny, come sit with us."

Several people around them chuckled, but Jenna still felt her cheeks heat with embarrassment. "Katie, inside voice."

Fanny's gaze was warm as she turned to face them again. "Are you sure that's okay?"

"Uh-huh. Mei mamm said it was all right. Right, Mamm?"

Jenna nodded. "We would enjoy your company, Fanny."

"In that case, I'd be happy to accept. Thanks."

After she joined their table, Fanny chatted with Katie about the kitten, school, and what she ordered for breakfast.

Katie was so engaged, Jenna was able to sit back and just listen. These days, it was a rarity for her not to have Katie's complete attention.

After their food came, the three bowed their heads and gave thanks. Then they dug in. Katie with her waffle, Fanny with a bowl of fruit, yogurt, and granola, and she with her eggs, bacon, and fried potatoes.

When Katie slowed down, a server brought over a children's place mat and a small set of crayons, explaining that she'd forgotten to bring it earlier. Katie eagerly opened the box and started coloring, giving Fanny and Jenna a chance to get to know each other better.

"Nelson talks about you often, Fanny."

"I bet. Does he tell you that his cousin drives him batty?"

"Not at all. He says that you do a wonderful-gut job. And . . . that people often underestimate you because you're young and chatty."

Fanny smiled as she lifted her cup to take another sip of coffee. "I suppose that might be true." She shrugged. "I do my best for Nelson. He's given me a lot of responsibility, and I don't want to let him down."

"I don't think you've come close to doing that. He's proud of you."

"Thank you for sharing that." Fanny smiled. Then, looking at her a little more closely, she added, "May I ask you something?"

"Of course."

"It's . . . it's about being a widow." She nibbled at her bottom lip, obviously worrying about Jenna becoming upset with her.

"You have me intrigued. What would you like to ask me?"

"Do you ever think you'll marry again?"

"Why are you asking?"

"Oh!" Her eyes widened. "This isn't about you. It's about a man I met. His name is Hank, and he's a widower."

"Oh!" she said, feeling far less defensive. "Well, to be honest, I don't think much about marrying again." Of course, her cheeks and neck felt like they were on fire just then because she was telling a fib. There had been more than one moment when she'd looked at Nelson and thought that marrying him would make her happy. And wished it were possible.

"How long does a person's grief last, would you say?" Lowering her voice, Fanny added, "I was married when I was just a teenager but got divorced less than a year after. Then, a few years later, he died. So I know a bit about grieving, but my situation doesn't really compare to his."

"It still had to be hard, though, yes?"

"Yeah. But this isn't about me. I . . . really like this guy, but I don't want to be too pushy."

"I can understand that."

"What do you think? If it's been a few years, do you think Hank is still pining for his wife?"

"I have no idea. I've never met him."

"You're right. I'm jumping to conclusions, aren't I?"

"I don't know if you are or you aren't," she said honestly. "But I do think you should ask him. Every person handles love and loss differently, I think."

"You're right." She lowered her voice. "I just wish I knew when the time was right."

"How about when he takes you out on a date?" Wasn't that how Englishers did things?

Fanny leaned back. "That's the problem. We're not anywhere near that point."

"You aren't dating yet?"

"Nope. I only see him occasionally when I need to visit his house. Alliance Millworks is doing work for him, you see."

"Ah."

Fanny wrinkled her nose. "Actually, you could probably just say that the only thing that is true is that I have a crush on him. Listen to me. Here I am, worrying about him falling in love when he probably doesn't ever think about me unless I ask him something about his house."

Jenna thought Fanny's confession was adorable. She was tempted to tell her that she knew all about unsuspecting crushes, but there was no way she could tell Fanny that without also sharing that her personal crush was on Nelson.

"It's been a while since I've dated, but I do seem to recall that telling the other person how you're feeling is never a bad idea."

"It is in this case. If I tell Hank I like him, he's going to never want to see me again."

"He might."

"And I don't want anything to jeopardize the family business. This guy is bringing us a lot of work."

"I see." She sighed. "Well, in that case I'll just tell you something that my mother used to tell me when I was Katie's age."

"What was that?"

"That never is a very long time." She winked. "Chances are good that this Hank will one day be ready to start dating again."

"And if he does, it might as well be me."

Jenna chuckled. She hadn't meant for Fanny to take her words that far, but what did it matter? "I hope that is the case."

"Me too. Until then, I'm going to try to be as happy as little Katie here."

"Miss Fanny?"

"Yes?"

"If you get married to Hank, can I come to your wedding?"

As Fanny's eyes widened, Jenna laughed. "Out of the mouths of babes," she teased. Turning to her daughter, she said, "If Miss Fanny ends up marrying Mr. Hank one day, I'll see if we can go."

"I'll do one better," Fanny teased, as she regained her composure. "You may be my flower girl if I marry Hank Arias."

"Yay!" Katie said, though Jenna was almost positive that Katie had no idea what a flower girl was.

Exchanging glances with Fanny, Jenna smiled. "Yay, indeed."

chapter twenty-two

After enjoying the rather eye-opening breakfast with Jenna and Katie on Saturday and then spending a relaxing Sunday doing little besides attending church and working on her tan, Fanny walked into work on Monday feeling refreshed and ready for anything.

It only took a few minutes, however, to want to turn back around.

"I didn't think you were ever going to get here," Nelson snapped as he paced back and forth from his office into hers with a cell phone to his ear.

She waited a moment to respond in case his call was about to end.

When it didn't and Nelson continued to look like he wanted her to say something, Fanny pointed to the small digital clock behind her desk. "It's five minutes to eight, boss. I'm early."

"Not early enough," he groused.

Needing a minute to settle down, Fanny pulled out her chair, booted up her computer, and put away both her purse and her lunch.

When Nelson only continued to stare at her without saying a word—not to her or the mystery person on the phone—she folded her arms across her chest and watched him pace.

"What?" he asked when he walked toward her yet again.

"I'm trying to figure out what's going on with you, boss. Are you on the phone or just pretending to be?"

He grunted. "Fanny, this isn't funny."

She wasn't trying to be. "How about you take a second and tell me what's going on?"

"I'm on hold with Premier Lumber," he bit out. "Things with them are going bananas."

"Bananas, huh?" Those were fighting words for her cousin. "Oh no."

"Oh yeah." When Nelson paced her way again, he tossed a file onto her desk. He'd obviously picked it up from her desk before she arrived. "Look at this, Fan," he added as he opened the front and picked up an invoice from inside it.

She took it. Scanned the sheet. And became even more confused. The order was for a shipment of mahogany, placed two months ago by her. And the deposit had also been marked as paid.

She remembered writing that check because it was a doozy. Mahogany was never a cheap product, but she'd found a vendor she liked in south Florida. Working with a vendor in the States seemed best. Premier charged more per unit, but shipping was far cheaper than if it came from Central or South America.

This order was fairly sizable because it was one of the

materials Big John was painstakingly carving and nailing into Hank Arias's study.

"What's going on with the order?"

"We are missing most of it," he said, each word sounding like a staccato beat.

"Huh?"

"It hasn't arrived, Fan." He frowned. Held up a finger, signifying for her to wait a second. "What? No. Don't! No, really. Hey, I've been holding!"

Nelson's face was flushed. Honestly, it looked like he was about to blow a gasket. There was only one thing to do. She stood back up and reached for the phone. "Let me talk to them before they hang up on you," she hissed.

"Gladly. Here."

After she held the receiver up to her ear and listened to some awful, tinny-sounding Muzak, she turned to him. "Tell me what exactly is going on and what I need to tell them to do."

"Yet again they are giving me the runaround. We just got the order, but it was only half the amount we ordered, and half of that was unusable. There are bores in the middle of it, some of the other boards are uneven, and some look almost rotten. I wouldn't put it in a barn, let alone in Hank Arias's study." Nelson shook his head. "Fanny, this order was a small fortune! They don't agree that the wood is subpar. Worse, they're saying they can't send out any on a flatbed anytime soon."

This was getting worse and worse. No wonder Nelson looked like he wanted to hit something. "I understand now." As the awful Muzak continued to play in her ear, she started to think of all the consequences. "Who have you told about this?"

"I haven't told anyone beyond John."

"Hank doesn't know?"

"Nope. I didn't want to tell him the news until I had a way to fix it." Looking pained, Nelson said, "Fanny, you know how much all those bonuses were."

"We had plenty of money to cover those," she said quickly. "The employees earned them."

"I agree. But more money is going to be flying out the door as we get the Wooster branch started."

"We're not talking about acres and acres of mahogany, boss. Relax."

"I would if we didn't have two other orders for it coming down the pike. Plus, if John can't work on his schedule . . ."

"Uh-oh." Big John was easygoing and relaxed . . . until he wasn't. Then he was known to get as out of sorts as a diva on tour.

"Uh-oh is right. I talked to him at six this morning, and then he showed me his calendar and told me that everything was going to be messed up." Nelson closed his eyes. "Among other things."

Fanny could well imagine what had been said. Most Amish never cursed, but they were also not saints. If they were pushed enough, any one of the men could stand up for themselves or allow their temper to snap.

And Big John was kind of known for his colorful outbursts.

"Hank wanted this woodwork done yesterday."

"I know."

Nelson blinked as if he'd suddenly remembered that she'd been the one going to his house regularly to check progress. "Listen. When you finally get someone over at Premier to talk to you, don't hang up until you either get a promise for the right wood to be delivered this week or our money back. We can't let them buy time and ask to 'look into it.'"

"You got it."

"You sure?"

Oh, she was very sure. "Go sit down, boss." Looking at her empty mug, she picked it up. "Better yet, go take a walk and get me a cup of coffee."

"Are you serious right now?"

"Uh, yeah. I just got to work. I'm dying for some caffeine." She batted her eyelashes. "Pretty please?"

"Fine." He picked up her coffee cup and strode down the hall.

Fanny hoped and prayed that someone in the plant had brought in donuts. They were Nelson's weakness. Pretty much everyone at the mill knew this, and many of the men's wives usually made six or seven extra donuts for them to take to the break room. Sure, they were supposed to be for everyone to share. But there was an unspoken rule that Nelson should get one of them if he was around. His mood seemed to improve with increased sugar intake.

Just as he was out of sight, a cheery voice came on the line. "Sorry about the wait, Nelson. We just wanted to try to get an answer for you."

Fanny frowned. The man's voice sounded far too lighthearted for the minor meltdown their bad shipment was about to create in multiple areas of their company. "You are now speaking to Frances Harper. I'm Nelson's personal assistant. To whom am I speaking?"

"This is Steve, miss." His voice turned slightly oily. "How are you doing today, dear?"

She gritted her teeth. "I'm really glad you asked, Steve. You see, as a matter of fact, I'm not doing well at all. Your company's mess-up with this order of mahogany has ruined my morning."

"Don't worry about it, honey. These things happen all the time." He took a deep breath. "As a matter of fact, once—"

"Oh no. We are not sharing stories. All I want to know is that the mahogany will be on its way today." She had no problem if someone she really liked called her "honey" or "dear." Honestly, she had a sneaking suspicion that if Hank called her either of those pet names, her knees might get weak. But this guy on the line saying it? Well, it made her teeth go on edge.

"Today?" He chuckled. "That's not possible."

"All right. Then I'm going to need you to FedEx a cashier's check for our entire deposit today. Or, better yet, you can wire it."

"That's not how we do things, hon."

When he dared to chuckle, she saw red. "First, my name is Frances, or Miss Harper. It is absolutely not 'hon' or 'honey.' Second, I'm afraid that those two options are exactly how we do things, Steve. I need that wood, and I don't care if you have to send people all over the state of Florida and put it on a train car. All that matters is that I will be able to tell the client, whose study your missing shipment is ruining, when it will be finished."

"Where is your boss? I appreciate you trying to help, but you really have no idea what you are asking."

Fanny was trying for patience. She really was. But what she was aching to do was pull a "Big John" and start cussing at Steve like she was a woman possessed.

"I do know," she said in a firm voice. "I know *exactly* what I am asking. Just like I know *exactly* what I will do if I don't receive either your promise the wood will be delivered this week or that money by five o'clock tonight." She lowered her voice. "I'm going to make it my personal goal to ruin your reputation. After that, I'm going to call a lawyer and sue you for breach of contract."

She took a breath. "Then, last but not least, I'm going to let my very important client know who, exactly, has tried to swindle his money."

Getting creative, Fanny lowered her voice even more. "And he's not a sweet Amish guy, Steve. He's far from that. In fact, I'm pretty sure that this man is used to getting things done in ways that have nothing to do with Google reviews and lawyers. He—or one of the scary guys who works for him—could show up at your doorstep tonight and make sure you understand how unhappy he is with you."

She felt slightly embarrassed. She didn't think Hank Arias had a team of bad guys at his beck and call at all. But she'd done her best to sound believable. At the moment, that was all that mattered.

There was silence on the other end of the line. For a split second, she was afraid they'd been disconnected, but then she heard a small sigh.

"All right," Steve said.

"All right, you'll find me the wood? Or all right, you'll be sending over a cashier's check?"

"All right. I'll find the wood."

"When should I tell the guys in receiving to expect to receive your shipment number? Because I can guarantee that they'll be tracking it every step of the way."

"I don't know. Give me a minute."

"Every day that this wood is late means that we're going to have to pay them overtime, Steve. Plus, half of the crew is Amish. I need to make sure they can let their families know that you've decided to ruin their evenings. That means I'm going to have to hire drivers to take them home too."

"You know, you're a piece of work." All traces of the earlier slickness had disappeared from his voice.

Fanny rolled her eyes. She worked with truckers, dock workers, and a whole bunch of carpenters and master craftsmen. Ninety percent of them were men. She'd been called far worse when she had to press someone to do their job. "I still need a timeline, Steve."

"You'll have your ship number and tracking information by five tonight."

"Are you sure?"

"Yeah." He cleared his throat. "I just remembered that we have several yards of mahogany in a back warehouse. It's going to take a bit of juggling to get it loaded and on a truck to your facility, but I'll make sure it gets done."

She smiled. "Thank you so much, Steve. I appreciate your help *sooo* much."

"Yes, ma'am."

When she hung up, Fanny was grinning ear to ear.

"Did you really just make that guy believe that I had a group of minions ready to go beat them up if I don't get that wood?"

Fanny inhaled. Closed her eyes. And felt pretty much every patch of skin on her body turn bright red.

When she turned around, Hank's blue eyes met hers.

What could she say? "Kind of."

His eyes were now lit with amusement. "At least you're not lying to me."

"I wouldn't lie to you." Not about work, anyway.

He pulled up a chair, crossed his legs, and grinned. "I can't wait to hear what's been going on, Miss Harper."

Fanny sincerely hoped that Nelson was about to appear with her coffee because, for the first time in her life, she couldn't think of a single thing to say.

chapter twenty-three

"Your cousin's a pistol," Hank told Nelson after Fanny had turned beet red, reported that the wood was on its way, and then scurried down the hall.

"Yeah. She sure is," he replied, watching as she disappeared from sight.

Hank had been watching Fanny's escape too. "Where do you think she ran off to?"

"I'm not sure. She's good at taking a walk when her temper flares. I'm guessing she probably needed a break."

Nelson had a feeling that Fanny was either going to seek shelter in the women's restroom or go find Big John and sit with him—if he wasn't at Hank's house.

Fanny and John had a close friendship, and she often sought him out when she was feeling stressed. It was almost a father-daughter relationship, but with a whole lot more ribbing and joking around. Most likely, John would get a kick out of Fanny's retelling of her phone call. Shoot, Big John might even go so far as to pat her on the head and tell her that she did a good job.

Hank was still looking down the hall, obviously hoping

that she'd reappear. Nelson wasn't sure why Hank was so interested in Fanny's departure, but it wasn't his business. All that mattered to him was that Hank wasn't going to be upset about a delay. "I'm pretty sure John can bring in another guy to help him make up any lost time. We have several men who are master craftsmen. Most of them apprenticed under John."

"That's fine. I'm sure you do."

"If you'd like, I can text you when the wood arrives. I don't want you to worry." Sure, he was going above and beyond what he'd normally do with a customer, but Hank Arias wasn't just any customer.

At last, Hank directed his attention away from the hall and back to him. "Nelson, I hear what you're saying but that's not necessary. I didn't come over here to tell you how to do your job. And believe me, I've dealt with plenty of shipping issues over the years. Those things happen." He folded his arms over his chest. "I only wanted to stop by to tell you how pleased I am with the progress."

"Okay. That's good. Thanks." Nelson knew he sounded a little scattered, but what else could he say? Hank could have easily said all of that in a phone call or a text. There was no real reason for him to come to the mill in person. Unless it had to do with a five-foot-seven-inch woman with an attitude.

"Do you think she's okay?"

Yep. There was now no question in his mind about Hank's appearance today.

The bit of confusion Nelson had been feeling was starting to meld itself into something more. Something like concern. But not for Hank, for Fanny. His cousin wasn't shy or timid, but that didn't mean she was all that worldly either. She was a small-town girl, and Hank was anything but small-town.

"I'm pretty sure she's fine," Nelson said at last. "I'd bet a nickel that she went down to Big John to fill him in on that conversation."

"John is that concerned about mahogany?"

"John is always concerned about his materials—but it's more that he's concerned about her. They're friends. Close friends." John had always had a soft spot for Fanny. Nelson added, "He used to make up little jobs for her to do by his side when she was a kid. She'd talk a mile a minute, and he'd listen. Whenever my uncle—her dad—would try to get her to stop bothering him, John would intervene and say he liked her company."

"Ah, okay." Hank's expression softened but he still looked worried.

Nelson folded his arms over his chest. "Why are you so concerned about my cousin?"

Hank blinked. "And you're worried that I'm worried about her?"

"No, I'm worried about your intentions."

To his surprise, instead of looking embarrassed or defensive, Hank started laughing. "Fanny seems like a lady pretty capable of handling her own affairs, Nelson."

Lady? That made it sound like she was a forty-year-old stranger. Fanny was not that. "She's really just a girl, you know."

"She's more than that, Nelson. She's a grown woman doing a great job at a company where there is a significant amount of pressure. I don't think of her as a girl at all."

"Yeah, I guess her job is hard to do. And she does it well." Nelson shook his head. "I mean, she's great. But still, she's been sheltered."

"I understand." Looking at him directly, Hank added, "Look, if you are asking about my motives, I think it's pretty obvious. I think she's gorgeous. She makes me smile. She lights up every single room she walks into. So much that I want to be around her more often." He took a breath. "But . . . no, we aren't dating. Not yet. I'm not even sure if she would be interested in dating me."

"I'll talk to her about that."

"Why? I mean, no offense, but you aren't her father. Maybe you should let her make some of her own decisions. I want what she wants. So if she's not interested, I'll abide by her wishes. But I want anything she does to be her decision. Not something she decides to do in order to make you happy."

As hard as that was to hear, Nelson nodded. Hank was exactly right. He couldn't treat her like the grown woman she was and a sheltered child at the same time. It wasn't fair to Hank, and it sure wasn't fair to Fanny. "I understand."

"Thank you."

"Hey!" Fanny called out as she walked down the hall toward them. "Hank, I didn't know you were still here."

He stuffed his hands into the front pockets of his jeans. "Yeah, I had a couple of things to talk to Nelson about."

She looked from one of them to the other. "Is everything all right?"

Hank glanced his way.

And for some reason, that made Nelson look at Fanny

again. This time, really look at her. Study her without allowing a bunch of memories of her playing softball—all braces and freckles—get in the way.

Instead, he looked at her as an adult.

Thought about how she'd dealt with Steve without skipping a beat. How she dealt with a dozen balls in the air all day without dropping a single one. She might be young and sheltered, but she was a competent, smart, attractive woman.

Then he noticed how Fanny was gazing at Hank, with the type of expression he could only hope Jenna would send his way.

Fanny really liked Hank. Not as a crush, but as a grown woman likes a man.

And then he realized that Hank was right. She was a grown woman, Hank was a good man, and they were both adults.

It was also obvious that there was something between them, and if he tried to get in the way of it, he wasn't going to make anything better. Actually, he was very likely going to make a lot of things worse.

"Yeah, Fanny," he said at last. "Everything is fine." Holding up his cell, he said, "If you'll excuse me, I just remembered that I need to go take care of something. I'll, uh, be in my office."

He walked inside, closed the door, and then sat down at his desk. Took a breath. And realized that he needed to let Fanny grow up.

After all, it was obvious that she already had.

chapter twenty-four

Three hours later, against his better judgment, Nelson stopped by the store and bought two dozen pink roses, a spiral-sliced ham, and a battery-operated bubble machine, then picked up a pan of freshly baked mac and cheese from Brenneman's.

Then, just as he'd done dozens of times before, he drove up Jenna's driveway, parked his truck, and knocked on the front door.

He spied Katie peeking through the window and waving at him before Jenna unlocked the door and opened it.

"Hi, Nelson," Jenna said with a hesitant smile. "I didn't know you were stopping by this evening."

"I was at work most of the day but wasn't quite ready to head home. Are you busy?"

She hesitated. "Well, um, as a matter of fact, it's not a good day for you to be here. I'm so sorry."

"Oh. I see." He noticed then that Jenna had dark circles under her eyes, her face was flushed, and her dress looked a little wrinkled. "What's going on? Are you okay?"

"Jah. I'm okay." Her smile was strained as she seemed to grip the door a little more tightly.

Katie wiggled her way under her mother's arm to stand in front of him. "Mamm is sick," she announced.

Ignoring the fact that Jenna was still standing right in front of him, he bent down slightly to speak to Katie. "She is?"

"Uh-huh. Mamm doesn't feel good. Not at all."

"Uh-oh." Focusing back on Jenna, he lowered his voice. "What's wrong?"

She shrugged. "It's nothing for you to worry about." When he continued to stare at her, she sighed. "Fine. I have a stomach bug. It'll pass."

It didn't look like it was passing anytime soon. He was kind of worried she was about to pass out. "Who's taking care of you?"

"No one needs to take care of me. I'll be fine. I'm just tired. Now, if you'll—"

"Wait." He reached out and pressed his palm to her cheek. She was burning up. "You have a fever."

"I doubt that. It's warm in here." But her eyes were averted.

"I didn't ever think you'd lie to me, Jenna."

"I'm not lying. Not really."

Stepping forward, he motioned for Katie to move out of the way. "Let me in."

"Certainly not. I'm fine." Catching sight of his narrowed eyes, she mumbled, "Okay, I'm not fine. But I'm not too sick."

"She's real sick, Nelson," Katie blurted. "Mamm was throwing up all night. I heard her in the bathroom."

Looking pained, Jenna closed her eyes. "Katie, you mustn't talk about things like that."

"How come? It's the truth."

"Jah. But it isn't something we speak of." Meeting his gaze again, she murmured, "I'm so sorry. I'd have been perfectly good if you had never heard that."

She was being silly. "There's no reason on earth for you to be embarrassed right now. I'm glad that Katie told me what's been going on." As he stepped inside, he added, "I'm glad one of you ladies has decided to tell me the truth."

"Nelson, I'm not in the mood to spar with you."

"I know you're not," he said as he closed the door behind him. Boy, Jenna looked under the weather. Concern for both her and Katie surged through him. Someone needed to be taking care of both of them. "Are you sick too, Kitty?"

"Nope." She smiled.

"Is your grandmother coming over?"

"I don't think so. My Grandma Amy had to be somewhere else today. I'm not sure where."

"What about your other grandmother? Mary?"

Katie shook her head. "My mamm doesn't like it when my grandmother comes over to help. Because she doesn't listen to Mamm, and that makes her mad."

Jenna closed her eyes. "Katie!"

"It's a good thing I'm here to take care of her, then." He winked. "I'm fantastic at following directions."

"Nelson, this isn't funny. Please go."

"Sorry, but I can't do that," he replied with another wink Katie's way. While the little girl giggled, he reached for Jenna's arm. "Come on. Let's get you back in the living room. You can sit down or lay down or whatever you were doing," he said in a tone of voice he usually reserved for guys at work.

"Why?"

"Because I have some things in my truck for you," he replied, deliberately sidestepping her protest. "I can't get them and watch you at the same time."

"Nelson, I'd rather not be around you right now."

He knew she'd probably get mad at him later, but he figured it was time he brought out the big guns. "I have two dozen pink roses for you in the cab of my truck, Jenna. They're wilting as we speak. Do you really want them to die because you're being so stubborn?"

"You brought me roses?"

"Yep, and I brought a bubble machine for Katie."

"You brought us a bubble machine?" Katie asked, her whole face lighting up.

He smiled down at her. "I did, and I think we're going to love playing with it. I even brought the batteries it needs."

She clapped her hands. "Yay."

When he dared to meet Jenna's eyes again, Nelson saw everything he was sure he'd see—irritation that he'd steamrolled over her wishes combined with a reluctant appreciation for the roses she hadn't yet seen.

"Come on." He walked her into the living room, rearranged two pillows for behind her head, and then helped her lie down. "How's that? Are you settled? I don't want you to fall."

"I'm not a child. I am not going to fall."

She sounded so full of herself.

He smirked at her before walking out the door. He left the front door open, which allowed him to make the two trips back and forth from his vehicle. One to get the roses and bubble machine. The second trip was to bring in the ham and mac and cheese. It was all going to be too rich for Jenna's queasy stomach but probably perfect for Katie and him.

He was sure he was going to be sticking around for a while and eating supper with her.

"What's that?" Katie asked as she followed him into the kitchen after he closed the door.

"A spiral-sliced ham. Do you like ham?"

"I think so."

He lifted the foil off the pan that was still warm. "And this is mac and cheese. I know you like this."

"I like it a lot." She grinned. "I'm really hungry too."

"Well, we can't have that. Let me get your mother settled, and then I'll fix you a plate."

"But what about the bubbles?"

"That comes last."

She frowned. "Can't we play first?"

"Not if you're hungry."

"I'm not that hungry anymore . . ."

He laughed. "Sorry, but I'm not going to change my mind. Take it or leave it, Kitty. What do you want to do?"

"All right. Fine. I'll eat first."

"Katie, you be nice," Jenna called out.

"I'm being nice." She turned to him. "Aren't I?"

"Yes, honey. You are being very nice. Now, can you sit down and wait for me while I get your mama settled?" When she nodded, he gently squeezed her shoulder, then headed to the more prickly female in the household. She was finally lying down on the couch. "Do you have ibuprofen?"

"Jah. But I can't keep anything down."

"Let's try. Do you have any soda, like Sprite or ginger ale?"

"No."

He pulled out his phone. "I'm going to get some over here." Remembering his mother's cure-all—saltines, popsicles, applesauce, and toast—he typed off a list of things for Fanny to bring over as soon as possible.

Deciding that water might be best for Jenna anyway, he filled a glass with cold water and handed it to her, along with two of the pills he'd found in her medicine cabinet. "Take this."

"Danke." She took the pills and sipped the water with a look of foreboding but seemed to handle it all right.

"Were you up all night?"

"Kind of," she admitted in a small voice. "This—this flu, or whatever it is, came up on me suddenly. It's been awful."

"It's time for a nap, then." Reaching for her hand, he said, "Come on. Let's get you in bed."

Her pretty eyes widened. "I can't leave Katie alone."

"You aren't. I'll stay with her. We'll be fine."

"Nelson, are you sure? She's five, you know."

"I'm positive, honey. I love spending time with her. I'll feed her some supper, and we'll play with the bubble machine. Plus, if she needs something, I'll wake you up."

"You promise?"

"Of course. I'm trying to help you, Jenna." He waggled

his fingers. "Now, come on. Take my hand, and let's get you back in bed."

At last, she took his hand. Then Nelson helped her to her feet but kept her hand securely in his own. Her skin was warm—too warm—but as he ran his hand along her knuckles, he noticed how smooth and soft they were. So feminine.

He was pleased when she didn't try to pull away from his grip, instead staying by his side and allowing him to walk her up the stairs and into her bedroom.

There were four pink walls, a stack of books, and a truly beautiful quilt over a white iron bed frame. A vase of flowers adorned her white dresser. The flowers were obviously from her garden and no doubt had been there a few days, but they still lent a bright, pretty contrast to her dour mood.

Her sheets were in disarray. Even her three pillows were scattered across the bed. Hoping to lighten the mood, Nelson chuckled. "It looks like you went round and round with the bedding, and it won."

"Yes. Unfortunately, I barely made it to the bathroom the last time."

"What time was this?"

"I don't know. Six, maybe? Seven? After I lay on the floor for a while, I moved to the living room couch."

"You really do need some rest." When she moved to straighten her bedding, he shook his head. "I've got this. Want to go to the bathroom or something before you lay down?"

"Jah. I probably should."

He reached for her. "Do you need help?"

"Nee, Nelson."

He didn't argue but he did hover until she walked into the bathroom and closed the door behind her.

"You okay?"

"Yes. Don't come in!"

Nelson grinned at her words as he pulled up her sheets, tucked in the light cotton blanket and quilt, and rearranged the pillows.

He'd just pulled down one side when she returned, her face damp from where she'd washed it.

"Look how nice you made everything."

"I've been making my own bed for a while now."

"Jah. I guess you have."

She crawled in and lay down with a sigh. "This feels gut. Danke, Nelson."

"You're welcome. Now close your eyes and try to rest. I'll come back to check on you in a while."

Jenna's eyes were closed and she was breathing softly before he was in the hallway.

Poor thing. She must have been exhausted.

Katie was coloring a picture on the coffee table when he came back. "I'm drawing some flowers for mei mamm for when she wakes up. She really likes flowers."

"That's a pretty picture. I bet she's going to love it."

"Uh-huh." She colored a little more before looking up at him. "What should we do now?"

"Eat."

"And then bubbles?"

"Yep. Come on."

Katie sat down at the small table in the kitchen and watched as he made her a plate.

"Do you want milk?"

"Yes, please."

After she was all set, he sat down across from her. "Okay, dig in for me."

Without his prompting, she closed her eyes and said a quick prayer. She moved her lips, but he didn't hear a word.

Nelson thought that was just about the cutest thing he'd ever seen. Once she started eating, he fixed a small plate for himself and ate across the table from her.

"This is pretty good, don't you think?"

"Uh-huh."

"Do you like the ham or the mac and cheese better?"

"I like them the same. What about you?"

"I feel the same way you do. The same," he said with a smile.

When Katie grinned back at him, Nelson knew that he'd been right to be so pushy. He was taking care of Katie and giving Jenna a much-needed break. He'd call that progress.

When they were both done, he washed their dishes and set them on the wooden drying rack. "You know what? Let's call your Grandma Amy, just to make sure she can't come over. She has a phone in her kitchen, jah?"

"Jah." Brightening, Katie added, "I even know her phone number."

"Aren't you smart?" He pulled out his cell phone and punched in the numbers that Katie recited. Jenna's mother answered on the first ring. "Amy, this is Nelson. I . . ."

"I know who you are. Is everything okay?"

"Not really." Briefly he explained about Jenna feeling poorly.

"I'll come over to spend the night, but I can't stay long in the morning. I've promised that I would help make fried pies early tomorrow for a benefit auction coming up."

"I can come get you and bring you here, then take you back in the morning."

"No need to do that. I have my bike. But I might not get there for an hour."

"That's fine. Katie and I have been having a good time together."

After he hung up, he explained to Katie what the new plans were. Amy would come over when she could and spend the night. He'd stay until she arrived and then return in the morning.

Katie seemed to take everything in stride.

"Ready to try out the bubble machine now?" he asked.

"Yes!"

"Come on. Let's go sit on the front porch and figure it out."

When she scrambled to her feet, she reached for his hand. As he held it while they walked outside, Nelson decided that he could get used to holding both of these women's hands. Taking care of them.

Doing whatever they needed in order to get through life. Jenna might disagree, but he was pretty sure they needed him.

He sure knew that he needed them.

chapter twenty-five

The first thing Jenna heard when she woke up the next morning was laughter drifting through the screen of her bedroom window. It was Katie's signature "very happy" laugh, which was sharp and shrill and so full of exuberance that anyone nearby couldn't help but smile.

It was loud and it was special, because that "very happy" laugh was something of a rarity for Katie. Her daughter giggled a lot and smiled often. She was a happy little girl and always had been. But it was unusual for her to completely let loose and laugh, no holds barred. Jenna had never been able to hear that laugh and not smile.

And here she was, smiling now. Even though Jenna felt weak and was in desperate need of a shower, Katie's laugh lifted her spirits.

Her heart lifted even further when she walked outside and spotted Katie sitting next to Nelson. He was holding Blue while the cat was pawing at the spray of bubbles in the air.

It was too good a picture not to admire. Jenna settled against the doorframe and watched the three of them.

As if Nelson sensed she was near, he turned his head. When he spotted her just behind them, he grinned. "You look better."

"Danke. I feel better."

"Hi, Mamm!" Katie waved but made no move to budge from Nelson's side.

"Hiya, Katie."

Still keeping a firm hold on the kitten, Nelson said, "I hope our antics didn't wake you up."

"Not at all." Moving closer, she added, "I'm starting to feel like I've been missing out, though. You two have been having all the fun."

"Mamm, come sit with us. This is really fun."

"I don't know if I should. I don't want you to catch whatever I have, Katie. Believe me, you don't want this."

"She might have a point there, Kitty," Nelson said.

Katie wrinkled her nose. "Jah."

"Do either of ya want to tell me how our indoor cat came to be sitting out here on the porch?"

"He was meowing something awful," Katie said. "He really wanted to join us."

"Katie."

"Jenna, I promise, Katie's telling the truth. Blue was very upset to have to watch the bubbles from the window."

She wouldn't have thought that, but what did she know? "He doesn't seem to mind you holding him now."

"You're right, though to be honest, I don't think Blue remembers that he's on my lap. All he cares about is batting at these bubbles."

"See?" Katie called out as another batch of bubbles flew

into the air and Blue got on his hind legs and batted them with his front paws.

It really was adorable. "It's a good toy, Nelson. Thank you for bringing it." Of course, she had about a dozen things to thank him for. The roses, the food, calling her mother to come over, then returning early this morning so she could leave.

He'd done so much, just so she could rest. It was humbling. "I don't know how I'm going to repay you for all these favors."

"It's a good thing I don't want you to try. We're friends, remember?"

"I haven't forgotten that."

"Good." He stood up, securely holding Blue in one arm while he bent down to turn off the bubble machine. "Let's go inside and see how you do with some soda and maybe a cracker or two."

She was surprised by the offer. "You were able to get them delivered?"

"Fanny ran to the store and dropped them off last night." He motioned for Jenna to walk inside first.

"Fanny is so nice," Katie said. "She brought me a sugar cookie from the bakery."

"Wow. That was nice of her to do."

Katie frowned. "Nelson wouldn't let me eat it, though. He said I had to ask you if I could have a cookie."

Surprised, Jenna glanced his way.

He shrugged. "You're the mom. Not me."

"Can I have that cookie now?" Katie asked. "I've been really good and quiet."

"You may," she said. Sure, it was Katie's laughter that

had woken her up, but she'd take that sort of wake-up call any day. Her daughter's happiness was good medicine.

"Yay!" Katie trotted into the kitchen while Nelson set the cat on the floor.

"Don't run, Katie," he warned.

"I won't." After getting her cookie, Katie walked over to the kitchen table and sat down.

"How are you feeling?" Nelson asked when Katie was out of earshot.

She knew he was asking about her health. He was concerned about her. He wanted to know if she was feeling less feverish. If her stomach was better. Less sour.

But all Jenna could think about was how at peace she felt. Or, maybe *peace* wasn't the right descriptor. It was more like she felt normal. Like herself. Less stressed. Less everything.

It came as a surprise.

Jenna realized then that she hadn't felt "normal" for quite some time. Maybe not since Jimmy died. Or . . . maybe she hadn't felt like this for even longer.

She and Jimmy had been experiencing a bit of a rough patch before his accident. She'd kept hoping he would change. Become a bit more stable. Less restless.

Not that she'd ever want to admit that out loud. But it was how things had been.

And after his death? Well, Jenna had just been trying to survive. The weight of being a single mother was heavy on her shoulders. The knowledge that she might be alone for the rest of her life was something else that she'd been trying to come to grips with.

Nelson's appearance in her life had made things brighter.

Easier. As they'd gotten closer, things had changed between them again. A friendship had developed, and now that he and Katie had become close, there was an ease between them that she appreciated.

Nelson helped her relax. He made her feel as if all the detritus, all the extra stuff that got in her head and took hold and seemed to constantly keep her up at night, didn't really matter.

Instead, it was a sunny morning, there was a smile on her daughter's face, and she had the comfort of a good friend who didn't seem to want anything besides her happiness.

"I'm good," she finally answered.

Nelson raised one eyebrow. "That took you a minute. Are you sure you're okay?"

"Jah." Choosing her words with care, she added, "It's going to sound funny, but I just realized that I'm good right now. Not because I feel better—though I do—but because I feel content. At peace. Almost normal."

Some of the worry lines around his eyes eased. "That's a good thing."

"Yes. It sure is." She smiled. "I think the Lord has finally helped me see that I still have much to be thankful for. Even though Jimmy died too young and his accident was a terrible thing, dwelling on it won't help me. And grieving his death for the rest of my life won't ever bring him back."

"It's nice to see you happy, Jenna," he said softly.

"It's nice to be happy," she replied. Unlike the night before, she was being completely honest. Putting her heart out there for him to see.

She secretly thought that was what he'd always wanted. For her to openly return his feelings. To want to date him.

And though she hadn't quite gone that far . . . she still thought he'd be pleased.

And he was. Almost. For a second, though, she thought he seemed a little uneasy. Something had flickered in his eyes. It looked a lot like doubt. Maybe worry.

Perhaps regret?

But when the moment passed and they started talking about other things, everything seemed to be normal again.

Most likely, that brief flicker of doubt had just been her imagination.

chapter twenty-six

It had taken Jenna almost a week to feel completely better. As soon as she got home from dropping Katie off at her parents' house, she sat down at her desk and opened up the day's mail. She'd received three letters from her pen pals that morning. One was from Liam in Germany, the second was from Laura Beth in Mexico, and the third was from Holly, her Amish pen pal in Pinecraft.

All three letters were full of news and inquiries about her. Holly, in particular, seemed concerned about how she was doing now that so much time had passed after Jimmy's death.

> *Have you considered eventually dating again, Jenna? I hope you will. I promise, there's nothing wrong with opening your heart to the idea.*

Jenna supposed it was only natural that Holly would seem so concerned. She was older and had lost her husband years ago. She'd occasionally written that she'd had a difficult adjustment to widowhood.

Feeling as if Holly had read her mind, Jenna decided to write to her first.

As a matter of fact, I have been wrestling with some unexpected things. Holly, the truth is that I think I've fallen in love with the best man I've ever met. He's kind to me, and he loves Katie too. But he's also unsuitable. He's an Englisher.

Jenna bit the end of her pen, then continued.

I honestly don't know what to do. My heart is telling me that the Lord must have brought him into my life for a reason, but my brain continually reminds me that I took my baptism seriously and shouldn't break those vows. I don't know what to do.

She'd just flipped the first sheet over to write on the back when she heard a knock at the door.

A little burst of happiness filled her. Perhaps Nelson had been driving by and decided to stop in for a spell. As much as she enjoyed the way he and Katie got along, it would be so nice to focus completely on him.

And, yes, to have his attention be solely on her.

As much as she tried to ignore the signs, Jenna knew she was really starting to care for Nelson. She liked him. She liked him a lot. Sometimes when he smiled at her, she felt goose bumps on her arms or a little shiver up her spine. It might be wrong, but she was anxious to feel that way again.

Plus, of course, she needed to thank him again for taking such good care of her when she was sick. She needed to repay his kindness and generosity somehow. Maybe she could ask him if he'd like to come over for supper one day soon. She could make some of his favorite dishes.

If she ever discovered what they were.

When she heard the knock again, she hastily pulled open the door. And then barely caught her feeling of disappointment as Doreen greeted her with a bright smile, an immaculate white kapp, and a rather pretty teal dress with no apron. On her feet were white leather Keds. If it hadn't been for her gray hair and fine lines around her eyes, the woman could have passed for a young bride.

"I'm so glad you are home, Jenna," she said as she walked right inside. "I didn't see all of the blinds up, so I wasn't sure."

"I just got home from taking my daughter to my parents' house for a visit," she explained as she hurried to pull up the living room shades. "I'm afraid I got so busy writing to one of my pen pals, I forgot to pull the shades up."

While she pulled them up on one side of the room, Doreen crossed and took care of the other set. "You have a pen pal?"

"I do. I've got four of them."

"Four? My word. Are they all friends of yours who moved away?"

"Not at all. Years ago, I came across a woman asking for prayers in *The Budget*. She was on her first missionary trip and was feeling lonely. I started writing to her. She happened to be in Germany. She moved on, but a friend of a friend started writing, mainly because he was interested in me being Amish." Realizing that she could talk all day about her treasured pen pals, Jenna forced herself to stop. "I started writing the others much the same way. They were friends of friends or other folks who enjoy letter-writing as much as I do."

Doreen smiled. "I love that I just learned about this from you. I feel that we're becoming good friends."

"I feel the same way." Feeling much better about her unexpected visitor, Jenna walked toward the kitchen. "Would you like a cup of kaffi?"

"I enjoy coffee, but it's warm outside. A glass of water would be most welcome."

"I'll be right back."

Doreen sat down. "Take your time, dear."

Jenna was a little embarrassed about how she was dressed. She was wearing an old work dress. The fabric was faded and even a little bit worn in places. It was also still a little too big, thanks to all the weight she'd lost in the last few years. "You look like a ragamuffin, Jenna," she muttered to herself as she filled a water glass for Doreen and a coffee cup for herself. Well, at least her bare feet were mud-free.

Maybe proper manners called for her to drink water too, but Jenna needed another cup of coffee in the worst way. She placed a few two-day-old cookies on a plate, summoned a composed expression, and walked into the living room. "Here you go."

Doreen brightened. "You brought cookies too." She picked one up. "What kind are they?"

"Monster cookies."

"Those are yummy. Why, I've been known to eat these for breakfast," she said as she pinched off a bite and popped it in her mouth.

Maybe it was Doreen's exuberance, or maybe it was because Doreen had seemed interested in her pen-pal hobby, but whatever the reason, Jenna felt herself relax. "Are you visiting members today?" she asked.

"Not exactly," she said around a second bite of cookie. "I mean, I was just visiting a woman out toward Dundee who's a widow, but I'm afraid she is not a gut candidate for the widows club."

That was surprising. "I'm assuming she's a recent widow?" What else did a woman need to be in order to join?

Looking more serious, Doreen nodded. "She is, but she's rather a sourpuss."

Even though the woman was a stranger, Jenna felt as if she should stick up for her. "Perhaps she's still grief-stricken. Grief can make a person act out of sorts."

"I don't disagree with you there. Grief takes all shapes and forms. But . . . in this woman's case, I got the feeling that her grieving is not what has soured her mood." She took a sip of water. "I might even go so far as to say, she's probably been unpleasant to be around for years."

The outlandish comment startled a laugh from her. Mortified, she covered her lips.

Doreen's own lips looked like they were trying hard not to curve up on the edges too. "Don't be embarrassed, dear Jenna. I know I sound shocking. But to be honest, I've gotten tired of always saying the correct thing. Sometimes I'd rather err on the side of . . ." She frowned as her voice drifted off.

"Honesty?"

"Exactly." She popped the last of her cookie into her

mouth, then leaned back and crossed her legs. "Anyway, after hiring the driver to take me out there, he dropped me back home, and then I started getting organized for tomorrow's meeting." She brightened again. "And that, my dear, is why I am here."

"Oh?"

"Beth Ann was going to host, but I'm afraid she got called out of town. One of her daughters is due to deliver her seventh babe. The due date was set for next month, but I guess the midwife and doctor are thinking that she's going to deliver early. As you might imagine, she needed a helping hand."

"*Sivva kinner*. That is a lot."

"I know! I was glad the Lord decided that three was enough for my body to take. Four more might have made me batty," she added with a wink.

"Or at least in need of earplugs." Katie's adorable laughter made her smile, but it could be shrill at times. Just imagining six other bodies creating noise made her wince.

"Right? Seven children must make for a loud and boisterous household. But a happy one too, I imagine." She smiled. "In any case, Beth Ann is now out of town and we are in need of a hostess for tomorrow. What do you think?"

"About what?" She took another sip of coffee, wondering how rude it would be to fill it up again.

"Hostessing, of course."

"Hostessing?"

"Indeed." Doreen looked around the room. "To be sure, your haus is small, but it has the benefit of being secluded. I bet you hardly see anyone driving by."

"I don't see too many Amish folks. Mainly vehicles." Mainly Nelson.

"See, that's a good thing for our almost-secret club." Sitting up a little bit straighter, she added, "Plus, the weather is supposed to be mighty nice. We could all gather in the backyard. I bet there's plenty of room there. Let's go look, shall we?" Doreen stood up. "Is the back door through here?" She pointed at the kitchen.

"Yes," she answered before she could stop herself.

"Wonderful." Doreen charged forward without waiting for Jenna to lead the way.

She followed slowly, grimacing as she spied both the morning's and last night's supper dishes in the sink. She really should not have lingered over her devotional that morning or been so anxious to write her pen pals when she got home from her parents'. She should've washed those dishes the moment she got out of bed.

Whether Doreen noticed the dirty sink or not was up in the air. Because she opened the back door and stepped right outside. "This will be so nice," she called out as Jenna hurried out to join her.

Nice? Looking at everything with an appraising eye, Jenna frowned. "I don't know if my backyard is suitable for company or not."

"No?"

"It's . . . um, much like a field." Sure, the man she paid to mow the grass had come recently, and a gardener had also stopped by last Saturday to trim some of her bushes. But other than short grass and pruned bushes, she didn't think the space had much going for it. "There isn't much here." No cove of shady trees. No firepit. No beautiful flower garden.

"I disagree, dear. Look at all the space! We could have a nice-sized gathering." Doreen pointed to her right. "We can put two card tables over there to hold drinks and snacks."

Jenna could maybe envision it. If she had two card tables. Or if she wanted to host a meeting. However, she did not. She couldn't exactly come right out and tell Doreen that, though. Could she? "I don't have any fold-up tables or chairs. Where would everyone sit?"

"That won't be a problem. I'll ask everyone to bring a chair."

"Women won't mind carting around a chair?"

"Oh, not a real one, child. You know what I mean. One of those folding contraptions one buys to take to the park." She clapped her hands. "It will be great fun. Like a picnic. But not."

It wouldn't be anything like a picnic. Like . . . not at all.

Turning to her, Doreen stared at her intently. "Jenna, I know this isn't something you're comfortable with, and you are probably feeling overwhelmed."

"Yes. Yes, I am." Somehow she was supposed to get everything together and host in a day?

"We really are in a bind. Desperate."

"Desperate?"

"We really want to have a meeting, dear. Plus, I think it would be good for you."

At the moment, all she could think was that this meeting was going to give her an ulcer.

"Everyone needs to get out of her comfort zone from time to time. This will shake things up a bit."

"This will certainly do that."

"I reckon it will," Doreen said softly. "Please say yes. And don't think you'll be completely responsible for setting everything up. I'll have Violet and Anne stop by with some card tables and water bottles and such. All you will have to do is offer some easy-to-carry-around snacks." She looked at her intently. "And a good attitude. What do you think, Jenna? You have such a pretty smile. Could you try to make sure everyone feels welcome?"

Doreen was making hosting sound so simple. "I could do that," she murmured before she could stop herself.

Triumph seemed to gleam in Doreen's eyes. "So, does that mean you'll host the next meeting of the Amish Widows Club, Jenna?"

Feeling like she was caught between a rock and a hard place, Jenna nodded.

"I'm so glad." Doreen reached out and clasped her left hand with both of her own. "Danke, Jenna. I'm so grateful."

What had she just done? Feeling as if she were looking through a foggy haze, she cleared her throat. "You are welcome," she replied. "I am glad to help."

The other woman released her hand and gave a little clap. "Well, now that *that's* settled, I must be on my way. Plus, I'm sure your mind is spinning with all the things you've got to do."

"Ah, yes. I suppose it is."

"I'll have the message about tomorrow's meeting on the recording within the hour, and I'll come over an hour before so I can help you get everything in order," Doreen added as she headed to the driveway.

Moments later, she gave Jenna a little wave and then climbed onto her electric bike.

Off she went, leaving Jenna's house in almost the exact shape as before. Only her head seemed to be in disarray.

Why had she agreed to host so quickly? She'd only attended a few of the meetings. She barely knew most of the women. What would they think of her small house? Or having to bring a lawn chair and sit in the backyard?

She gazed up at the sky. Plus, what if it rained? What would she do then?

"I suppose if it rains, you will get wet," she murmured to herself.

The idea of all the women coming over with lawn chairs in hand, then having to seek shelter in her house while it poured was almost laughable. They would be packed inside like sardines.

But there was no need to dwell on that, Jenna decided as she walked back inside her kitchen.

She couldn't stop the rain any more than she could stop the sun from rising. When Blue began walking in a figure-eight pattern between her legs, taking care to rub his glossy black-and-white coat against her calves each time he made a pass, Jenna picked him up and cuddled him in her arms.

"Why didn't you show yourself while Doreen was here? She might have been allergic to you and scurried away to the next unsuspecting widow."

Blue studied her face with his lovely silver eyes. "Mew."

"Mew, indeed, cat."

Returning to the couch, she sat down and ran her hand along Blue's back. Listened to him purr. Thought again about how easily Doreen had convinced her to agree to hosting.

But maybe it hadn't been much of a decision anyway. She'd known from the beginning that the women took turns hosting the group.

Sooner or later, it would've been her turn.

Or maybe she'd agreed *because* Doreen strong-armed her. Maybe Doreen—and the Lord—were determined to remind Jenna that there were other women who had been going through some of the same things she was.

She didn't have to handle everything on her own. She could find their support . . . if she allowed herself to receive it.

Maybe that was what was going on.

After all, it wasn't like she could ever have a future with Nelson. She needed to remind herself about that.

chapter twenty-seven

So many things were going wrong, Jenna didn't think she could count them all. First of all, neither Violet nor Anne showed up at her house until four o'clock. Two hours before everyone was due to arrive. Both apologized but didn't seem too flustered. "There's always a storm before the meeting starts," Anne said with a grin. "Don't worry, everything will get done."

Unfortunately, some of their good spirits faded when they admitted that they hadn't known they were supposed to bring card tables. Anne had only the lists of members and a small tray of snacks. Violet had brought a bag of paper cups, napkins, and plates. That was it.

"You don't have a set of lawn furniture to put everything on?" Violet asked.

"Not a one."

"Hmm. This is going to be a problem, I fear."

Jenna thought so too. Desperate, she hurried to her kitchen phone and called Nelson. After explaining the situation to him, she said, "I know it's a lot to ask, but do you have any folding tables I could borrow?"

"It's not too much to ask. I'll get some guys to help me load up two long tables and twenty-five chairs."

Asking for tables was one thing, asking for an additional twenty-five chairs seemed like too much. "Chairs aren't necessary."

"Jenna, I know you don't want to be a bother, but I think we both know all the ladies that are coming would prefer to sit in chairs."

"I guess you're right. They are supposed to bring their own, but . . ."

"I know I'm right. And this isn't a bother. If I couldn't help you this afternoon, I would tell you."

"All right."

"I'll be there within forty minutes."

"Danke."

After she explained to the ladies what was going on, Anne suggested they go inside and get the drinks organized. Luckily, Jenna did have two pitchers ready to go, as well as five ice-cube trays.

"All we have to do now is make kaffi," Violet said with a smile.

That smile faltered a bit when Katie joined them in the kitchen with Blue in her arms.

"I want to help too," she chirped.

Violet immediately sneezed and then her eyes started watering. "I'm sorry, I'm allergic to cats."

"Oh. I didn't even think." Jenna leaned down. "Katie, go put Blue in your room."

Her daughter's smile vanished in a heartbeat. "But he likes being out here with me and you too."

"He's going to have to make do with being in your

room." Noticing that her usually eager-to-please daughter was frowning, Jenna kept her voice firm. "Katie, do as I say. He'll be all right. Plus, Mammi Mary will be here soon to pick you up."

"Nee! I don't want to go over to Mammi Mary's haus. I want to stay with you and go to the party."

Anne, who had been unpackaging the paper goods, frowned at Katie.

Jenna prayed for patience. "I'll be right back," she called out to Anne and Violet as she guided Katie out of the kitchen. When they were in the living room, Jenna said, "Katie, what is going on with you?"

"I don't want to leave. I want to be with Blue and you."

"But this is a party for grown-ups. Not little girls."

"Nee. I want to stay!"

Just then, there was a knock at the door. "That's probably Mary now."

Katie turned her back to the door. Frustrated, Jenna hurried to open it. "Mary, I'm sorry— Oh! Nelson!" She took a breath. "I didn't expect you to get here so fast."

"Curtis was free, so we decided to run all this out to you before an emergency popped up."

"They always do, ain't so?" Curtis murmured.

She'd known Curtis a long time. Jimmy had worked for him for years. "I suppose that's true. Thanks for coming out here. You two have saved the day. Would you take it all to the backyard? You can go around the side of the house."

"We're on it."

"Thank you again. I'll go tell—"

"Hi, Nelson!" Katie said. "Look at Blue."

Nelson stopped mid-stride and turned to Katie. "My, he's getting bigger."

"Uh-huh."

"Sorry, but I can't stop to chat now, Kitty. Curtis and I have to carry some tables and chairs to your backyard."

"Blue and I will help ya with the chairs."

Jenna had had enough of her daughter's antics. "Nee, Katie," she said in a firm tone. "You will only get in the way. Go put the cat in your room and stay there until Mammi Mary arrives."

"Nee!" Katie was staring at Nelson as if she were never going to see him again.

"Katie, do as I say. Now."

"What is he doing here?" a new voice asked.

Jenna's insides knotted as she turned around. And, sure enough, there was her mother-in-law. Mary seemed to be glaring at Curtis, Nelson, Katie, and her all at the same time.

Could things get any worse?

Knowing there wasn't a thing she could do, she cleared her throat. "Hi, Mary, I didn't see you there. Won't you come in? I think Katie is almost ready."

Of course, that was an obvious lie. Katie was standing in the middle of the room, on the verge of having a full-blown temper tantrum.

Mary didn't return Jenna's half-hearted smile, and she didn't even reach out to give Katie a hug like she usually did.

Instead, she remained at the front door and glared at Jenna. "I can't believe that you've continued to ignore my wishes about that man. You should be staying as far away from Nelson Harper as possible."

"Mary, stop," she whispered.

"I will not stop. Jenna, he's responsible for your husband's death!"

From the back of the room, Violet gasped. Nelson froze, and even Curtis was staring at Mary in shock.

She had no idea how to fix the situation, but she had to try. "No, Mary, Nelson is not." Aware that Katie was listening intently, Jenna lowered her voice. "Now is not the time or the place. You must stop saying such things."

"I will not."

"Please. You're upsetting Katie."

It was as if Mary didn't even realize that she had an audience. "What is going on with you and Nelson, Jenna? You are always so quick to defend him. To be with him." She narrowed her eyes. "Are you having an affair?"

"What? Nee!"

"It sure looks like it. I've tried to excuse your unseemly behavior because of your age, but now I must admit that nothing can excuse it. You've obviously fallen for this man."

Nelson, who'd been standing off to the side with Curtis, strode forward. "Jenna, let me speak to her."

"Nelson, do something," Katie said with a cry as she pushed her way past Jenna, past Mary, and ran into Nelson's arms.

Nelson immediately knelt down and picked her up. Katie still held Blue and was crying noisily in his arms. Clinging to him. He was whispering to her.

Jenna felt everything inside her shift. Almost every emotion she was currently feeling—embarrassment, confusion, anger, dismay—shuffled. And then, at last, she could see everything more clearly. The way her in-laws really were, not the way she was hoping they could one day be.

She knew she had a choice, but as she met Nelson's expression, she realized that there was no choice to make. "You are right, Mary. I have fallen for this man. I've fallen in love with him."

"Nee. You love Jimmy."

"I did. I loved Jimmy with my whole heart. But he is gone now. He's been gone for some time." Taking a deep breath, she added, "I didn't plan for it to happen, but I've fallen in love with Nelson. And . . . as you can see, Katie loves him too."

Still holding Katie in his arms, Nelson met her gaze. "Jenna?"

She was sure she'd stunned him. Maybe almost as much as she'd shocked Jimmy's mother. "It's true," she whispered.

"Nee," Mary said. "No."

"I love you too, Nelson," Katie announced as she buried her face in his neck.

Watching him whisper words of reassurance to Katie, Jenna knew that the timing might have been terrible, but the choice had been made.

After that? Well, everything seemed to move at lightning speed. Mary turned around without another word and got into her buggy.

Nelson said something to Curtis. As he started to carry chairs to the backyard, Nelson strode to her side.

Then, with Katie still cradled against him, he wrapped

his free arm around Jenna. "I love you too. I love you both."

Tears pricked her eyes. His expression was so sweet. The moment was so sweet. "I'm sorry that I blurted it," she said in a rush. "I don't know what came over me . . ."

"I'm not sorry. I wouldn't take a second of what just happened back."

"Ah, excuse me. Jenna?"

Violet and Anne! Pulling away from Nelson's arms, Jenna hurried over to Violet. "I'm so sorry." Inwardly, she cringed. How many times was she going to apologize that afternoon?

"Um, no apology needed," Violet whispered with a smile. "I just wanted to remind you that everyone will be arriving in thirty minutes." She winked. "Even though I'm pretty sure you aren't going to be an Amish widow too much longer, we have a lot to get done for tonight."

Jenna was sure her face was beet red. "Yes. Of course, you're right. Let's get to work."

Nelson put Katie down. "I heard," he said with a smile. "Listen, I'm going to help Curtis set up the tables and chairs and then get out of here. How about you call me when your meeting is over? I'll come back, and we can talk."

She chuckled. "Yes. Yes, I'll do that." Turning to Katie, she held out her hand. "Katie, we need to keep Blue in your room for now. Do you think you could help Violet and Anne and me set up for the party?" There was no way she was going to make Katie stay in her room now.

Katie nodded, her face full of hope.

"Then, come on. We've got a lot to do." She hurried to

the kitchen, picked up a tray of brownies that she'd made earlier in the day, and went out the back door.

To her amazement, even though all her plans had just fallen apart and her personal life was in complete disarray, she couldn't have been happier.

She couldn't have been happier about a lot of things.

chapter twenty-eight

As they headed back to the office, Curtis was unusually chatty. Usually, the guy was pretty reserved with him. Nelson figured it was because he was Curtis's boss and the guy liked to watch his words.

But now Nelson was wondering if Curtis had been biding his time while he was waiting for a topic that interested him. Which, to his surprise, was Nelson's relationship with Jenna.

"You know, I'm real pleased that you and that sweet Jenna Graber have hit it off so well."

"Thanks. It was unexpected, but I feel fortunate."

"I'm sure you do, but Jenna would be a fool not to see a good thing right in front of her. You're as steady as a rock, Nelson."

He supposed Curtis meant that as a compliment. He chuckled. "Hopefully she sees me as something more than that."

Curtis shrugged. "I've learned that there's no telling what women are looking for. My wife said she fell in love with me when she discovered that I always wanted to go on a cruise."

"Really?"

"Rhonda hates camping." He snickered before saying, "In all seriousness, Jimmy was such a hothead, I reckon you're a nice change from that."

Even though Jimmy was always in the back of his mind, Curtis bringing up his name brought forth another wave of doubt. "There's a part of me that is having a hard time handling that Jimmy's accident at Alliance happened under my watch and now I'm somehow benefiting from it."

"Boss, Jimmy was a grown man, and he reported to Paul, not you."

"You know what I mean."

"Okay, how about this? There isn't a man in our company who would appreciate you acting as if he needed a babysitter. You hired us to do jobs. We do them." He waved a hand. "And sure, accidents happen, but they're not your fault, Nelson."

"I hear you. Sorry."

"If you heard that, then I hope you hear me tell you that Jenna has her own mind too. If she wants to be in a relationship with you, then that's her choice. She's falling in love with you, and you are falling in love with her, right?"

"Right."

"Then focus on that, boss. Don't twist up love."

When they got back to the mill, Curtis's words of wisdom replayed in Nelson's mind as he headed back to his office.

Fanny wasn't there. She'd gone out to visit a couple of clients. He was glad to have a few moments of peace and quiet.

To think about Jenna's declaration.

And his, of course.

Sure, he would've never planned to declare his love in that situation, but he decided that he didn't care. All that mattered to him was that Jenna felt the same way he did. Somehow, some way, they were going to have a future together.

Eventually, he buckled down and got back to work instead of going home to wait for Jenna's call. It would keep him busy.

Then, just around half past six, it started raining. Nelson supposed the farmers were pleased for their crops, but all he could think about was that Jenna's backyard party was going to have to be moved indoors. Poor thing. He bet she was just about at her wit's end by now.

"Oh, don't look so sad about a little rainstorm, Nelson," Fanny teased. "You won't melt if you get a little wet."

"I don't mind getting a little wet, I just wish that it would've held off awhile longer. Jenna's hosting a party in her backyard this evening."

"Not anymore. What a bummer, though."

"Yeah. I feel terrible for her. This shindig was kind of thrown at her, and she wasn't sure what to do. Curtis and I took over a couple of tables and two dozen chairs this afternoon."

"I'm sorry I wasn't here to help. I would've been happy to go with you and help her set up or something."

"Believe me, it's just as well that you didn't."

"Why? What happened?"

Briefly, he filled Fanny in on Mary's accusations, Katie's

tears, and Jenna's declaration. "To make matters even worse, Curtis heard the whole thing," he finished.

"Whoa." Looking completely stunned, Fanny said, "I don't even know where to start."

"It was a lot. A whole lot."

"What's going to happen next?"

"I told Jenna to call me when the party ends. I'm going to go over there and make sure she knows that I meant what I said."

Reaching out, Fanny clasped his hand. "I'm so happy for you, Nelson. You two are going to be perfect together."

"We've got a long way to go before we start planning happily-ever-afters, Fan. Don't forget, she's Amish."

"If she marries outside the faith, it's going to be bad, isn't it?"

"Yep. I'm not even sure if it's allowed."

"You might not want my advice, but I'm going to offer it anyway." She took a deep breath. "Concentrate on the two of you tonight."

"You think so?"

She nodded. "I don't have a lot of experience in this, but I'm pretty sure that falling in love with someone is something to celebrate. It doesn't happen all that often."

"You're exactly right. Thanks."

"Anytime. I'll see you tomorrow." She picked up her purse off the top of her desk. "Don't forget that we have a load of lumber arriving at seven, and you've got a meeting with the bank at nine."

"I'll be here. See you bright and early, Fan."

"Yeah, you too. Careful going home."

After she walked out the door, Nelson checked his

phone. Since he still hadn't gotten a call from Jenna, he did a walk-through of the plant to make sure everything was shut down and the security guards who worked the night shift had arrived.

Then he strode out to his truck.

The rain was coming down in sheets, and the wind had picked up, making it almost impossible to see. For a moment, he considered following Fanny to her apartment. Sure, she was a competent driver, but it was really awful out. He wouldn't be surprised if some of the traffic lights started malfunctioning because of the wind.

When he pulled out onto the state road that led toward his house, he decided just to go on home. Fanny wouldn't appreciate him following her around. Instead of being glad that he was worried about her safety, Fanny would think he didn't trust her driving.

Besides, he was anxious to get home and wait for Jenna to call. He couldn't wait to see her. Not only did he want to reassure her about his feelings, but they had a lot to discuss about the future. And maybe . . . a few overdue kisses to be had.

After hearing on the radio that there had been a multi-vehicle accident on the state route he usually took, Nelson decided to take a detour. Usually, he hated driving on the hilly, winding roads in the evening. The route took twice as long and was often occupied by the Amish. Every time the road turned, he feared that he'd come upon a horse and buggy or one of the more popular electric bikes.

However, with the weather being the way it was, he figured navigating around Amish vehicles was the least of his worries. It was rare to see many buggies or bicycles in this type of weather.

Turning his brights on, he slowed and crept along in the dark, glad he recognized some of the intersections and houses since there weren't any streetlights around. As the radio got scratchy, Nelson turned down the volume and thought about Jenna.

If she loved him as much as he loved her, they were sure to have a future together. He wasn't sure what it would mean to her, though, to break her baptismal vows. Was she worried about what her parents—or even Jimmy's parents—would say? Or how she'd be treated in the community? Then, too, was the fear that she might eventually regret leaving her faith. He would hate if she one day felt she'd made a huge mistake by marrying him. But eventually—if Jenna was still willing and the Lord helped things along a bit—she would be his wife. Maybe one day, he'd be driving home on another night like this. Tired from work, but anxious to see her.

And when he pulled into the garage, she would be waiting for him. So pretty. So fresh and sweet.

He could pull her into his arms, try to carry her inside—just to make her laugh. And then he would kiss her like he wanted to. Kiss her until she was clinging to him, responding to the heat in his gaze, silently promising that she was just as anxious as he was for the night not to end.

Just imagining it, Nelson felt a shudder run through him as he guided his truck up another hill. He'd wanted Jenna for so long. He'd hoped and prayed that one day she'd let him in. At least a little bit.

And now—

His mind froze as the scene before him jerked him into action. There was a buggy. And an electric bike. And a car attempting to weave around them into his lane—just as the road started to curve again. Every instinct encouraged him to jerk the steering wheel to the left because there was a deep ditch on his right. But the car was weaving, attempting to miss the bicycle. He had no choice. Nelson slammed on the brakes, jerked his truck to the right, and practically leapt off the road. The tires screamed against the wet pavement and metal crashed. He could have sworn he heard someone in the distance call out, but he wasn't sure. His truck rolled, the airbags deployed, and every muscle in his body braced for impact.

At last, the vehicle came to a stop.

At least, he thought it did. It was impossible to tell because there was nothing to see.

The only thing in front of his eyes was red.

chapter twenty-nine

It was raining and Fanny was stuck behind what had to be the longest train in the state of Ohio when her cousin Heidi called.

Ever since Fanny, in a moment of weakness, had confided that she had a bit of a crush on their richest private client, that seemed to be all Heidi wanted to talk about. Fanny hoped she could steer the conversation toward something better.

"So, what are you doing now?" Heidi asked.

"Beyond sitting at a train crossing in the rain?"

"Obviously."

"What do you think I'm doing? I'm heading home after working eight hours." Actually, it was more like nine.

"I'm so jealous. I'm home, but I have to put address labels on something like a hundred catalogs. It's taking forever."

Heidi was a receptionist at a small company in Medina. As the train continued, moving slow as molasses, Fanny pictured her cousin lounging on the couch, watching television while putting stickers on catalogs. "At least it's not hard."

"I guess. I wish it was exciting, though. You're so lucky. You get to do all kinds of fun things in your job."

"Yeah, fielding calls and organizing paperwork for Nelson is loads of fun."

"You know that's not what I meant. I mean—you get to see *Haaank*," she said in a singsong voice, followed by a giggle. "He's so hot, Fanny."

He was, but no way did she want her cousin thinking that. "Don't talk about Mr. Arias that way."

"Oh, so it's Mr. Arias now? Before, it was Hank."

"Heidi, stop. Sure, he's, um, gorgeous, but he's an important client. That's all he is to me." Which wasn't true, since she kind of lived for his every-so-often texts. Feeling even more self-conscious, she added, "And don't make my visits to his house into anything weird. All I do when I'm there is discuss orders and designs with him."

"Uh-huh. What's he like? Is he a jerk?"

"No. He's nice."

"Sooo . . . this Mr. Arias is good-looking, super-suave, and has a ginormous bank account, but you don't feel anything for him at all."

It would be so easy to lie, but she couldn't. "I didn't say that." Sure, she sounded weak, but whatever. When would this stupid train ever end?

"Come on, Fan," Heidi said in a soft voice. "It's okay to admit it. The guy's a catch."

"Okay, fine. He is that."

"At last! You admit it."

"Heidi!"

"Sorry, I couldn't help but tease you. I mean, it's not like you could ever have a chance with him or anything."

"He isn't married, Heidi. He's a widower," she added before she could remind herself to leave it alone.

"I didn't know he was a widower. That's sad. Well, I hope he finds happiness with someone one day. Someone suitable."

"Suitable?"

"Yeah. No offense, but we both know a man like that isn't going to go out with you."

"What's wrong with me?"

"Beyond the fact that you're a lot younger than him and a personal assistant to the guy in charge of building his fancy house? A friendly small-town girl? The truth is that you two probably don't have anything in common." She chuckled. "I mean, a date for him probably means fancy restaurants or expensive concerts or something. A date for you and me is going to an actual restaurant for pizza instead of getting it delivered."

"Hey. Heidi, I can't believe you're saying all this."

"Wait, you're not upset with me, are you? Fanny, come on. You know I love you, but some things just don't go together. Like peanut butter and mayonnaise, parkas and Hawaii . . . and you and Hank Arias."

As she continued to stare at the slow-moving train, Fanny felt tears form in her eyes.

The sad thing was that she knew Heidi truly wasn't trying to make her upset. She really had thought that Hank was Fanny's fun secret crush. A bit of excitement in an otherwise boring job. But the truth was that he'd become something more to her than that. He'd become her friend, and he'd made her feel attractive and like she was worth something.

Maybe even worth his time.

"I think I finally see the end of this train. I need to go."

"Okay." After a pause, Heidi said, "Hey, are we okay? I feel like I hurt your feelings."

"We're fine."

"Are you sure? Fanny, you know I think you're pretty. And I'm as small-town as you are! I wasn't trying to put you down."

Fanny wasn't so sure about that, but she was able to admit that Heidi hadn't been wrong in her description of her. She might tell Nelson that she wanted to be called Frances and try to come across as sophisticated and smart, but that wasn't really what she was. She really was just a small-town girl blessed with good hair and a decent figure who worked for her cousin. It was nothing to be embarrassed about, but it sure wasn't anything to attract a man who could probably have his pick of any woman in the state.

But . . .

What if she hadn't mistaken the look of interest in his eyes? What if he really did like her and didn't see her as "just" anything?

As the train finally passed and a car behind her beeped its horn, she realized she didn't want to go straight home.

It wasn't all that late either.

So, instead of heading straight at the next stoplight, she turned left. Hank's house was only ten minutes away.

She had a perfect reason to stop by too.

Nelson had agreed to give Big John and his team of

workers overtime pay now that the shipment of mahogany had arrived. Checking in on everyone was as good an excuse as any.

As she parked at Hank's, Fanny stewed some more. She thought about Heidi's words, and then she thought about Nelson's ex-girlfriend Emme.

Nelson and Emme had dated for almost a year just after Nelson took over the reins of Alliance from their dads. Fanny had still been in high school, but even she remembered how stressed out he'd been. The older generations had taken a step back but were watching Nelson's every move.

So were most of the workers—including Big John.

That wasn't to say that no one thought Nelson was going to do a good job. They did. But he needed to prove himself. Some weeks, everyone joked that he should buy a cot and put it in his office because it seemed like he lived there. Well, everyone but Emme. She complained to anyone who would listen that Nelson was ignoring her. When she made the mistake of talking badly about him at a family barbecue, more than one person had told her she was out of line. As far as most everyone in the family had been concerned, Nelson and Emme couldn't break up fast enough.

No one had come right out and told him that, though. Instead, they watched and waited and hoped Nelson's infatuation with Emme would run its course. Everyone thought that was the kindest thing to do for Nelson. Only later did they all realize that he'd been so confused. He'd stayed with Emme longer than he should have because he believed that everyone thought they were good together.

After they broke up and the truth came out about just how much everyone disliked her, Nelson mentioned that he wished someone had told him how they really felt about the relationship.

Fanny bit her lip. Maybe that was why Heidi had decided to share her feelings?

Shaking her head, she put her phone and tablet in her tote bag, opened her umbrella, and hurried to the front door.

Only to find Hank Arias standing on his front porch, leaning against the door and watching her with those blue eyes of his. He was wearing old, faded jeans, work boots, and a snug gray T-shirt that advertised some surf shop.

"Hey," she said. "What are you doing out here?"

"Currently, I'm wondering if everything is okay with you."

"I'm all right." Now that she was under the porch, she shook out her umbrella and closed it. "Boy, it sure is raining."

"It is at that. Cats and dogs."

"Yeah. It's a little better out here in Wooster, though."

"When I saw you drive up, I was going to help you out of your car, but you looked like you were upset about something. I decided to stand here for a second or two, just to watch you."

He was leaning a little bit closer. She could smell his cologne now. That woodsy, dark, addictive scent that wreaked havoc on her senses.

She needed to get herself together. "That sounds kind of rude, Hank."

"Yeah, maybe. But I've got a good reason. I was starting to get a little worried about you."

Hank was using that tone of voice again. The one that sounded like it was halfway between teasing and truth. She never knew how to respond to it.

So she opted for being safe. "I'm sorry I kept you waiting. I thought I'd just check on the progress."

Confusion, accompanied by a little bit of something else, flashed in his expression before he cleared his throat. "Don't apologize to me, Fan. There's nothing for you to apologize for."

She nodded because she realized that she'd been on the verge of apologizing yet again. Work. She needed to concentrate on work.

"Listen, if I was frowning, it was because I was thinking about another conversation I had a few minutes before I got here. It's nothing to concern you."

And . . . she was pretty proud of herself for keeping a straight face. Because that chat she'd had with Heidi had everything to do with Hank.

"Who were you talking to?"

"No one you need to worry about."

"I didn't think you were dating anyone. Are you?"

"I'm not." Desperate to get done with the conversation, she blurted, "Right now. I meant to say that I'm not dating anyone right now."

"Gotcha." Now he was the one smirking.

And honestly, she couldn't really blame him because even to her ears she sounded like she couldn't string two sentences together. "Hank, it's getting late. I'm going to go ahead and see how everything looks."

Hank gave her a once-over, then he started walking to the house. "No problem. I'll be happy to do a walk-through with you."

"That's . . ." *Awful. Annoying.* "Great."

Hank knocked twice and yelled "Incoming!" as he cracked open the door.

"Incoming?" she asked.

Big John answered before Hank could. "Ack, after I almost got smashed into the wall, Hank decided that anyone about to walk inside should announce themselves."

"Hmm. Well, that makes sense." Kind of.

Hank's lips twitched. "I'm afraid everyone's gotten kind of silly with it. I'm glad you haven't been here to hear everything the guys have been calling out."

Thoroughly entertained, she leaned forward. "Let me guess, they aren't just yelling 'incoming'?"

"I'm afraid not," Hank said. "Some of it has been . . . a little off-color."

"He means not fit for a young girl's ears, missy," John added.

"Maybe so, but now I kind of feel like I've been missing out on all the fun."

Whether he was shocked or intrigued, she wasn't sure. But when Hank met her eyes again, there seemed to be more of an interest than usual. She felt a little bolt of happiness charge through her.

"I've been sweating something awful this afternoon. You ain't missed much."

Fanny laughed as she turned to examine his work. "Oh, John," she gasped. "This is beautiful." She ran a finger along a section of the intricate design John had been hand carving. "Are these maple leaves?"

"Jah."

Each leaf was between two and three inches long. They were lovely. So lovely and detailed that she couldn't imagine why John would choose to carve them in place instead of in the shop. "Why didn't you want to make them back at Alliance?"

"I made three, but I didn't like how they looked when I nailed them in. By the time I put in putty and such, it looked like the leaves had been made with a machine." Big John exchanged a look with Hank. "The boss and I decided that it would be better to do the carving here."

"I tried to change his mind," Hank said. "I've witnessed how challenging it can be to carve these right here—even when he doesn't have to worry about getting hit by the door."

"If I'm going to do this, I'm gonna do it right, Fan," Big John murmured.

His voice was quiet, but there was an unmistakable thread of iron in it. He was no pushover.

"Well, I'm impressed. John, is it okay if I take a picture for Nelson?"

"No need to ask, Fanny. It's your job."

"Thanks, John." She smiled at him before snapping multiple photos from different angles. If Nelson was as impressed as she was, then Fanny knew they'd be putting at least one of these pictures in a brochure for future clients. The workmanship was remarkable.

When she stepped back, Big John released a heavy sigh. "I need to get back to work now, girly."

"I hear you. I'm getting out of your way this minute."

"Danke."

"Ready to see the progress in the rest of the house, Fanny?" Hank asked.

"Sure, though I can go by myself. You don't need to escort me."

"I've got the time. Besides, there's a couple of things I want to ask you about."

"All right. Well, um, lead the way."

She ignored Big John's chuckle as they walked away. She suspected he was vastly entertained by the tension that was looming between her and Hank. She really hoped he didn't go back and tell everybody else at work. They'd enjoy teasing her about her crush for years to come.

Hank led her into the kitchen. "I've got appliances in here now. What do you think?"

The appliances were high-end, all stainless steel. They were likely every chef's dream. "I think they look amazing. I hope you like to cook," she teased.

He grinned. "I do."

"Now you surprised me."

"Oh, I don't cook anything fancy. Pork chops, chicken, steak, salmon." He smiled, and the room lit up. "I can make a mean omelet."

"That's more than I can."

"I guess that means that I'll have to have you over for dinner one day."

He was looking at her intently, and they were close enough that she could smell what was left of his cologne.

Her insides jumped. He was so . . . so everything.

Reminding herself that he probably didn't mean the

invitation in the way she was taking it, Fanny joked, "I never pass up a free meal."

He stepped closer. "If I asked you over, would you come?"

"Yes." Unable to stop herself, she whispered, "Though I might wonder why you would ask."

"Why?"

Oh, those blue eyes of his. Piercing. Intense. Warm. Though it was tempting to look away, she forced herself to meet his gaze. "Yes." She swallowed. Cleared her throat. "I mean, as a thank you . . . or something else?"

"If I asked you to dinner, Fanny, it would be because I thought you were an attractive woman and I wanted to spend time with you. I know I'm old, but we used to call them dates."

"I might be younger than you . . . but I call that a date too."

"So are you saying yes?"

Oh yeah. She was saying yes to a lot of things with him in her mind. Not that he needed to know that. "Hypothetically, yes," she replied. It was too bad she sounded so breathless.

Hank noticed. His eyes lit up. "I've never met anyone like you, Frances Harper."

Just as she was about to tell him she felt the same way, her phone rang.

"I'm sorry. Let me see who it is." She frowned when she saw a number she didn't recognize. "Hello?"

"Is this Frances Harper?"

"Yes. Who is this?"

"This is Deputy Evan Pierce from the Holmes County

Sheriff's Department, ma'am. Your name was on Nelson Harper's contact list."

"Nelson is my cousin. What's going on?"

"I'm sorry to let you know that Nelson was in a vehicular accident this evening. His injuries aren't life-threatening, but he is in an ambulance on the way to county hospital."

"I'll be right there. I mean, I'm on my way. Thank you for letting me know."

"Yes, ma'am. Drive careful. It's still pretty bad out there."

"I will. Thank you."

"What happened?" Hank asked as soon as she disconnected.

"Nelson was in a car accident. He's in an ambulance on the way to county hospital. I need to go."

"I'll drive you."

Meeting his gaze, Fanny saw everything she'd ever hoped to see in his eyes. Reassurance. Compassion. Strength.

She could lean on him and never worry about falling. No matter what Heidi thought.

chapter thirty

Friday morning arrived with a blast of bright sun and humidity. Jenna groaned as she walked into the backyard with her first cup of coffee. The air felt like a sauna. It was sure to make cleaning up the ravages of last evening's meeting even more of a chore.

Glad she'd taken a dish towel outside with her, she wiped off the seat of one of the chairs and sat down. "I don't know where to even begin," she muttered.

That was the truth too. Last night's storm had blown chairs everywhere. The tables were still in place, but they were covered with water and debris.

In addition, the pretty floral arrangements that Anne had made from flowers in her garden and two glass pitchers had fallen on the ground. At least one of the pitchers was broken.

"At least everything wasn't broken," she joked to herself.

She, Violet, and Anne had just gotten everything in the backyard set up when the first wave of women showed up. Only about half had brought a fold-up lawn chair, so Nelson's idea to bring chairs had been a good one.

Jenna had still been rattled by Mary's visit and her own announcement about falling in love with Nelson. It had taken everything she had to push aside her chaotic thoughts and welcome everyone to her home.

It had started well enough. Doreen gave her a hug, and several women declared that they thought hosting the meeting outside was a charming idea.

But then the rain started to fall. Followed by lightning in the distance.

And then, with a clap of thunder, the storm arrived. Everyone rushed inside, only some thinking about bringing in the trays of food.

Once inside, the women were wet, their feet were muddy, and the space was cramped. Jenna passed out towels so everyone could get dry, but even the most easygoing ladies were visibly uncomfortable.

As the rain continued, Anne helped Jenna retrieve the rest of the food from outside. A few other women attempted to set things to rights in the kitchen.

But it was obvious that everyone wanted to leave.

Eventually, someone used her kitchen phone and called for a driver, who arrived in a van and drove six women home. Then several others decided to just walk home in the rain. Jenna lent them her two umbrellas.

Finally, just before nine, the rain had almost stopped, and those who had ridden bicycles left. By the time she closed the door, she was exhausted.

Katie had fallen asleep in her room earlier, so the house was quiet and still. After collecting the plates and cups that had been left scattered around, Jenna had picked up the phone and tried calling Nelson. It was too late for him to come over, but she wanted to hear his voice. When he didn't answer, she was disappointed but not completely surprised. It was rather late. She left a quick message and asked him to call her in the morning. She was sure he would.

But he still hadn't, and she'd begun to fear that he'd changed his mind about her and him.

Jenna heard a car out front. Was it Nelson? She went back inside, and as she looked out the front window, she saw a black Suburban drive up her driveway too fast, the expression on the man's face serious and grim. Her brain knew what that look meant. Another tragedy had happened to someone she knew. After reminding herself that Katie was home safe, she took a deep breath and opened the door as he arrived on the doorstep. "Yes?" she asked.

The man—the very tall, confident-looking man—took off his dark-gray cowboy hat before directing his blue eyes at her. "Ma'am, are you Jenna Graber?"

It was bad news. It had to be. No one appeared at a doorstep with such an expression if it wasn't. Imagining the worst, her heart started beating faster. "Yes." Feeling a little lightheaded, she gripped the door more tightly. "May I help you?"

"My name is Hank Arias, ma'am. I'm a client of Nelson Harper's. I believe you know him?"

This wasn't about her parents. Her parents must be all right. But why was he talking about Nelson? This made no sense. Feeling even more confused, she nodded.

Looking relieved that she finally responded, he cleared

his throat. "All right. So, um, I'm one of Nelson's customers, but I know him better than that. I . . . well, Fanny and I are friends. I believe you know her as well?"

"Yes. I know Fanny, and she's mentioned you." Feeling more impatient, she said, "Even though I do know both of them, I don't know anything about Alliance Millworks. I mean, not beyond the fact that my deceased husband used to work there."

"I'm sorry to be so confusing, ma'am. I just didn't . . . well, I didn't want you to think I was just some man off the street."

"What is it that you wanted to speak to me about?"

He took a deep breath. "There's no easy way to tell you this, but Nelson was taken to the hospital last night."

"Nelson? My Nelson?" Before he could answer, the tears started to fall. "Is he okay? What happened? Is . . . is he hurt? Oh my word. Was there another accident? Did a machine malfunction?"

The muscles in his throat worked. "There was an accident, but not at the Millworks. It was on his drive home."

"It was raining something awful."

"Yes, ma'am. From what I understand, there was a car swerving around a buggy and an Amish guy on an electric bike. The driver of the vehicle was going too fast and driving recklessly on the curve. Nelson had to swerve in order not to hit them. He ended up in one of those deep ditches off Miamiville Road. He got banged up pretty good."

She frowned. "Banged up?"

"He sustained some injuries, but none are life-threatening," he said in a soft voice. "He's going to be all right, ma'am. An ambulance took him to the hospital."

He'd been in an ambulance. He was in the hospital. Tears filled her eyes as Hank's words registered at last. Nelson had been in a car accident and was in the hospital.

Unbidden, this news kept getting muddled with that from another visitor, that one from about two years ago. A man from Alliance had rushed over to pick her and Katie up and take them to the hospital.

Jenna knew Hank was speaking about Nelson and not Jimmy, but her body couldn't stop itself from reacting as though the man she'd fallen in love with was going to die. A wave of dizziness flowed through her. She felt as if she was about to faint.

"Jenna, Nelson is going to be okay."

He's going to be okay. Relief seemed to burn a hole through her fog at last, allowing the tears to fall.

Mr. Arias looked a little alarmed, no doubt because she was rapidly losing her composure. "Please don't cry, ma'am. The good news is that no one else was hurt. From what Fanny found out, it was Nelson's quick thinking that saved several people. Both the man in the buggy and his horse are just fine. The Amish guy on the bike is too. Nelson's a hero."

"A hero." She'd murmured the word.

"Yes." He folded his hands behind his back. "Like I said, he helped a lot of people, and he's okay. But he is a little worse for wear. The doctors told Fanny that he'll probably be in the hospital for a day."

"Okay. Thank you for telling me." Staring at him, she wasn't sure what she was supposed to do. She wasn't Nelson's wife. Few people realized that they knew each other well. Was she supposed to pretend that she felt nothing but concern about him?

Or was she allowed to rush to his side?

Did it even matter what everyone thought?

Obviously seeing her distress, Hank lowered his voice. "Ms. Graber . . . ma'am . . ."

"It's Jenna, please."

"All right." He took a breath. "Jenna, the first thing Nelson did when he regained consciousness was ask for you."

"Me?"

"Yes, ma'am. He wants you to come to the hospital, Jenna. He wants to see you. If that is all right with you."

Relief poured through her. "It's all right with me." She shook her head. No, she wasn't going to do this. She wasn't going to pretend that she wasn't eager to see him. "I mean, I'd like that. I would really like to go. Would you mind taking me?"

"That's why I'm here." Hank darted a look behind her. His gaze softened before he focused on her again. "Fanny asked if I could come over here and pick you up and take you to see Nelson. I'm happy to do it." He hesitated. "But, ah, I wouldn't think that a hospital waiting room would be the best place for your daughter." He wrinkled his nose. "It's a very small room, I'm afraid. There's not even a television on the wall."

"Katie." Thinking quickly, she said, "Would you mind if we drop off Katie at my parents' house? They live in Walden." Sure, Mary and Peter lived closer, but she didn't want to think about Jimmy. She didn't want Katie to hear anything about Nelson that wasn't positive. It would upset her too much, and just as importantly—Nelson didn't deserve anything negative to be said about him.

"Walden won't be hard to get to. We'll pass right by there on our way to the hospital."

So it was all settled. Katie would be safe and happy with Jenna's parents, and Hank would drive her to the hospital. She had no idea what would happen after that, but Jenna realized that she didn't care. God would make sure she was in the right place, whether it was staying by Nelson's side or returning home to take care of Katie.

Suddenly, she realized that they were still standing in her doorway, and the July sun was hot and probably beating down on his back. "Oh my goodness. I'm sorry to keep you out here. Please, come in. I'll gather Katie's things and be ready in just a few minutes."

"Yes, ma'am." Hank walked inside and closed the door behind him. He was a big man and seemed to take up her entire entryway. Or maybe that was his personality?

"Here. Um, let me get you a glass of water or something and introduce you to Katie." Feeling in a dither, she added, "Is water okay? Do you need—"

"Hey, Jenna?"

"Yes?"

"Don't worry about me. I can get myself a drink of water if I decide I need one."

"Oh. Okay, then . . ." She froze again. Pressing a hand to her face, she groaned in frustration. When she looked up at him again, she said, "I'm so sorry. I don't—"

Suddenly, he held out an arm and enfolded her in a quick, sideways hug. "Take a deep breath. Now take another one." After she did as he asked, he bent slightly to be even with her eyes. "Better?"

"I think so." She inhaled and exhaled again for good measure.

Hank seemed pleased that she was following his directions. "There you go."

"Danke. I mean, thank you. I—"

"No apology needed. You can say whatever you want and do whatever you want. You'll receive no judgment from me. But just try to keep positive, okay? I promise, Nelson is going to be okay. He might be sore and hurting for a while, but he's not in danger."

"You sound so sure about that."

"That's because I am." Sobering, he added, "I would never tell you that he wasn't if the doctors and nurses hadn't assured me otherwise."

"Okay. Well, um, I'll hurry."

"All right, but take whatever time you need. Everyone knows that you've got to take care of yourself and take care of your daughter. Me too."

"You are making me feel better. Danke." She shook her head, frustrated with herself. "I mean, thank you. So much."

"If I'm helping, I'm glad." He straightened. "Now, if you don't mind, I think a drink of water sounds like a real good idea after all. I'm going to go take myself into your kitchen, help myself to a glass of water, and sit down until you're ready. I'll also introduce myself to Katie and get her anything she needs while you get settled. Okay?"

She'd never met anyone like this man. Hank was assertive and calm and maybe even a little pushy. God must have known he was the perfect person to come get her because everything Hank was doing soothed her nerves.

He was expertly taking every doubt from her head and putting it to rest.

"Okay," she said at last.

"Good." He lowered his voice. "Go on, now."

"Yes. Of course."

"Mamm?" Katie said as she hurried out of her bedroom. "What's wrong, and who's he?"

"Katie, dear, this is a friend of Nelson's and Fanny's. His name is Mr. Arias. He's going to be our driver this afternoon. Will you please keep him company while I change clothes?"

"Uh-huh."

When Jenna was walking to her bedroom, she heard Hank say, "I know your mama said to call me Mr. Arias, but most everyone I ever met calls me Hank. You can too, if you'd rather."

"My name is Katie. Everyone but Nelson calls me Katie."

"What does Nelson call you?"

"Kitty." Her voice lifted. "And guess what? He got me a kitten! His name is Blue."

"Blue? You got yourself a blue cat?"

Katie giggled. "He's not really blue. But he's cute. Do you want to see him?"

"Of course I do. It's been quite a while since I've gotten to see a kitten. He doesn't bite, does he?"

Katie burst into laughter. A bright, happy sound. "Nee, Hank! He won't bite you at all."

As the conversation continued, Jenna felt her body relax. She was still very worried about Nelson, but she now believed everything was going to be all right.

Mr. Hank Arias was certainly a miracle worker.

chapter thirty-one

Nelson figured no one liked being in the hospital, but he was pretty sure that no one should be forced to rest in a hospital bed if they could do it just as easily at home.

Looking around the room with its faded blue walls, drab shades, and white Formica tile flooring, he frowned. "This is the kind of room that's bound to make a person feel worse instead of better, Fanny. I need to get out of here."

"No, you don't. You need to stay in bed and let the nurses help you."

"All the nurses have done is poke and prod me. I hardly got any sleep last night."

"They also checked your vitals, monitored your concussion, and x-rayed your ribs and wrist. You've been given top-of-the-line care, and you should be grateful for it."

"I am grateful. I just want to go home."

"As soon as the doctors give you the okay, you're going to be discharged." Sitting back down in the plastic chair next to him, she added, "You would know that too, if you'd ever stop fussing and listen to them."

"I listened."

"Not very well." She folded her arms across her chest. "And don't even try to tell me that you've been a good patient. I talked to the nurses before I came in here."

Nelson would probably be embarrassed about how much he'd fussed . . . if he wasn't the one sitting in the hospital bed.

"Have you noticed what this place smells like, Fan? It's like a combination of pine cleaner, bleach, and lavender."

"It smells clean. You'd appreciate that if you weren't in such a snit."

"I'm not. I've been in this bed for twelve hours, and it already feels like two days. I can't take much more."

"I've never known a grown man to whine as much as you are doing, Nelson Harper," Jenna said from the door.

Feeling like a little kid who got caught sneaking a snack, Nelson gulped. "Jenna. You came!"

"Mr. Arias was kind enough to come get me and bring me here." She smiled at Hank, who was standing by the door. "And just in time, I think."

"Thanks for getting her, Hank," he said.

"Of course." Hank had replied to Nelson, but he was looking at Fanny.

Actually, it was pretty obvious that he had gone over to retrieve Jenna as a favor for Fanny. The way Hank was staring at Fanny told him everything. Fanny was important to Hank. That was perfectly clear.

Just like Jenna had become so important to Nelson.

"Nelson, you really shouldn't be giving everyone here such a hard time." Jenna had moved to the side of the bed and was straightening the sheet and blanket around his chest—all while lecturing him like he was Katie's age. He'd tease her about it if he hadn't just noticed that her eyes were a little puffy and red. She'd been crying.

She'd been crying about him.

"Why don't you take my seat, Jenna?" Fanny asked as she stood up and headed to Hank's side. "I think the rest of our family is about to arrive. I'm going to head them off before they all come in here at once."

"Mom and Dad are here?" He wasn't surprised, but he wasn't ready to have his dad ask him a dozen questions about the accident and the company.

"They're on their way," Fanny said. "My parents are heading over here too. But don't worry, I'll tell them they need to give you and Jenna some privacy."

"I owe you. Thanks."

"You're welcome, but I wouldn't count on getting more than a few minutes, boss."

He would have grinned if his head wasn't hurting so badly. When he noticed that Hank closed the door after he and Fanny left, Nelson focused on Jenna again.

"Hey," he whispered.

"Hey." She reached out and fussed with his blanket again.

She was still worried and stressed. Instead of asking her to relax, he decided to redirect. "How was the rest of your meeting?"

"Oh, you know . . . chaos, but I survived."

"I knew you would." He smiled at her.

Jenna licked her bottom lip. "I was surprised when you didn't call back this morning. I thought you'd forgotten."

"I didn't forget." He was tempted to tell her that she

was his priority. That he would never ignore her wishes or forget to give her something she needed—even if it was just a phone call.

"That accident, Nelson! I heard that you are something of a hero."

"I'm not. The weather was bad. I'm just glad that no one else was hurt." He frowned. "At least, I'm pretty sure no one else was."

"No one else was. Only you, Nelson." Her bottom lip trembled. "When Hank told me what happened, I thought I was going to faint. I was so scared for you."

"I'm sorry. I guess it brings back a lot of memories, doesn't it?" He was only just now thinking about how hard it had to have been for Jenna to rush to the hospital again.

"It did bring back memories, but I'm okay."

"Are you sure?"

"Jah, Nelson. You see, I didn't lose you."

Could her words be any sweeter? "I'd give anything to hold you right now."

"That is going to have to wait. From what I understand, you are pretty banged up and bruised."

"I'm going to be okay, though."

"I know." She still looked troubled, though.

"Jenna, take my hand, would you?" The hand next to her had an IV attached to it, but it wasn't wrapped in a bandage.

When she gently slipped her hand into his, he immediately was soothed by the feel of her smooth skin next to his.

"Jenna, there's something I need to tell you. Something about Jimmy's accident."

"All right." Her brown eyes clouded, whether it was from confusion that he'd brought up Jimmy or because she didn't like thinking about the accident, he didn't know.

Taking a deep breath, he forged ahead. "Jenna, there's something I've been keeping from you. You see, the day Jimmy died, he . . . he ignored a lot of protocols. He was mad at his supervisor, in a hurry, and refused to get help when the machine jammed."

She shook her head. "Nee, Nelson. It was the machine."

"The machine did jam, but it was because of Jimmy's mistakes." Before she could protest again, he continued in a rush. "I'm sorry."

"For what?"

"He'd been written up several times. I kept giving him another chance, though. I knew that you and Katie were depending on him." Hating how hard it was to admit the complete truth, he added, "But after the accident, I thought if I had fired him, he wouldn't have had that accident. If I had fired him, he would still be alive."

Jenna gaped at him. Her entire body seemed to tighten before she exhaled. "Oh, Nelson."

"I know it's a lot to ask, but do you think you could ever forgive me?"

"Nelson, I canna believe you've been holding on to this guilt all this time. I wish you hadn't kept it a secret."

"I didn't want to cause you any more pain."

"Why?"

"You know why," he whispered. "I meant what I said last night, Jenna. I love you."

"I meant it too."

"I know we've got a lot to work through, but I figure if

we start with love, then everything else will fall into place. I want you to be my wife one day, Jenna."

When she gasped, he quickly added, "Can you? I know that's asking a lot. I'm asking you to put a life with me ahead of your traditional way of life. Because of that, I'm willing to wait until you are ready."

"Are you sure?"

"I'm positive. I've waited this long. I'll wait another two years for you if that's what it takes. All I need to know is that you want to be my wife one day. Whether it's in a couple of months or not until a couple of years, I don't care."

"You can't mean that," she whispered.

"I mean every word," he said. "I don't want to pressure you, though I guess I am. I . . . well, this car accident made me realize that I need to tell you the words. I need to stop waiting. What do you think?"

When she didn't say anything right away, he was pretty sure his pulse started racing.

Please, Jenna, he begged silently. *We've come so far. Don't give up on us now.* He held his breath as he waited for her to speak.

"I think that it's time I let my heart lead the way instead of everything else. I feel the same way. It's time to stop waiting and say how I feel. Before it's too late."

He smiled at her just as his hospital room door opened and Fanny, Hank, his parents, and his aunt and uncle all poured into the room.

chapter thirty-two

Jenna had met much of Nelson's family at Jimmy's funeral. Because Alliance was a family-owned company, Nelson's father and uncle had both known Jimmy.

So, as she stood up and hugged everyone hello, she wasn't hugging strangers. She also quickly realized that her sitting next to Nelson in his hospital room didn't come as a surprise to them. They all seemed to know that he'd been looking after her and Katie for a long time.

When a nurse came in to tell everyone that Nelson was going to need to get his vital signs checked and possibly be taken down the hall for another CT scan, Jenna knew it was time to leave. As much as she would've liked to be there for Nelson, she felt anxious about staying too. It was a blessing when Nelson took the decision out of her hands.

"Jenna, thanks for wanting to stay here, but all I want to do is sleep. Why don't you go get Katie, go home, and get some rest too?"

"Are you sure you'll be all right?"

"I'm more than sure," he said with a tired smile. "There's nothing you can do for me now."

"Come on, Jenna," Fanny said. "Nelson's right. He's probably going to be asleep before we get to my car."

Noticing that his eyes were already drifting shut, Jenna finally agreed.

Luckily, it wasn't a far drive from the hospital to her parents' farm. When Fanny pulled up to the house, she gasped. "Oh! This is a lovely place! Look at the garden. It's gorgeous."

Fanny wasn't wrong. Her mother had the prettiest garden she'd ever seen. It was a cross between a manicured English garden and a field of wildflowers—a riot of hydrangeas, vincas, daisies, and black-eyed Susans mixed with Queen Anne's lace, marigolds, and zinnias. Perhaps it didn't need to fit in either box. Everywhere one turned there were flower beds, bird feeders, sitting areas, and glorious smells.

"My mother is a master gardener," she said. "This is her happy place."

"I think it could be everyone's happy place," Fanny said as she parked the car.

"If you have a moment, I'd love for you to meet my mother."

"Thank you. I'd like that."

"Mamm!" Katie called out as soon as Jenna got out of the car. Running closer, she said, "Mammi has a new bird nest, and there are blue eggs inside."

"Robin's eggs are very pretty, aren't they?" she asked as she gave Katie a quick hug. "Do you remember Fanny?"

Katie nodded. "Hiya, Fanny."

"Hello, Katie." Pointing to Katie's boots, she said, "I like your yellow rain boots."

"Me too." She smiled. "These are so I can help Mammi in the garden and Dawdi feed chickens and not get the kitchen floor dirty."

"They sound like a very good idea."

Seeing her mother approach, wearing a light-pink dress with a matching apron and flip-flops on her feet, Jenna smiled. "Hi, Mamm. Thank you for watching Katie."

"No need to thank me. Katie's been a big help."

"This is Fanny. She's Nelson's cousin. I don't think you've met."

"I think we met at Jimmy's funeral. You were there, yes?"

"Yes, I was," Fanny said.

"Well, it's gut to see you again," her mother said with a kind smile.

"I was just admiring your beautiful gardens."

"Danke. It's a lot of work, but I enjoy it." Sobering, she said, "How is Nelson?"

"He'll be going home soon, but he's going to be sore for the next few days," Fanny said. "And that's if he behaves himself."

Her mother's eyebrows rose. "Behaves himself?"

"He's not a good patient, Mamm."

"Few men ever are," she replied. "Would you like to come in for a glass of lemonade, Fanny?"

"Thanks, but I need to head on home. I'm happy to drive you and Katie to your house, Jenna."

"Thank you, but I'm going to visit with my parents for a little while."

"Katie?" Daed called out.

"Oh! I gotta go!" Katie said. "Dawdi knows where a

mama bunny had her babies. We're going to go see them," she added before running back into the barn.

"As you can see, I might be here for a while."

"I'd want to stay too. Baby bunnies would be hard to resist." Reaching out, Fanny gave her a tight hug. "Thanks for everything you've done. Nelson is lucky to have you."

Feeling her mother's piercing gaze, she smiled nervously. "Please tell him that I'll be over to see him either tonight or tomorrow."

"Will do," Fanny said as she walked back to her car. "Good to see you," she said with a smile before climbing in and driving off.

"She is a nice woman," Mamm said. "So bright and cheery. Like the sun."

Jenna grinned at the comparison. "You're right. I like her a lot."

Her mother gave her another long look before looping her arm around Jenna's elbow. "Let's go get some lemonade and sit down. You can tell me what you've been doing."

A pool of dread formed in her stomach. She knew that tone of voice. Her mother hadn't missed Fanny's comment about Nelson, and she wanted some answers. They went inside, filled tall glasses with ice and lemonade, and then Jenna followed her mother back outside. She had a favorite sitting area in the shade.

"Every time I am here, I am amazed that you ever have time to sit."

"We don't always have Katie here," she said.

"She looks like she's been having a good time."

"I reckon she has been. It's hard not to when you're a

little girl like Katie. She even seems to enjoy weeding." Mamm sipped her lemonade. "She has also been a wealth of information."

"What has she been talking about?"

"Nelson this, Nelson that. Sounds like Nelson has been over a lot. And that he now hugs you hello and goodbye? And . . . that you have fallen in love?"

"Wow. She has had a lot to say."

"Is it true?"

Jenna figured she had options. She could deny it, say that he was a good friend, and insist there was nothing more, or she could tell her mother the truth.

Briefly, she filled her in on the commotion before her club's meeting and the spur-of-the-moment declarations that had happened. As she expected, her mother was horrified by Mary's outburst, shocked about Jenna's declaration, and moved to tears when she learned about Katie holding him close. "It sounds like I missed quite the event," she teased.

"Oh, Mamm. I haven't even gotten to the part about the storm and everyone running into the house!"

"I do want to hear about that . . . but I want to backtrack to you and Nelson. Did you mean what you said, Jenna?"

She nodded. "I did. I really have fallen in love with Nelson, Mamm."

Her mother's eyes widened. She pursed her lips before looking out at the garden. "You sound so sure."

"That's because I am. Nelson's sure too, Mamm. Neither of us planned on falling in love . . . but it still happened."

"I see." She picked up her glass and took another sip.

Jenna stared at her mother. Panic gripped her as she prepared herself to listen to a lecture about how everything she was doing was very wrong. How everything she felt was very wrong.

"I guess I should've seen this coming," she said after a long minute passed.

"What?"

"This man looked out for you even during your darkest days. He's looked out for you and Katie for months and months. Over a year, yes?"

"Almost two."

"I suppose it's a shame that Jimmy worked for him. That Jimmy's accident was at his family's mill."

"Jimmy was at fault," she blurted.

"What?"

"All this time, Nelson hadn't wanted to hurt me, so he's let me believe that it was just a bad accident. And it was, but Jimmy wasn't following the protocols he should have. Jimmy was the one who made all the mistakes."

"But . . . no one ever said anything."

"I think everyone wanted to preserve Jimmy's memory. They didn't want to tarnish it."

Her mother's expression had gone slack with shock. "This paints a whole other scenario, doesn't it? Nelson cared for you so much, he was even willing to shoulder the blame so you wouldn't hurt so much."

Jenna nodded. "I think there's always been a part of me that thought there was more to the story than I was being told."

"I don't know how Mary and Peter will ever be able to handle you marrying again, Jenna."

"I know. I don't want to hurt them, and I want them to have a relationship with Katie." She took a deep breath. "But Mamm, they have to realize that even if Jimmy had been completely innocent and someone else at the mill was to blame, Jimmy is still going to be gone."

"What are you going to do about Nelson?"

"I want to marry him one day."

"If you leave the faith, you'll be hurting yourself," she warned. "Breaking your vows is a serious thing."

"I know. But there's not going to be anyone else, Mamm. I believe that God meant for us to be together. Just as importantly, I want Nelson in my life. I want to marry him."

When her mother remained silent, Jenna continued. "I mean, sure, I could raise Katie, see my new friends at the widows club, and spend time with you and Daed. But it isn't enough." She reached out for her mother's hand. "Pushing away Nelson Harper is not something I can do."

Her mother studied Jenna's expression. Looked down at their clasped hands. And finally nodded. "All right, then. Daed and I will go with you to speak to the bishop."

"You'll support me, Mamm? Even if you don't agree?"

"Darling girl, didn't you just hear yourself? That's what love is, right? It's loving another person so much that you're willing to put their needs above your own. It's what Jesus did for all of us. If He can die for our sins, I think I can still love you even if things between us will be different."

Unable to help herself, Jenna launched at her mother and hugged her tight.

"I love you, Mamm."

"I know." She stood up. "Now, let's go see those baby bunnies and speak to your father."

"Now?"

"No time like the present, dear."

"You're right. There's no time like now."

chapter thirty-three

So much had happened during the last month. After she and her parents spoke with the bishop, Jenna made her decision. To her surprise, neither the bishop nor her parents attempted to get her to change her mind about leaving the faith.

"You are a young woman who has been through so many difficult years," Bishop Burke said. "Only you have walked in your shoes, not me."

"Danke. This isn't an easy decision."

"I can't help but think that your life's path has been so challenging because the Lord has been leading you. Maybe He's known that you needed to be strong in order to be with Nelson."

"He's the best man I know," Jenna said.

"Then you should hold tight to that, for that is what matters."

Jenna had held tight to those words ever since. It had felt strange to take off her kapp and imagine a future with electricity, but she realized that neither the clothing nor creature comforts would make a difference to her. She still loved the Lord, and she still loved Nelson. That was what mattered to her the most.

Nelson, of course, had been overjoyed by her decision. They decided not to make any immediate plans. Instead, he would heal and she would wrap her head around their future together.

When September came around and the first leaves were starting to change, Hank invited Jenna, Nelson, and Katie over for supper with him and Fanny.

Just as things had been changing for her and Nelson, Fanny and Hank had become a couple too.

After hearing so much about the house and all the work that Nelson's company had done inside it, Jenna had been excited to see it. Her first impression exceeded her expectations. The house was large and beautiful and the woodwork inside was exquisite.

While she and Fanny sat in Hank's sunroom and played cards with Katie, the men grilled hamburgers and hot dogs. Then, just as they were all about to sit down, Nelson reached for Katie's hand and smiled. "Ready?" he asked.

"Yep."

"Ready for what?"

"To get married!" Katie shouted.

"What?"

"Nelson got you a ring!"

She gaped as Nelson knelt down at her feet, pulled out a ring, and gazed into her eyes. "You know I love you, Jenna. You know I'll wait as long as you want until you are ready, but I don't want to wait any longer for everyone to know you are mine. Would you wear my ring? Will you be my fiancée until you are ready to be my wife?"

This was it. This was love. It was messy. Unscripted and in disarray, and she wouldn't have it any other way.

"I love you so much that I'd marry you tomorrow."

When he slid the ring on her finger, she decided that the weight felt good. The ring felt right.

It all felt right.

It was the right moment. It was the right time.

It was the right forever.

—Epilogue

SIX MONTHS LATER

Jenna supposed some things would never change. Looking around her house, with the many boxes in disarray, the collection of new clothes that Nelson had bought her when they'd gone shopping in Columbus, and the few leftover toys and crayons that Katie had forgotten when Fanny picked her up, Jenna knew that she should get busy and put everything in order.

Instead, she was writing her pen pals. Her excuse was that she needed to give them her new mailing address. That was important. After all, she'd already filled them in about Nelson's dreamy proposal, when he'd knelt down on one knee in the middle of the barbecue and given her a lovely ring with a beautiful, understated diamond.

Glancing at her left hand, Jenna had to smile. She'd never understood why English women liked wearing a set of wedding rings. It seemed like a waste of money and far too fancy.

Now, however, she thought she finally got it. Her engagement ring would always be a symbol of Nelson's love and promises to her. She found herself wearing it with pride.

So, all her correspondents knew all the important stuff. But she still felt a need to write just one more letter.

Holly, do you remember all those months ago when I shared how worried I was about the future? I was petrified to move on because I didn't want to hurt Katie, my family, or even Jimmy's family.

But then, there you went, telling me that love is what is important. How love overrules doubts and worries. And that it shouldn't be taken for granted.

You were absolutely right. Loving Nelson hasn't brought conflict into my life, instead it's brought me peace.

So, thank you for that.

Jenna smiled. Took a fortifying breath and scanned the room again.

Now for the important stuff. You wanted to know if I was going to wear a wedding gown, and the answer is yes! And, Holly, you should see it. It has long sleeves and goes to the floor, and it's made of the most shimmery, beautiful white silk. At first I thought it was too fancy, but my mother said that the pretty material made up for the fact that there isn't a speck of lace to be found on it. It's all simple, clean lines with a lovely sweetheart neckline. And yes, I had no idea such a neckline existed until the lady at the shop told me about it.

Finally, there's a long line of buttons on the back. I think I counted twenty.

And between you and me, Holly, I've gotten a little misty-eyed thinking about my wedding night, when Nelson carefully unbuttons each one.

"Oh!" Jenna pressed her hands to her cheeks. She wasn't going to cross out what she wrote . . . but it was surely time to end the note.

When I write you again, I'll be Mrs. Nelson Harper. Jenna Harper to you. It has a nice ring to it, doesn't it?

Now, I had better go. I have a bunch of things to put into suitcases. And I need to finish boxing up all my Amish clothes. I'm not going to give them away quite yet.

I think I want them on hand, just in case Katie wants to ask me about the life we used to have. The woman I was before I became the woman I am now.

That was a person I was proud to be, and I have a feeling I'll even miss her simple life quite a bit.

Those boxes will serve as a reminder that I haven't completely changed.

That's what life does to us, doesn't it? It twists and pulls and stains and embellishes. And the fact that we're still standing at all? Well, that's something to celebrate.

Thanks for teaching me that.

I love you, Holly.

Warmly,
Jenna

Author's Note

Dear Reader,

I often tell people that I have the best job in the world. Not only do I get to spend my days making up stories, but my publishers have given me the opportunity to write the kind of stories I love to share. Stories about good things happening to people I would like to know.

As I was going over *The Forbidden Caller* "just one more time," I reflected on how much this book is an example of that. I enjoyed getting to know the entire cast of characters. From the moment I first imagined Nelson showing up at Jenna's doorstep, both characters had my heart. I loved the secondary romance with Fanny and Hank too. Then, of course, there was Doreen, the founder of the Amish Widows Club. In many ways, she's become the heart of this series. I hope and pray that one of the storylines or characters in the book appealed to you.

Sometimes folks ask about my writing process. I'm a little embarrassed to say it's very imperfect. I write fast and am always happy to let my characters lead the way. Though this means I've yet to make a timeline that I couldn't mess up, it also allows me a bit of freedom. All kinds of things happen to characters that are unexpected. Jenna's many pen pals are an example of this. Although I loved the idea of a pen-pal support system, I worried that her letters might be a distraction. When I turned in the novel, I fully expected my editor to kindly ask me to give Jenna a new hobby. Instead, she encouraged me to add more snippets of her pen pals throughout the book.

Thank you for picking up this book—which is something like my 140th published novel! I hope you enjoy the story as much as I enjoyed writing it. Thanks for your notes and library visits and continued support. Thanks for giving me a wonderful reason to wake up in the morning.

With my blessings,

Shelley

Read on for a sneak peek
at the next book in

the
AMISH WIDOWS CLUB SERIES

*Available
March 2027*

chapter one

JANUARY

She was late. Guiding her buggy horse into the back of the middle school parking lot, Cynthia Byler attempted to ignore the beads of perspiration forming between her shoulder blades. Ever since she was a teenager, she began to sweat whenever she got frazzled. It was embarrassing, but she couldn't seem to help it.

The only things that did seem to help were to breathe slowly and count her blessings. There were a few days in her past when both of those things had been difficult to do.

Luckily, today wasn't one of them.

For sure, she had many blessings now. She was thankful for still having a horse and buggy, even though the buggy was old and smelled faintly of mildew. She was thankful for her twins, Nora and Danny, who for some reason were still kind and considerate to her and to each other instead of being disagreeable teenagers. She was also grateful for her job at Cornerstone Bakery. It was a good job, and Tricia, her boss, was both dependable and kind. Cindy even appreciated the unusually good weather they were having in January. It made driving a horse and buggy so much easier.

"You are fine. Relax," she whispered to herself as she set the parking brake, secured Vanderbilt to the hitching post, and crossed the parking lot.

But even after successfully dodging three vehicles in the pickup lane and making her way toward the school's gymnasium where her twins were playing volleyball, Cindy knew the truth.

No matter how many deep breaths she took or blessings she counted, the truth was that she was not okay. She was tired. She was frazzled. She could use a fifteen-minute break from her life.

But most of all, she really wanted to go take a hot shower. And not for the usual reasons either. Sure, her back was now damp from her latest panic attack, and her shoulder muscles hurt after spending eight hours working at the bakery. No, today was rather special because she was currently splattered with two cups of chocolate glaze. It was as sticky as it was unsightly.

The accident hadn't been her fault either.

Rachel Weaver—Tricia's newest hire—had been scatterbrained yet again. Lost in her own world, Rachel had picked up a hot, heavy pan from the stove too quickly, nearly walked into Tricia, turned on her heel, and then splashed Cynthia with two cups of warm glaze.

Her white kapp, apron, and much of her dress were stained. The sticky substance was difficult to wash from her skin and even more uncomfortable to wear.

Though Tricia was usually rather kind, she didn't offer

to allow Cindy to go home early. After giving her a few minutes to clean up, she put everyone back to work.

Cindy supposed she couldn't blame her—they'd had a big order for the Rotary Club. Tricia had promised to deliver several dozen cupcakes, frosted brownies, and cookies to the organization by five o'clock. By the time Cindy was able to leave, the glaze had soaked into the fabric of her gray dress and dried.

Now here she was, walking into the gym of the public middle school, smelling like a stale chocolate cake and looking like . . . well, there was no good descriptor. Calling her a mess was an understatement.

Cindy's only hope was that Danny or Nora would spot her quickly, notify the other, and hurry to her side. If that happened, there was a chance that she could leave the premises without too many folks noticing her current state.

"Hi, Mrs. Byler! I was just about to ask Nora if she thought—oh my gosh! What happened to you?"

Cindy gritted her teeth. Miss Mayson was Nora's favorite teacher in the seventh grade. She taught art and was fresh out of college.

She also was bright, cheerful, and had afternoon duty for all the students who chose to stay after school to play intramural sports. Miss Mayson also happened to have the loudest voice in Alliance, Ohio.

Okay, sure. That wasn't very nice of her to think. But given the way half the population of the gymnasium was now staring at her, it sure felt that way.

Rushing to her side, sweet, oh-so-loud Miss Mayson patted her arm. "Oh, Mrs. Byler. You look a sight. Are you okay?" she asked.

Though Cindy was tempted to answer her honestly, she did what she always did. Smile and deflect. "Jah. Sure. Someone at the bakery had an unfortunate accident with a pan of chocolate glaze. I'm afraid I got the brunt of the spill."

"I'm so sorry. Did you get burned?" The young woman truly was a sweetheart.

Cindy took a deep breath. "Nee. I mean, not really." She glanced at the game in progress. It was hard to see every player. There had to be at least thirty adults and children watching the game from the sidelines.

The teacher frowned as worry clouded her eyes. "Not really? Do you need—"

"Do you happen to know where Nora and Danny are?" she interrupted.

"Oh. Uh . . ."

"We're coming, Mamm!" Danny called out. "Give us five minutes."

Turning, she saw that both twins were playing volleyball on the far side of the gym. They were mixed in with several English students, and everyone seemed to be clapping for Nora, who'd just served.

"Go, Nora!" one of the kids in the crowd yelled.

Miss Mayson grinned at Cindy. "Your daughter can rock a mean serve."

"Ah." She hoped that meant Nora was a good player.

Her children were safe and happy. Playing a game. Allowing them to go to the public middle school for seventh and eighth grade had been the right decision.

The knowledge made her smile for the first time in hours, and she relaxed at last.

Miss Mayson's posture eased as well. "I'm sorry you have to wait, but your children really are well-liked, Mrs. Byler. That's across the board too. Everyone—teachers and students—enjoy them very much."

"Thank you. That is good to hear."

Miss Mayson looked as if she was about to add something else but was summoned by another parent. "I better go see what she needs. See you later, Mrs. Byler."

Folding her arms across her chest, Cindy sagged against the wall. It could be worse, she told herself. They could be troublemakers or getting picked on. Instead, they were happy, well-adjusted children. It was a miracle, really. Their father had died seven years earlier, when they were only six. They'd been too young to experience death.

Unfortunately, Adam's death hadn't been the worst thing they'd ever experienced. She swallowed. Life with him had been fraught with pain too.

Her skin prickled as the memories that she fought so hard to block threatened to surface. Cindy breathed deep. Exhaled.

"Are you waiting for the game to finish too?"

She turned to the voice. An Amish man had walked to her side while she'd been having her mini panic attack. She thought she recognized him, but she couldn't place his name. That made her almost as uncomfortable as her dirty dress.

Though she would've loved to ignore him, Cindy realized she didn't have a choice. He was waiting for a response. "I am."

"Which one is yours?" He wasn't looking at her. Instead,

he was watching the white ball continually fly back and forth over the net.

"I have two children over there. A boy and a girl."

"Two? Which ones?"

She pointed. "They're on the left. My son just served, and my daughter is in the front row. She's the one wearing the dark-green dress."

The man scanned the group, then grinned when he seemed to spot them. "Ah, I should've guessed. They look just like you."

"I suppose they do." She'd always loved that they had her blue eyes and light-brown curls. Adam had had dark hair, ruddy cheeks, and matching dark eyes. It hadn't been displeasing. He'd been handsome at one time. Before life and years and hardships got in the way and seemed to sour both his looks and his disposition.

"My son is the tall one in the back with the blond hair. His name is Roy."

"Ah."

"So, your son is Danny. What is your daughter's name?" There was humor in the man's voice. It was obvious he was amused by her prickly attitude.

She didn't appreciate that.

Reminding herself that she was already covered in chocolate and didn't need to embarrass her children further, she cleared her throat. "Her name is Nora."

"Which one is in eighth?"

"Neither. They're both in the seventh grade. They're twins."

"My Roy is fifteen and he's in eighth grade."

Fifteen? "That seems old for middle school."

He nodded. "That's probably because it is."

He didn't seem flustered, but her rude statement pricked her consciousness. "Forgive me. I spoke out of turn."

"Did you?" He shrugged. "I think you were more likely stating a fact. Roy is old for his grade. It couldn't be helped, though. He had to repeat third grade. He missed a lot of school that year. We'd already kept him home an extra year too." He shrugged. "I used to feel guilty, but it doesn't seem to have done him any harm." Looking almost amused, he added, "I've been told by my parents that one can't go back in time. Therefore, I should agree that it is what it is."

He'd just told her a lot of information that Cindy hadn't asked for but now couldn't help but think about. She wondered why. "I see."

"Do you? Hmm."

Feeling a bit embarrassed, she turned to watch the game again. What was wrong with her? She was usually more circumspect. Always a lot less judgmental. Roy's educational development was none of her business.

She should probably apologize again. When she glanced his way again, she was caught off guard. The man had his hands stuffed into his front pockets and was humming a tune of some sort under his breath. Why was he in such a good mood?

And why was he persisting to speak to her? She had on a shapeless gray dress and probably smelled like an old chocolate bar.

"Hey, I just realized that I never introduced myself. My name is Monroe Cross. What's yours?"

She turned back to him. Noticed that his brown eyes

were light. Leaning toward hazel. "I am Cynthia Byler. Most everyone calls me Cindy, though."

He held out a hand. "It's good to meet you."

She shook it gingerly. She would have preferred not to touch him. But his grip was gentle. Nothing like Adam's used to be.

It was the second time in this gym that she thought of her husband. She sometimes went days without thinking about Adam. Why was this happening?

Ignoring Monroe's concerned expression, she placed her hands over her face and breathed deep. Attempted to clear her head.

"Hey, are you all right?"

Quickly she put her hands back down. "Of course. It is gut to meet you as well, Monroe."

"Sorry you had to wait so long, Mamm," Nora called out as she hurried forward with her backpack on her back over her thick green dress. "But did you see how good that spike was of mine?" Her happy expression faded as she turned to face her. "Wait, what's all over you?"

Aware that Monroe was still standing there and no doubt eavesdropping, Cindy lifted her chin. "Chocolate glaze."

"Wow, Mamm. It's everywhere."

"Believe it or not, it was worse." Touching her eyes, she added, "For a moment, I could barely see."

Sweet Nora's expression filled with sympathy. "Let me guess . . . Rachel struck again?"

"Your guess is correct."

"She's a menace, Mamm."

"She's a nice young woman. But she is accident-prone."

"What's on Mamm?" Danny asked Nora.

"Chocolate. From Rachel." Nora shrugged as if Cindy wasn't standing directly in front of her and Monroe couldn't hear every word that was being said. "At least she smells good. Kind of."

Her embarrassment was now complete. "Danke, Nora." Turning to her son, Cindy added, "Hello, Danny."

"Hi." Looking her over from head to toe, he frowned. "You should have said something. We wouldn't have made you wait if we'd known you were covered in chocolate."

"I'm glad I got to watch your game. Besides, there's nothing you could've done. I'm afraid the accident happened hours ago."

"I guess not. At least you got to meet Mr. Cross," Danny said. "Oh. Mamm, this here is Roy."

The fifteen-year-old. "Hello, Roy. I'm Danny and Nora's mother." She prepared herself for a moment of awkwardness when he realized what a mess she was.

His pleasant expression didn't fade a bit. "Hiya, Mrs. Byler. It's nice to meet you." He smiled at her, but his gaze almost immediately darted to Nora, who was gazing at him like he was one of the seven wonders of the world.

Nora had a crush on Roy! The sight shook Cindy up a bit. Summoning what she hoped was a friendly expression, she said, "It's gut to meet you, Roy. And, children, I'm sorry, but we should go."

Nora nodded. "I'm ready."

"See you later," Danny said as he started toward the door.

"See you. See you tomorrow, Nora," Roy said.

"Okay. Bye, Roy," Nora said in a soft, sweet voice.

Nora was blushing. Great. She had a crush on an older boy.

Appalled, Cindy glanced at Monroe. His lips were pursed, but he looked more amused than horrified.

Why, he probably saw nothing wrong with his son flirting with a girl who was two years younger than him. She was going to have to put a stop to that. Her mind began to spin as she headed to the gymnasium's door.

"Hey, Cindy?" Monroe called out.

She stopped. Turned back to him. "Jah?"

"I hope you have a good evening."

"Danke. You as well."

She put her head down as they walked out the door. Picked up her pace as the chilly air enveloped them.

By the time she reached the buggy, Nora was already standing next to Vanderbilt and kissing his nose. The horse was leaning toward her. Nora had always been the horse's favorite.

"Let's get going, children."

"I'll drive the buggy, Mamm," Danny said.

Happy to give him the control, she allowed him to get in the driver's side. Then she untied the leads and helped him back Vanderbilt out of the covered space. Only after Danny turned the buggy so it was facing forward did she climb in on the other side of Nora.

Ten minutes later, they were halfway home.

"Mamm, you sure smell like chocolate," Nora teased.

"Believe me, I know."

Her daughter continued. "I can't believe you were standing with Roy's daed."

"Why? He was waiting for the game to end too."

"Did you like Mr. Cross?"

Like? "I didn't speak to him enough to have an opinion, child."

"Oh. Well, he's been nice to Danny and me. Every time we see him, he says hello."

"That's gut." It didn't seem unusual, though.

Danny chuckled. "Nora's only saying that because Roy really likes her, Mamm."

"He shouldn't." The last thing Nora needed was to be thinking about a boy.

Nora stiffened by her side. "How come?"

"You're too young to like a boy, Nora."

"Nee, I'm not. A lot of girls have boyfriends."

"You don't need to be one of them."

"Mamm, come on. Even the girls who decided to stay in the Amish school have beaus."

She knew. Long ago, she'd been a teen with a crush too. "I realize that, but it isn't a good idea, Nora. You should put Roy out of your mind."

"That's impossible."

Danny snickered.

Cindy didn't feel like laughing, though. "Nora, mind your manners."

"Mamm, I'm allowed to have an opinion."

"Hmm."

"Are you always going to be like this?"

"Like what?"

"You know, mean to men?"

What was her daughter saying? "I wasn't mean to anyone."

"You know what I mean." Nora paused. "You know. Are you always going to push men away because of Daed?"

She was pretty sure she was starting to sweat again. "We are not going to talk of your father," she bit out. It was difficult to even say that much.

"That's what you always say." Her daughter sighed in a way that let Cindy know exactly how she felt about that.

Cindy knew she needed to say something. She needed to defend herself. And, yes, chastise her daughter for being so mouthy. But she was suddenly too tired to do even that.

Ironically, even though she was very relieved that her husband was no longer hurting her, there was a part of her that missed the way he would tell the children when it was time to stop pushing. It was so difficult to be the only parent of two teenagers.

After the silence stretched the entire time Danny drove the buggy through the intersection, he spoke. "Come on, Nora. Give her a break. You know why Mamm feels that way."

"I know. But Roy isn't like him." Lowering her voice, she added, "He's not like Daed at all."

"I don't want to talk about this, daughter."

"We need to, though. Danny and I are almost fourteen. We're not little kids. You can't keep pretending that we're not going to want to be in relationships."

Cindy inhaled sharply. Felt like jumping out of the buggy. It would be better than what was currently happening, which was that she was trying not to cry.

Though, she wasn't sure why it mattered.

Her tears had never made a lick of difference when Adam was alive. They certainly weren't going to help her now that he was gone. All they would do was upset her children.

She sure didn't want to do that.

Shelley Shepard Gray is the *New York Times* and *USA Today* bestselling author of more than 100 books, including *Unshaken*, *Unforgotten*, and *Unforgiven*. Two-time winner of the HOLT Medallion and finalist for both the Christy and the Carol Awards, Gray lives in Ohio, where she writes full-time, bakes too much, and can often be found walking her dachshunds on her town's bike trail.

Learn more at ShelleyShepardGray.com.

Meet Shelley

Find her at **ShelleyShepardGray.com**

AND ON SOCIAL MEDIA AT

ShelleyShepardGray ShelleySGray Shelley.S.Gray